Do You Wish You Never Met Me?

LAURA MAY

Also by Laura May

The One Woman

I See You in My Dreams

Published in the United States by Creative James Media.

www.creativejamesmedia.com

978-1-956183-22-1 (trade paperback)

First U.S. Edition 2024

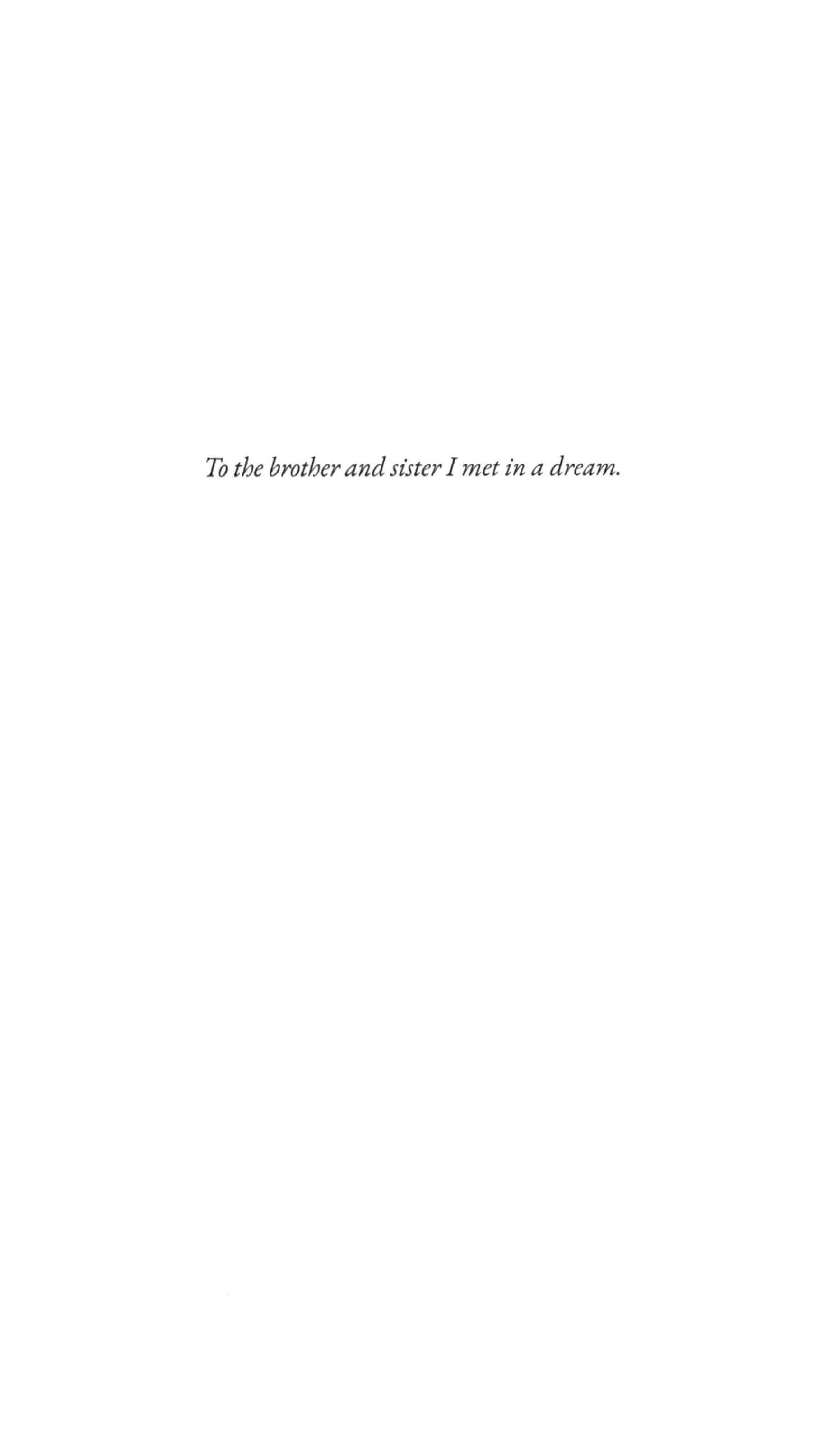

To the brother and sister I met in a dream.

Part One

Chapter One

The neon sign of the *Sapphire Duck* bar loomed at the end of the street. I pulled my jacket tighter to stop the unusual chill of an early September night.

People stood outside, smoking, laughing, hugging. I could hear the roar of voices and music inside. I dragged myself to that place every Friday, trying to socialize. Miranda said I needed it, but every time the cacophony of noise offended my senses and I was reminded how much I preferred silence.

I pushed the greasy door open and spotted them immediately. Brian's arm was draped over the chair Miranda sat on, her head thrown back in a laugh. Brian was chuckling, and she pressed her forehead to his shoulder, just for a second.

Every Friday I watched how those two lived in a separate world made only of them, oblivious to everything around. I got to see how comfortable they were in each other's arms.

"Emily!" Miranda cried when she saw me and rushed to my side.

In a second, she had draped her arms around me and tugged me to the table. Brian smiled and scooted over to free a place for me.

"Beer?" he asked, standing up.

I nodded. "Thanks."

"No one is here tonight, yet," Miranda said. "How's your new room, by the way?"

Miranda and I had been roommates for the first three years of university, but for the final year, she and Brian had decided to rent a small house off-campus, which left me with the prospect of a new roommate, and I just couldn't handle that at that time. I started working part-time in a bookshop to allow myself a separate room.

"Quiet as a cave," I said. "I like it that way."

"Of course you do," Miranda said, a small shadow darkening her features for a moment.

I knew that look. It was not pity; it was worry. Miranda understood me best. She had seen how I had crumbled the year before, and she stayed by my side, guiding me, helping me to find a way back.

"Here you go," Brian said as he set three glasses down in front of us.

I wrapped my fingers around the icy jug. It was a nice distraction from the stifling hot air of a bar. I took a gulp; the bitter liquid was freezing on my tongue.

Miranda leaned closer. "So, we finally booked our plane tickets to Canada," she said, her voice raised trying to be heard over the buzz.

"It's time for my doom," Brian said, and I laughed.

"My parents are going to love you, you'll see," she retorted.

"Or hate me and will ban you from seeing me," Brian shot back, taking a sip of beer.

He put the glass down and looked up, to my right.

"No way," he mumbled and stood up.

"What ..." Miranda said, confused, but he was already elbowing his way through the crowd to the entrance.

I looked back to where Brian was going just to see him

stopping in front of a tall guy in a white shirt. In a second Brian's face lit up and they embraced warmly, both laughing.

"Who is that?" I asked Miranda, who eyed the encounter with a suspicion.

"I have no idea."

I shrugged and took one more numbing gulp of beer. Honestly, I hated the taste. I was not a fan of this place either. It was a sticky, weird-smelling bar close to the campus where Miranda and Brian insisted on meeting with friends. They said they liked the vibe.

"Girls, meet Jake," Brian said right behind me.

Before turning to Brian, I registered how Miranda's eyes grew wider when she faced the stranger. I twisted back and froze.

My eyes met with the dark blue of high seas for a moment before they turned away to Miranda. The man had a light brown wavy shag, light skin, and the warmest smile. He was tall, but all I could focus on was his face. He was the most handsome creature I had ever seen in my life—including in my dreams and imagination.

I felt a kick on my shin under the table and was jerked back to reality.

"Hi Jake, I'm Miranda."

"She tricked me into dating her and now we live together," Brian said.

"And this is Emily." Miranda smiled, kicking me again.

"Hey," was all I managed to say.

His eyes lingered on me, turning all my thoughts to milky glue.

"Nice to meet you both," Jake said in a velvety voice.

"So, what are you doing here?" Brian questioned, moving closer.

"We transferred here for this year."

"We? Is Alice here too?"

Jake nodded.

"Do you want to step outside for a couple of minutes? It's deafening here," Jake asked Brian, looking around.

"Sure," Brian replied and turned to us. "I'll be right back."

Jake waved goodbye and they disappeared into the waves of people.

Miranda snorted as I watched them go.

"You can close your mouth now," she said, laughing.

Was I gaping?

"What ... who was that? Was he real?" I asked.

"He was," she said and laughed again, a tinkle of a sound. "Let's wait for Brian and ask. I've never met the guy before."

"I need to use the restroom," I said and bolted away before she got a chance to say anything else.

The blur of bodies, a mass moved around me as I almost ran into the bathroom door. Once inside, the music faded away, the voices muted. I was alone.

A flushed face looked at me from the mirror, dark eyes darted to my shamefully rosy cheeks. I put my hands under the cold water and took a shaking breath. I was embarrassed by my own reaction. I didn't want to remember how my body leaned in the direction of that stranger. What was that? A hormone craze? I splashed cold water on my face to calm the blaze under my skin and looked back at the mirror. The water glistened on the black nose ring I wore.

I took a paper towel and noticed how my hands were trembling. Something was not right, something had happened to my body and I wanted to bolt away from there, to run back to my dorm room and hide.

"Stupid," I murmured as the door to the restroom opened and three giggling women filled the space.

One last look in the mirror and I headed back.

Miranda was beaming when she saw me. Her dark auburn hair glistened like a rainbow in the colorful light of the bar.

"You're getting back to life, girl," she said.

"Stop it," I murmured, but her smile was infectious.

We were always different. Miranda surrounded herself with colors and light, but I was always monochrome. We shouldn't even have been friends, but there was something between us I didn't have with anyone else anymore. Trust.

"Oh, there's Brian," Miranda said.

In a moment his hands rested on her shoulders and Brian kissed the top of her head. He took a sip of his beer and looked at us.

"So ..." Miranda started, "who is he?"

"Jake? Oh, you're going to love him. He's one of the smartest people I've ever met, reserved, but once he knows you, he's such an interesting person to be around."

"Does he have a girlfriend?" Miranda asked and looked at me.

Brian followed her gaze and coughed. "No, no, no, don't even think about it. He doesn't date."

"Is he gay?" Miranda asked, raising a brow.

"No, he definitely isn't. All the girls from our school swooned over him, from the most popular ones to the smartest, to the plainest. Every girl, but he chose no one. For some time he dated a girl from a neighboring town, but it ended abruptly. It's not about you, Emily, trust me, you're gorgeous," he said, and Miranda nodded.

"I'm not, but thanks." I laughed.

"But Jake isn't interested in relationships, and he never was. He always reads, studies, or travels with his sister."

"Alice?" I asked.

"Yes, they're very close," Brian said.

Miranda tilted her head. "How do you know so much about him?"

"We were neighbors 'til my family moved to Florida. His family has an interesting story, our moms were close when they were younger." He paused awkwardly before continuing.

"When everyone was popping out kids, Jake's parents just couldn't. They tried everything, even some magic when medical stuff didn't work, so eventually, they decided to adopt. Jake is adopted. But a month into happy family life, Jake's mom realized she was pregnant, so here comes Alice. I've never seen such a strong sibling bond as between those two. They do everything together, Jake even transferred here along with Alice because the art program at our university is much stronger."

"What does he study?" I asked.

"Biomedical engineering."

"Wow," Miranda murmured.

"So anyway, Emily, I suggest you don't even spend a second thinking about Jake. He's a hopeless case. Just don't," Brian said. "Sorry."

"Yeah, sorry," Miranda chimed. "I already imagined them together, such a sexy couple."

I shook my head and smiled.

"Stop it," I said. "I was not even *that* interested."

What a shameless lie.

Chapter Two

In a week the weather cleared up, back to the warmth of summer—though it was likely to be the last. The balmy wisps of evening breeze hugged my uncovered arms and ankles as I walked slowly to the bar. Friday. My black dress went down to my knees and I realized that that was probably one of the last times I could wear it that season. I often preferred black then, or white. It was like I was trapped between those two colors, my mood somewhere in between.

I forbade myself to think about those dark blue eyes, about those brown curls, but they crept into my dream that night. I didn't need it, I didn't need to dwell on something unreachable. I had to prepare myself for life after university. The money that was coming from renting out the house would help a bit with my student loan, but then I would be on my own.

Stepping into adult life would be abrupt and I hoped that my Computer Science degree would sustain me.

Before, I had loved university life, I had loved meeting new people, but as it was coming to an end, I was almost relieved and terrified at the same time.

Again, those sticky doors, and the maddening roar of a Friday evening bar. I noticed the auburn immediately; Miranda stood at the bar and recited her order.

I touched her elbow and she turned and hugged me. It was always so easy with her, she was so at ease with her body, her movements.

"Lots of people here tonight, Jessica prepared a *Friends* quiz, it should be fun, you know how she's crazy about the details. And ..." Miranda said as she tried to lift a huge tray with snacks, "Jake is here with his sister. Wait 'til you see her. I don't know what their parents took or did, but I'm sure many couples would like to know the recipe."

I shook my head as I watched her balance the tray. "Do you need help?"

"Nah, I'm fine. Grab your drink and come to the table, I saved a seat for you."

I ordered a glass of beer and took a deep breath. Waiting for it to be poured, I looked outside to the dark of the evening. One thing about that night I knew for sure would make me happy, was that I loved *Friends*.

Cradling the glass as I stepped through the crowd, I walked slowly to our usual table. Jessica and her boyfriend were laughing with their friends. I'd seen them there a couple of times before but never managed to remember their names. Brian was bent over talking with Jake, who looked at me for a second before turning back to Brian. Miranda was chewing a mozzarella stick, her face turned to a blonde woman sitting by her side.

Miranda noticed me and, as always, her face lit up.

"Here she is. Alice, meet Emily," Miranda said.

When the woman turned to me, I immediately saw what Miranda meant. She looked at me with bright gray eyes, a smile open and welcoming. The smallest black mole hid on her cheek. Alice shook my hand, her skin warm against my cool. Her long blonde hair cascaded down open shoulders. There was something comforting about her, in the way she moved, flowing.

"Hello," I said and smiled.

And, for a second, I turned to Brian, just to find Jake's eyes on me. He held my gaze, steady blue, and looked away. I sat between Miranda and Alice.

"How do you like university?" Miranda asked Alice. "Brian said you're an art student."

"The professors are much more practical here, and I like it. They insist that being a broke and drunk artist is not a goal for us and that we should all learn something that could bring us a constant flow of money—get a job that is well paid and not too time-consuming." She paused for a moment, thinking.

"They also really emphasize that in our free time we can create experimental art, that our jobs need to provide the resources to really create. So that we aren't in a constant hunt for means."

"That's smart, what would you like to do in your day job?" I asked.

Alice smiled at my question.

"I'm deep into graphic design and animation. Honestly, I think there's something really rewarding about contributing to pop culture. I'd like to be a part of a team who creates visual effects on blockbuster movies," Alice said and tucked a golden lock behind her ear. "That being said, my true passion is still live art in baroque style," she laughed, almost sadly, "and there is zero chance to monetize that skill."

"That's unusual," Miranda said. "Do you have photos of your work?"

Alice nodded and fished out a phone from her handbag. She unlocked it, and I saw strings of nature photos when she scrolled down.

"Here are some of the recents," she said and turned the screen to us.

There were canvases that would easily fit into any historic art museum. Details, small strokes of the brush created the volume of the fruits, jars, and glasses. Alice slowly swiped to the left, revealing more and more.

"Were you Bosschaert in a previous life?" I asked and Alice laughed, a warm sound filling the space between us.

"I wish," she said and swiped one more time revealing the modern-looking graphics of a girl standing on the cliff, blue ocean below. You could not see her face, only her back, but her hair and the fabric of her dress were made with such detail.

"Did you create it?" Miranda asked.

"Yes."

"I'm not an expert in still life art, but this is ..." Miranda faltered, clearing her throat, "good. Do you have more?"

Alice tapped the screen and a grid of the same style graphics appeared.

"When I visit the place I love, I paint myself there," Alice said, blushing.

The collection of twenty or so pictures revealed the blonde girl in fields, by the seashore, in cafés, and among skyscrapers.

I leaned closer. "That's beautiful."

And it was. She had a talent, massive. There were feelings in her art. She didn't only show an image, she showed emotion. Longing.

Involuntarily my eyes moved to Jake, and my heart skipped a beat when I found his eyes on me again. This time he held my gaze, and I got lost in his eyes, my cheeks warming. He smiled and shook his head, turning to Jessica who rose at the end of the table and clapped her hands.

I was still looking at his face, his brown curls hiding a part of it while he tried to keep a straight face, looking anywhere but me. The smile on Jake's face was the most exquisite thing I had ever seen.

Don't even think about it, I heard Brian's voice in my head, and switched my attention to Jessica. I had met her a couple of times before, and every time she was a whirlwind of motion and activity. She was the girlfriend of Brian's good friend, Alec, who was also constantly on the go. Being in their company for too long made my head spin.

"There are nine of us here today, so let's divide into pairs," Jessica said looking around at us, "random pairs. We will draw names. The questions' difficulty grows with each round, four questions in each round, five rounds total. I'll lead."

After an intricate system of pulling the names and lots of shuffling of chairs I was sat by Jake, Miranda was with Alec, Brian with Alice, and two guys I never caught names of were placed together. I saw how the two of them watched Alice's every move, but she never looked twice in their direction.

I still tried to appear as nonchalant as possible, even when my heart beat faster and faster, the staccato rhythm vibrating through my veins.

"So, are you a fan of Friends?" Jake asked, that deep voice making something tingle inside me.

I nodded raptly. "Yeah, honestly I can't even say how many times I've watched it. My dad loved it, and I remember how excited he was when they aired it for the first time. I joined in when he rewatched them when I was older."

A deep ache in my chest always appeared when I talked about him, the memory still raw. I was used to hiding it, but Jake noticed.

"Thank God, because I'm not an expert. We'll need to work together if we want to have any chance of pulling this. Will you help me?" he asked quietly. His eyes softly looked at me, easing the ache.

When I smiled back, he whispered, "Please?"

I nodded, and he nodded back, both of us beaming.

"Let the biggest fan be revealed," Jessica said, imitating a boxing referee.

The questions started simple, like: What was the name of a dancer Joey lived with? Miranda almost tripped over the table screaming "Janine." We were all struck by fits of giggles when Alice tried to imitate his "How you doing?" and when Jake and I tried to remember any moves from the famous dance of Monica and Ross, The Routine.

I pretended not to pay attention when our bodies grazed. At the end of the routine, I had to jump and Jake caught me, pressing me close. I could feel his muscles under the fabric, the faint smell of citrus washed over me, and his hand settled on my waist when we almost tumbled down at the end, panting and laughing.

When we slowly returned to the table, bowing, I noticed Brian's brow going up looking at Miranda, Miranda winking at him and looking back at us, and Alice's flushed face as she looked at me and Jake, beaming.

Needless to say that Jake and I won. We were given two celebratory fire shots which we drank to the hoots of the crowd. The liquid burned my throat and the edges of reality when I looked at the tall guy standing by my side, his ocean eyes meeting my gaze again and again.

"We should get going," Jake said. "Thanks, guys. That was fun."

Alice stood up by his side.

"It was great meeting you all," she said, smiling gently.

We all chanted goodbyes, waving. I looked at their backs, as they moved through the thinning crowd. When Jake reached the exit, he turned and looked in my direction, and when our eyes met, he shook his head lightly, a faint smile reaching his lips, and stepped through the threshold. I was still looking at the place where he stood a moment before when

Alice paused, her hand on the door, and looked around. Those gray eyes found mine, and she smiled so stunningly, so warmly that my thoughts formed one word—home.

When Alice saw the emotion on my face, her smile grew, and then she too disappeared into the night.

Chapter Three

I dreamed of a blue sea and gray sky that night. And when I opened my eyes to the string of fairy lights on the wall of my dorm room, I smiled. I knew I should not have been thinking about him, but I failed.

I failed at it the whole next week. I tried to shift my focus to my lectures but was generally unsuccessful. I tried working on assignments at night, but I was too distracted to get very far. My fingers stomping on the keyboard echoed around my room as I thought of him.

I almost ran to the bar the next Friday, putting extra care into applying eyeliner and choosing a dress. All that just to find my heart sinking at Miranda's words.

"Jake won't be here tonight," she said. "He and Alice went back to see their parents for the weekend. I see you've decided to ignore what Brian told you." She smirked.

I huffed. "No, I'm working on it."

"Maybe you shouldn't, there was a chemistry between you two last Friday."

"I don't know what you're talking about," I assured her.

Brian joined us at the table, kissing my cheek briefly.

"Miranda's right," he said. "But don't get your hopes up."

"I'm not," I grumbled.

"Good girl." He smiled and turned to Alec, who had just reached the table with two other guys.

I finished the night early, promising to meet Miranda the next day for HIIT in the park.

In the morning, we decided to skip the workout and, like many Saturdays before, we arranged to meet in the coffee shop instead. The feeling of guilt over missing the workout needed to be lessened by a buttery croissant.

The Corner was a tiny coffee joint just outside the campus with only a handful of tables inside, which were always occupied by students. They baked croissants that melted on one's tongue and they served them with napkins saying *Better than in Paris*. The coffee was also surprisingly good. The place attracted crowds on Saturday mornings and I was soon stuck standing between a groggy couple, two girls who—from the looks of it—never reached their beds the previous night, and a group of women who held colorful yoga mats.

Miranda flung her arms around me, almost crashing us both into the couple in front of us. She wore coral yoga pants that hugged her lean legs and a caramel hoodie.

"I have news," she said, panting.

"Next please," the cashier called.

We moved closer and I started reciting our order while Miranda bounced on her feet by my side. In a few moments, she was practically jumping. She pulled me aside while our coffees were brewing.

"Jake called Brian and asked for your number," she said, her face flushed.

I almost dropped the bag that held our croissants.

"What?"

"And Brian, God save his sensitive soul, gave him your number. Sorry we didn't ask you. Wait, not sorry." Miranda was ecstatic.

"You look like a madman," I said, trying to process what I had just heard.

The most handsome man I had ever seen had asked for my number. Jake had asked for my number.

"Okay," I said.

"Okay? That's it?"

"It doesn't have to mean anything," I said.

"Yes, right. He probably just wants to ask you to borrow that fascinatingly boring book you were discussing."

"That sounds more believable than what you're hinting at. Brian said Jake didn't date," I said.

"Yes, *didn't*, maybe now he does," Miranda said, wiggling her eyebrows.

"You're impossible." I laughed.

We took our coffees and went to a circular park trail that started just a few steps from The Corner. The trees were already all shades of fall, a kaleidoscope of golden red and brown. The sweet smell of fallen leaves filled the air and birds were singing farewell songs. As we walked, I tried not to check my phone more often than usual.

The text came on Monday morning.

Hey, it's Jake. Would you like to grab a coffee sometime?

I would like to say that I just read it and tossed the phone to the side, nonchalantly. But no, I jumped up and down in my tiny dorm room, grinning, and scratched my shoulder on a hanging IKEA shelf in the process.

<h1 style="text-align:center">Chapter Four</h1>

Jake stood by the park lamp post, two steaming cups on the bench by his side. He was looking at the sunset that had erupted in all shades of purples and pinks above the treetops.

"Beautiful, isn't it?" I asked, stopping by his side.

He smiled and turned to me, coming back from the world of his thoughts.

"Hi," he said and then hugged me.

Just like that, as though we were friends who hadn't seen each other for a long, long time. I froze, lifting my hands feebly. He smelled of citrus and my body leaned in, while my brain short-circuited.

"Hi," I murmured.

He released me as though nothing had happened and stretched out a cup for me.

"Decaf," he said. But when he noticed my expression he laughed. "Okay?"

"Okay," I said, and it was.

I took a sip of my decaf latte and our eyes met again, for a silent moment. It kept happening: me drowning in his steady gaze.

"Brian told me you're studying Computer Science," Jake said as we started walking. "Do you enjoy it?"

"Honestly, that was my dad's doing. He was that old-school developer who started when everything was nulls and ones, and he stayed on top of evolving technology. He always said that the future lies within computers, and I should do computer studies," I said, looking down at the pavement, putting one leg in front of another, and trying to mask the pain which always bled in my chest when I talked about him. "He said that with the right degree I would always find a well-paying job."

I felt Jake looking at me, but I could not turn my head to his side, not yet. I swallowed hard.

"But you don't really like it?" he asked tentatively.

"Not really. I only went there because I was my father's girl, I listened to everything he said. And even though he kept saying how a career is important for a woman, he never really converted his knowledge into a steady income. I was always good with books. I liked hiding in the worlds literature could create, but I followed his suggestions and here I am."

"What major would you choose if you had a choice now?" he asked.

"It's easy, English or Comparative Literature," I said and finally looked at him. "But they provide a very limited selection of jobs afterward. And with the digital world around us, my current major can supply me with not just a massive range of choices in terms of what I want to do, but also in terms of where I want to do it."

"Do you mean working from anywhere?"

"Exactly. I won't romanticize the popular images painted by the media, a freelancer sitting in a bikini under a palm tree with a laptop and surfboard by her side, no. I don't really believe in it. But the freedom of working from any place in the world, just having a laptop is one of the most crucial points for me."

"Do you want to travel?" he guessed.

"Yeah, another mainstream goal."

The shadows of the evening played around us in the trees, but the path we were taking was brightly lit. Jake listened to me, and I was immensely grateful that he didn't ask the question that was there from the first moment I started talking. The answer to that question had torn my life in two.

"Have you traveled a lot?" I asked.

He smiled and ran his hand through his curly hair. And I honestly tried not to follow his moving fingers.

"Alice was always a fan of Eastern Europe." He smiled. "All the money she ever earned, starting with mowing lawns, walking neighbors' dogs, she always said she was saving for a trip. Of course, she persuaded me to come with her. Actually, I didn't need strong persuasion, I always wondered how different nations lived, and Eastern Europe was as good a place to start as any."

"Where did you go?" I asked.

"The longest we spent in Ukraine, but we also visited Poland, Moldova, Hungary, Slovakia," he said, bending his fingers. "On her twentieth birthday, we finally went on the trip she had always dreamed about."

"And what did your parents say?" I asked.

"They encouraged us to go. As they had us pretty late in life they were avid travelers before, so yes, I think it runs in the blood. The only condition for us to go was not to pause our education, so we spent one summer there, hopping from hostel to Airbnb to couch surfing."

"How was it? How did you even speak there?" I asked.

"Because of Alice's fascination with that region—"

"That's really unexpected," I interrupted.

"That's Alice. She is what she is," he said, a warmth slipping into his words. "She started learning Ukrainian at age fifteen. So by the time we went, she spoke it pretty well, and it helped a lot. I mean tremendously. If in the big cities, you could find young people who spoke English, but in the smaller towns and everything in between it was impossible. She also tried really hard to mimic their accents. Overall, we got by."

"What was the most fascinating thing you saw there?" I asked.

"I think it was the people. They're different, they hide their smiles and hearts deep, but when you reach it, it blooms on their face. They are harder on the edges, many people struggle in places far from the cities. We went there to see different things, and Alice got what she wanted, a share of museums. You probably heard how she is fascinated by still art, architecture, food, and language. And I watched people, and that was the most captivating for me."

Jake was looking straight ahead, his mind lost in faraway places.

"So that's why I understand the need to travel," he said quietly.

I nodded. We walked in silence for a few minutes.

"Would you like to go back there? To live there?" I asked.

He shook his head, the curls falling to his eyes.

"To live there? No. To go back? Only to one place, maybe. What do you know about Kyiv?" he asked.

I searched my mind.

"Not much," I said.

He pulled his phone out of his pocket and scrolled through the gallery. And as we stood in the light of a park lamp, Jake took me to a place I had almost never heard of, showing the golden domes of churches, the long nine-story houses that looked like boxes with glued-on balconies that created an unusual kind of charm, people laughing, bridges, the wide river with green shores, Alice with a flower wreath in her silky hair. In those photos, I met the capital of a country so very far away. And it was beautiful.

Chapter Five

The next Friday I practically ran to the bar again.

Jake and Alice are here, Miranda texted me.

I had read plenty of times about butterflies in the stomach but had always regarded it as fiction—something that existed only on the pages of novels. As I walked the path to the bar, I felt my skin prickling, the air around me crackling with anticipation.

Jake texted me a few times after we met in the park. He asked how my day was, he wished me good night. That was the most romantic thing anyone had ever done for me, and my heart sang with unfamiliar songs.

When I entered the bar I saw Alice and Jake sitting at the usual table, though none of the usual faces currently joined them.

I walked slowly toward them.

"Hey," I said.

Alice looked at me with her huge eyes and a warm smile lit up her face.

Jake just stood, and a few moments later I was in his arms again. He hugged me, murmuring a greeting into my hair.

That was a most peculiar way of saying hello. And I felt my cheeks turning crimson as I leaned into him.

He released me and without saying a word pulled out a chair for me, next to him.

"Excuse my brother," Alice said, "he becomes too comfortable too fast with a person he likes. And I keep telling him that it's not always returned."

My face was burning already, but after her words, I think even the tips of my hair blushed.

"It's okay," I said, my voice trembling a bit.

Miranda and Brian stood in the far corner of the bar talking to a group of people. When I noticed them, Miranda gave me the dirtiest smile I had ever seen and a wink. A nervous laugh escaped me.

Brian motioned to our table, and the group made their way across the bar to us. In a blur of names that I immediately forgot, they seated themselves around us.

"Emily, come help me at the bar, please," Miranda said.

I stood and walked with her.

"How's your boyfriend?" she asked.

"He's not my boyfriend," I said, blushing again.

Miranda winked. "What was about that hug? Just so you know, you look sexy together."

"It's just his way of saying hello," I tried to justify.

"Just lift your head next time he says, hello, and it'll be a perfect kiss. God, I am so happy for you. All these firsts, so exciting."

"You say that as though you and Brian have been together for fifty years."

"Sometimes it feels like it, and I love that about us. But the firsts, will you tell me everything? I'm going to live my fantasies through you," her voice pitched up in excitement and she looked to me with a cheeky smile.

"Is it me or is everyone trying to embarrass me today?" I asked.

"It's you," Miranda replied and laughed.

Back at the table, Brian was talking to Jake, a determined look on his face as he waved his hands trying to explain one of his mad theories. Alice was cornered by the two men who had joined us, the raw hunger evident in their eyes. Miranda landed between them when we went back, like a mothering hen, and almost shooed the men away. Alice looked relieved.

I imagined how difficult it was to be so beautiful, always attracting attention for your looks, not the person behind them. Even when she was wearing a plain black shirt and jeans, her long silky hair wafted down her shoulders and her gray eyes flashed like a stormy sky.

"Jake told me you speak Ukrainian," I said as I sat across from her, by Jake's side.

Alice turned to me and something flickered in her eyes, her features relaxing almost immediately.

"Yes, and I'm learning Polish too," she said. "I even try writing in Ukrainian, mostly poems."

Finally. Somebody but me was blushing.

Miranda scooted over to us.

"You're like an onion," Miranda blurted.

I burst out laughing.

"You write poems in a different language, and Miranda hasn't even learned how to express herself in her mother tongue," I said.

"Oh sorry, I didn't mean the smell. I just meant, I bet you've made many men cry," Miranda continued.

"You see, she's awful with words," I said to Alice who blushed even more.

"I mean that every time I meet you, more and more layers of you appear," Miranda said quickly. "Like studying design is the first one, then still art and those beautiful photos, and now Ukrainian poems. What will be the next revelation?"

"I'm not that layered," Alice said, pushing a lock of hair out of her face.

"Can you read one of your poems to us? I'm sure no one here will understand a word you say, but I'm curious how it sounds," Miranda said.

Alice looked at me for a second.

"Please?" I begged.

She nodded and retrieved her phone, tapping on the Notes app. Alice cleared her throat and started to read, softly, so only Miranda and I could hear. But in a few moments, the whole crowd gathered around us, hushed, looking at Alice. Her voice lulled in unfamiliar flow, the words I had no idea the meaning of, rhymed, her quiet voice growing stronger. I looked at her, the impossible beauty of the woman, full lips forming the words in a foreign language and everything around dimmed, as I listened to the spell.

When she finished, the air boomed into a roar of applause. And when Alice looked up, she looked directly at me. I clapped hard as a warm feeling pumped in my veins.

Chapter Six

Good morning. Would you like to go for a walk?

That was the message I woke up to on Sunday morning. Jake never put any emojis into his texts, never shortened words. It was as though his texting skills were rusty or had never had a chance to develop in the first place.

Sure, I texted back.

I remembered Friday night, how our knees grazed under the table, how each touch sent a prickling sensation down my spine.

Jake was waiting for me at the same place; this time the sun shone through his curly hair, and he looked like a surfer— strange to see so far from the ocean. He hugged me as usual and Miranda's words echoed in my mind. I could lift my head and our lips would be impossibly close. I almost did it, sending my heart racing. But in a second, Jake released me and I took a shaky breath.

"Let's go," I said, my voice feeble, trying to hide the turmoil boiling inside me. I turned and started walking.

He asked me about books; I asked him about his degree in Bioengineering. He asked me about the places I wanted to visit; I asked him about his childhood. When I got back home my smart watch showed that we had covered ten miles on foot.

In a few days we met again, and a few days later, again.

We walked and, as all those miles died under our feet, I learned about Jake more and more, and each time I got more comfortable around him. He became a constant presence in my life.

My daily strings of texts with Miranda started revolving around my relationship with Jake. She kept bombarding me with questions.

Did he kiss you??? This text from Miranda came right when I stepped over the threshold of my dorm room after one of our walks.

No (sad emoji)
Did you kiss him?
No (crying emoji)
I'm worried, what do you do when you are together?
We talk.
Emily, I don't know if you're too romantic or too boring.
Maybe I should skip wearing a bra on our next walk... (blushing emoji)
So, when he hugs you ... oh, finally some spice, baby (pepper emoji)

And these strings were endless. Sometimes Miranda made me blush so profoundly with her dirty texts, I was sure my cheeks shone brighter than the red of a traffic light.

Jake stood at our usual meeting spot, his eyes on his phone. When I came closer, he lifted his head and his smile was dazzling.

"Has someone invented something new?" I asked.

His arms wrapped around me and he grazed the back of my neck with his fingers.

"No, it's you," he murmured before letting me go.

"Ah, just me," I said, shrugging. "Today we're doing something different."

"Are we?"

His eyes slid down to my black dress and gray tights and stopped on the Timberland boots, before going back up.

"Yes, but first, we need food," I said, pulling him out to the park exit.

When we joined a crowd at The Corner, Jake shifted from foot to foot, looking suspiciously at the croissants everyone was devouring with the coffee.

"What? Don't tell me you don't like pastry," I said, jokingly. "And you've been here, right?"

He shook his head.

When Jake registered that shocked expression on my face, he said quickly, "I'm new here, remember? And I'm not really into eating out."

"It's easy to fix. You must try their croissants. And afterward, we are going to explore the town."

Before he could say anything it was our turn to order. When I recited the order of croissants and coffee and took out my card to pay, Jake snatched it from my hand right before the cashier did and shook his head. He pulled out his wallet and gave his card.

"My treat," he said, giving back my card.

"But I dragged you here."

"You didn't, and it's not like I need to be *dragged* to go anywhere with you."

My face felt impossibly hot when I turned to take our croissants from the barista.

It was unbelievable luck that we found a free table to sit outside, the Sunday afternoon was busy as always. I watched closely as Jake unwrapped his croissant from the paper bag. The wrapping was already stained with butter, and he nibbled at the side of it, studying the dough.

I shook my head and caught his arm. "Just eat."

And I opened my mouth in the most unsexy way and took a huge bite of my croissant. I closed my eyes for a second as a savory-sweet sensation exploded on my tongue.

"I could eat these every day, three times a day, instead of every meal," I mumbled. "Unfortunate side effect would be that I'd turn into a ball, but sometimes I don't care."

Jake finally bit his croissant, chewing cautiously. But then he grinned and took another bite immediately.

"It's good," he said, his mouth full. I raised an eyebrow, and he corrected himself. "Okay, it's much better than good."

"It's as though the gods cried happy tears and golden sea nymphs wove the dough from their tears, taking the butter from the milk of holy cows," I said.

Jake chortled but took another bite.

"Where next?" Jake asked when we finished and freed the table for a non-stop chatting group of three girls.

I scratched my chin and turned to the left. "There. Let me show you my favorite places."

As I started walking, something warm touched the inside of my palm, and in a few seconds, his long fingers laced with mine. I looked down at our entwined hands for a moment and squeezed back lightly.

"So, this is an entrance to Diagon Alley," I said after five minutes of walking.

Downtown was pretty small, all my favorite spots huddled close to each other, a walking distance from the campus.

My heart skipped a bit as I silently prayed he knew what Diagon Alley was.

"Fortunately I have my wand in my pocket," Jake said and I let out a breath, chuckling.

"A wizard never goes anywhere without his wand," I replied and opened a door to *Dragontail Bookstore* for him.

The pleasant dry scent of paper coated us as we stepped inside. Shelves with books went up high to the ceiling, the dingy light enough to read the book covers gave a feeling of a library in a dungeon. A stand in the corner was full of brightly colored bestsellers, but the rows of books to the back were hidden in shadows. Soft Celtic music played in the background.

"It's a completely different bookstore from the one I work in," I whispered.

Jake nodded and stepped into the shadows, his finger gingerly caressing the spines of the books.

Our time in the bookstore turned into a contest of pointing out who had read what book. After an hour of shuffling the books, I was leading the count.

"I've never met anyone who's read so much," Jake whispered.

In the misty light of the bookshop, his blue eyes glinted of a storm, the calmness of the books around us a contrast to the inner turmoil I felt being so close to him. We were alone, the store manager lost somewhere among the rows.

Jake stepped closer, his eyes never leaving mine, and trailed his fingertips down my cheek. His thumb brushed my cheekbone as I took a step closer.

The bell chimed. A group of students walked into the bookstore, the quietness breaking with their loud voices.

I stepped back. Tucking my hair behind my ear, I looked down shyly, my heart hammering somewhere high in my throat.

Outside, I blinked into the blinding sun, the latest mystery novel by one of my favorite authors pressed to my chest. Jake insisted on buying it for me after I spent ten minutes arguing with him on the benefits of various genres.

This time as I took his hand in mine, we walked to the edge of downtown where behind a gas station stood a barn decorated with vintage signs. A plump rusty red Ford from the fifties stood in front of the entrance below big curly letters saying *Antiques*.

The musty smell of old upholstery hit us as the bell chimed when we walked in. Rows of mismatched furniture, dishes, carpets, books, boomboxes, cards, and stationary loomed in front of us. Jolly music played quietly as people roamed the shop. It was never deserted there, the things getting a second, third, or even fourth life as hands sorted through the stacks.

"Oh." Jake breathed loudly and turned to a corner with old music equipment where a light shone off the needles of record players.

We spent hours shuffling the records, browsing through creepy toys, ending with Jake buying an extremely old, ugly clown the size of his palm. I could not stop sneezing after we touched a stack of Christmas cards. And Jake chuckled when I murmured along with the words of a country song playing on the speakers.

It was almost dark when we exited the shop. We slowly made our way to the small park on the edge of the campus, our legs buzzing. The pond in the middle of the park sat just a few feet away when we settled on the huge flat boulder that was polished by hundreds of people before us. The question I had dreaded that first time we spoke finally came.

"Why don't you ever talk about your family?" Jake asked.

I looked away, curling my fingers into the moss on the side of the stone.

"Because there's nothing left but pain," I said.

"I'm sorry," he said and I felt how he touched my right hand, covering it with his, how he entwined his fingers with mine. His skin was callused, but it radiated heat which slowly slipped into me.

"My mother died when I was born. Her parents never got a chance to warm to my father, and they blamed him for her death." I sighed bitterly.

"I never even got to meet them, they just vanished, saying they wanted nothing to do with us. Dad was never close with his parents, they removed themselves from his life as soon as he left for college. So, for a very long time, it was only me and Dad, and we had a perfect time together," I smiled back tears for a moment before continuing. "He was this computer geek who found himself with a tiny baby crying in his arms. Later, I turned into more of a friend. We cared about each other, creating a world that worked for us."

I struggled to get the next words out. "Fifteen months ago, he was diagnosed with cancer. We didn't even get a chance to blink. He withered away by the second, and three months later he died in his sleep. He just kissed me good night one evening, never to open his eyes again."

Fat tears ran down my cheeks, blurring my vision. Jake draped his arm around my shoulders and I leaned in.

"I miss him so much," I whispered.

"I'm so sorry," Jake said again. He had a sympathetic frown etched into his brow.

"That's why I never talk about my family. One person kept me sane a year ago, Miranda. My Dad asked her to care for me. He loved it when she came to visit with me during the holidays. And he made me promise that I wouldn't drop out of university because of him. In the end, he begged Miranda to save me. I think he could see what his death would do to me. And Miranda did, save me that is. I was drowning and she and Brian dragged me back to the shore."

Jake kneeled in front of me, his ocean eyes shining bright, and he slowly drew a finger over my cheekbone.

"You don't need to drown anymore, you're not alone. And if you would allow me, I want to care for you too."

I just nodded. Now would have been the worst time to kiss, me sniffing, eyes puffy, nose running, but he slowly moved closer just to kiss my cheek.

"Thanks for ..." my voice trailed off, "for you being you."

And I meant it.

Chapter Seven

After that talk by the pond, something shifted in our relationship. It was as though the last walls that were built around him were crumbling, that the space between us shrank, pulling us together.

My phone chimed. *Usual place at 7?*

Yes.

I wore my sneakers that had walked hundreds of miles during the past weeks, black leggings, and a gray hoodie as I walked to the park. It was becoming chillier; winter loomed on the horizon.

Jake sat on the bench, a book in his hand. Something about robotics. I slowed and watched him, the view taking my breath away. That man made me forget how to breathe. His eyes lowered to the page, his curls covering his features.

It was as though he felt me watching him because he lifted his eyes and looked at me. There was a pause as he dropped the book onto the bench and walked to me. His eyes locked on mine and then moved down to my lips. I stopped, my heart hammering, and there he was, scooping me into his arms and drawing my chin up.

The world muted as our lips met, as his hand got lost in my hair, eventually landing on the back of my neck. And I was lost, a quiet sound escaping my mouth as his tongue grazed my upper lip. I was letting him in. The twilight closed around us as two merged into one, as his strong hands held me while my legs could not. A hot feeling stirred in my stomach.

"Breathe, Emily," he said, just an inch from my lips.

Because I didn't remember how, I didn't need to breathe anymore, only melt there, in his arms.

I took a shaking breath when his lips moved down my jaw to my throat, just to crash his lips into mine again.

After what felt like hours, we slowed.

That was how we started dating. It seemed so easy, merging into one another. But as it always is with life, it's never that easy.

Chapter Eight

We became a couple, and I could not believe my luck as I spent countless mornings and evenings with Jake by my side. He kept his promise, he cared for me. For the first time since my father had died someone chose to put me first. Jake said I fit right into his life, the missing puzzle piece he never knew existed.

A week after our first kiss, Jake invited me to the house he was renting with Alice. It was raining cats and dogs outside, the drops slicing at my skin like icicles, so our usual walk was out of the question.

I'm outside, the text pinged on my phone.

Through the glass of the dormitory entrance door I saw two lights piercing the waterfall of a rain. In a few seconds, I ran from the door to the car. The fabric of my hoodie was soaking wet. Jake looked at me, a smile cracking into his gaze.

"You look nice," he said and caught a wet strand of my hair between his fingers, planting a kiss to my jaw and sliding his finger down the nape of my neck.

Before shifting into gear, he cranked the heater up and I

shivered when the hot air blasted in my face, drawing me back into reality.

"Alice will get you something dry," he said, eyeing my outfit.

I nodded.

"You didn't mention that you have a car," I said.

"It's useless on campus, we get everywhere on foot. It's handy while grocery shopping and when we need to drive back home."

"I never got a chance to become a comfortable driver, since I always caught the train from here to my hometown, and it's not like I need to go there anymore," I said and I felt Jake's warm fingers find mine and squeeze lightly. "But my dad did leave me a car. It just sits there, covered by the house."

"Why don't you use it?" he asked.

"I guess I'm afraid."

"Of the car?" he asked.

"Of driving, the responsibility. I'm not sure I drove more than ten times after I got my license."

"You just need practice. You can drive this rusty old thing for starters and then we could go and fetch your car if you want," he said, his eyes on the road. The rain was easing a little.

"Actually, I would love that," I said, beaming.

"But I must warn you, I'm the most boring and slowest driver in the world," he said.

"That's good. Miranda and Brian drive as though they're invincible, that's why I never asked them to coach me."

"Oh, yes, I remember how our trash cans were always crumpled from Brian's bumper. He always thought it was a marvelous idea to drift at full speed into the driveway."

"Were you close when you were neighbors?" I asked.

"Not really," he said and scratched his nose. "It's difficult for me to become close with anyone, and when I was younger it was even harder. I was shy and awkward with kids my age. I guess if I wasn't that into sports in school, I would have been an easy target for bullies. But I blended, always participating just as much as needed to be able to get away with wandering off in the quietness of my own world."

There was a pause, as I processed his words. That tall, handsome man, so impossibly attractive and kind—one of the smartest people I had met—had difficulty interacting with people.

"Is it easier with me?" I asked quietly.

He looked at me for a second and turned back to the road, something warm playing in his eyes.

"It's natural with you."

And that was more than enough.

Jake pulled into the driveway by a tiny white house, just behind a canary yellow Volkswagen Beetle.

"It's Alice's," he said. "And she's an awful driver, never ask her to teach you if you don't want to receive regular speeding tickets."

While we were driving through the piercing rain, the wind picked up, and it was difficult to even open the car door, the draft pulling the door inward just to throw it out again. I caught it on time and was soaked when a gust of wind blasted rain into me. We ran to the porch and stood there panting and laughing.

The light brown of his hair got darker when wet and his curls stuck to his forehead. I lifted my hand to his cheekbone, catching the rain drops under my fingertips.

And suddenly I was not cold anymore, as warm lips pressed into mine and a slow fire lit inside me. As rain poured just feet away, slashing at the air, he sheltered me in his arms. It felt so natural to stand in his arms. Perfect.

Slow jazz music filled the house when we stepped inside. Alice sat on a red monster-sized sofa, reading. She looked up and smiled when she saw me.

"Finally, he's brought you here," she said.

"That's her way of greeting," Jake said. "Could you please give Emily something dry to wear while I put her clothes into the dryer?"

"Sure, come with me," Alice said and stood up, her movements graceful.

She was wearing burgundy yoga pants and a white silky kimono, her hair up in a messy bun. Even at home, Alice managed to look chic. We climbed the narrow staircase to a small corridor with three doors.

"The house is tiny," Alice said, leading me to the right door.

She opened it and a faint smell of vanilla hit me. The room had white walls. A big window opened toward the swinging tree outside. A wide bed with blue sheets filled almost all space, a big white dream catcher hung above it, the feathers swaying.

An ornamental rug covered the floorboards and a tiny white desk stood in the corner of the room, different prints of still art, video game graphics, and digital illustration were pinned to the white wall above it. A bookcase ran up to the ceiling, the familiar covers catching my eye.

The room was a direct reflection of Alice's personality. Her interests scattered here and there. She opened the door to a walk-in closet, which was the size of a usual cabinet and only held shelves.

"It's so cozy in here," I said.

"Thanks," she said and smiled at me, dimples playing on her porcelain cheeks. "This should be comfortable."

Alice put the clothes on the bed.

"You can change here." She brushed past me out of the door, and with a light touch on my elbow, she was gone.

I peeled off my soaking hoodie and put on a soft wool sweater, which smelled like her. The black pajama pants had a rope belt, which was perfect because I was wider in hips than she was. I looked around, feeling like Alice in Wonderland. Her sweet vanilla scent hung in the air, on the clothes I was wearing, between the books and pillows. She was all light, while I was all dark.

I shook my head, grabbed my wet clothes from the floor, and shuffled downstairs.

They were both in the kitchen, which was also tiny. Any other two would not have managed to operate there simultaneously, but their movements were oddly synchronized and they flowed past each other. Alice was brewing a glass pot of tea, while Jake spread cookie dough onto an oven tray.

"Hope you like herbal tea," Alice said, balancing a tray with three cups and the pot on a wooden serving board.

"I'm not sure I've had it more than twice in my life," I said. "Let's find out."

Alice put the tea on the table in front of the TV, poured three cups, and passed one to me. The smell wafting from the pot reminded me of mountains and green hills. She climbed onto the sofa and sat in a lotus pose, taking a sip of her tea silently.

I sat on the edge of the couch and hugged the cup with both hands, the warmth finally reaching my fingertips.

Alice scooted over to me and wrapped her fingers around mine for a second.

"You're freezing," she said.

I didn't get a chance to react to the touch because she stood up and went upstairs. In a few moments, she was back with a cream-colored fluffy wrap.

"You need to drink that while it's hot," she pointed to the steaming cup in my hand. "It'll warm you up."

I nodded and wrapped the soft fabric of the wrap around my shoulders, immediately getting even more comfortable.

The rain was slashing at the windows, the wind beating the walls of the house. As I looked at Alice, who was leafing through movies on Netflix, and as Jake came back in and wrapped his hands around me, I felt at home. Surrounded by the roar of nature and the smell of cookies and vanilla and herbal tea, I wanted to pack that moment away and save it in my memory forever.

We watched a comedy from the nineties, all of us laughing, Jake's hand always touching mine, and Alice sat on the other side of the sofa, her long legs just inches from my thighs.

"Let's make a pizza," Jake said after the movie ended.

"Like order pizza?" I asked.

"Like make it from scratch," Alice said, groaning.

"I have the dough ready in the refrigerator. You don't need to help," Jake said to her. "Alice hates cooking. But you," he said and looked at me, "can help."

I stood up, following him to the kitchen space, that in a moment filled with ingredients from the fridge. Before I even washed my hands, Jake was already rolling out the dough on a floured surface. So that's why he didn't eat out a lot.

"Wow," I said as I watched his hands working. "What should I do?"

"It seems Emily is more like me," Alice said, standing on the threshold. "I'm useless in the kitchen, I can only wash dishes. While Jake is a god of cooking."

"If you want, you can slice mozzarella," he said.

I took a brick of mozzarella, a knife, and a cutting board and stood in the corner.

"I had no idea you liked cooking," I said.

"I have a lot of secret talents and you have plenty of time

to find them out," he winked, and it was the sexiest wink I'd ever seen. It made my cheeks pink. But there was also one more thing that made my cheeks scarlet.

"Alice is right, I have no idea how to cook anything more difficult than fried eggs," I said.

"It seems that I'm cursed with women in my life who are awful at cooking," he laughed. "Just slice it and cut the slices in four. And Alice," he called her because she retreated to the living room, "you can wash arugula."

She made a funny face at him, but took a bundle from the counter, cut the rope that was tying it, and went to the sink. Our bodies almost pressed together in the tiny kitchen.

"Can you believe that every Saturday he goes to a farmers market ten miles out of town to buy fresh groceries?" Alice whispered. "How boring is that?"

I laughed.

"That *boring* helps you save your health, and that figure of yours," he grumbled.

"Okay, I know. You're going to eat so healthy with him. He's perfect, wait 'til he explains how he sorts the trash," she whispered to me and opened the drawer under the sink, where seven containers with different labels stood.

"The planet is dying and we need to live sustainably to save it. Anyway, are you ready with the mozzarella and arugula?" he asked and looked at us, three uneven slices lying on the board, and Alice only a few leaves in. The perfectly shaped pizza was lying in front of Jake, white dough covered with tomato sauce, slices of prosciutto, olives, and dried tomato.

"Yeah, the two of you are hopeless," he said and took the knife from my hand, cutting perfect slices while I backed away.

We ate pizza while watching the latest movie about superheroes, the olive oil sprinkled on arugula dripping down our fingers.

"I'm going to bed," Alice said after the movie ended, "miles to run in the morning."

"Are you a runner?" I asked.

She nodded. "Well, I'm trying to be. I'm preparing for a half-marathon."

That explained her well-defined calves, narrow hips, and perfect body. I almost said that out loud, and Alice watched me for a second longer, as if reading my thoughts.

"Bye, Emily, or," she said and looked at Jake, a sly smile forming on her lips, "maybe I'll see you in the morning."

"Bye," I said, blushing.

She waved and disappeared upstairs.

"I can drive you home, if you want, or you can stay here," Jake said, and his fingers found mine, waking a light tingle down in my core.

He moved closer, pressing his lips to the nape of my neck and biting my earlobe lightly. "If you wish to stay I'm not sure I can keep my hands away from you tonight."

I swallowed hard, as the tingle turned to fire.

"I'm staying," I whispered.

"Perfect," he said, his hand tracing the hem of my pajama pants, my breath hitching inside. He tugged on the rope, making the waistband go slack around my hips, his fingers touching the soft skin above my underwear. I lifted my eyes to him, and he found my lips, his tongue scraping mine.

"Let's go upstairs," I said, my voice shaking.

He slipped his fingers just an inch inside my panties, my heart hammering in my chest as he planted a kiss to my collarbone.

Then he stood and pulled me up. Jake tied my belt, grazing the skin below my navel. A sharp need ignited every inch of my body. My bra was suddenly too tight, the seams of my lingerie cutting my skin. I wanted to take it all off, I wanted his lips in the places that burned. I needed it.

I touched the fly on his pants, sliding my hand up and down his jeans.

"We'd need to wait 'til the morning," Jake said, "when we're alone. This house doesn't hide any noise."

I saw how difficult it was for him to say those words, my hand still on his jeans, his eyes half-closed as he rubbed back against my palm.

"Okay," I said and stepped back, bending down to pick up the plates from the table.

Jake crossed his arms and took in the view from behind. I made an effort to concentrate on the task at hand, but I'd never felt so hot, so wanted. His face was serene, but his eyes were on fire.

I picked up the plates and went to the kitchen, quickly turning on the tap and bringing my hands under the icy water.

Jake brought in more plates and stood behind me. He found my fingers and turned off the water.

"Don't make a sound," he whispered, scraping the back of my neck with his teeth. His left hand crawled under my sweater, finding my bra, his right went down between my legs, the fabric pressing into my hot flesh. My hips started moving, my back pushing against his chest, I felt him pressing me into him.

"I'm not sure I can wait 'til the morning," I whispered. I needed him under that fabric.

"God, this is difficult," he said and stepped away. I was breathing hard, my fingers still gripping the countertop.

"How are you doing this?" he asked, looking deep into my eyes.

"Doing what?"

"Pulling me, I physically can't stay away from you," he said.

Something wild threatened to tear away my composure. One more moment in those eyes and I'd be lost.

"I don't know," I managed to say.

We went up the stairs. Jake opened the left door, revealing light gray walls, a bed with dark gray sheets, a bookcase similar to one in his sister's room, a table with a laptop and open books, and a leather chair by the window.

"Can I take a shower?" I asked.

He gave me a towel and his shirt and showed me to the bathroom, the middle door at the end of the upstairs corridor.

I sat on the edge of the bathtub and took a shaking breath. The fire of burning desire was new to me. The few times I had had sex before, it had been awkward and flat, nothing like the heat that cracked between us any time our bodies met.

My thoughts scattered when I imagined the night ahead in his bed, close, almost naked.

It took time to calm the fire as I stood under the scorching hot water of the shower. The scent of his shower gel filled the room and I did my best not to bask in it.

When I entered his bedroom, Jake sat in the leather chair, a book in his lap.

"Never before has a book been so boring," he said and slowly looked me up and down.

I wore one of his numerous white shirts, it went down to my hips, revealing my naked legs. His gaze stopped at my painted black toenails.

Jake stood up and walked to me. He lifted his hand and gently pulled my hair tie. My dark strands cascaded down the white shirt.

"I'll be right back," he said.

In a few moments, I heard the shower running. I unhooked my bra and dropped it to the leather chair he was sitting in before. The crisp sheets grazed my bare thighs when I dove under the covers. The bed smelled of citrus. I realized how distinctly different the smells of the two people living in this house were, how I shed the soft sweater which smelled of vanilla, and draped on the lemon-scented shirt, how just a few feet away that girl was sleeping, and how my body ached to be touched.

Jake wore a black shirt and black briefs when he came back. I gulped audibly when my eyes landed on his bulging underwear, and he groaned when he saw my bra on the chair. He turned off the main light, sinking the room into the glow of a bedlight.

Jake stepped closer and pulled away the blanket. He bent down to kiss my knee, his fingers curling up around my black panties when he kissed his way up my inner thigh. My hands were lost in his curls, the bright blue fire of his eyes meeting mine just to move an inch higher. But when his lips were dangerously close to the place that burned, he straightened up.

"Tomorrow," he said, his voice breaking.

With shaking fingers he clicked off the switch of the bedlamp, plunging us into darkness.

I could barely breathe when he laid down by my side, still. God, that was difficult, the taunting need.

"Please touch me," I whispered.

And for a humiliating moment, he was still, only rasping breaths.

"Jake, please." I was begging.

And his hand landed on my thigh, his fingers squeezing my flesh lightly, just to move up, so, so slowly under my shirt. He took a sharp breath in when his fingers wrapped around my breast, when he found my nipple with his fingertips, when his fingers roamed. My heart was hammering just inches from his fingers when he went to slowly trace down my abdomen. He pulled my panties away, rubbing his fingers in my wetness.

A moan escaped my lips, and his left hand covered my mouth, gently. His fingers were slow, mocking, but I was losing myself anyway. I brushed against his fingers, rotating my hips, pressing his hand with mine. As he moved faster, drawing the maddening circles around the spot that burned, my moans died in his palm.

My nails dug into his thigh, and with my other hand, I was touching my breasts. I could not feel my legs as numbness spread from the tips of my toes, and with his final move, I came with a cry his hand did little to muffle.

He found my lips and I moved my hand down to touch him, but Jake caught it and pinned it above my head, his fingers wet against my skin.

"Tomorrow," he whispered and kissed me again, deep and slow. As I pressed my ear to his chest, I slipped away into sweet delirium.

Chapter Nine

I woke up to a bang. The bang of the front door. The bed by my side was empty, sheets crumpled, the sun shining on an empty space. I closed my eyes to remember his touch, how shamelessly I wanted it again, and more. Oh, so much more.

The water was running in the bathroom next door and I knew what it meant. Alice was away.

A light tingle was vibrating inside me already when I stood up and walked to the window, looking outside. The small space of a backyard was neatly maintained. Two chairs stood under an old oak, the leaves all yellow, and glistening from yesterday's rain under the fall sun.

A door opened behind me.

"You're up," he said.

A towel was draped around his hips, showing his abs. I followed the lines forming a *v* that disappeared beneath the fabric. I walked silently to him, running my fingers across the muscles when I reached him.

"Give me a minute," I breathed and ducked around him into the bathroom.

As I studied myself in the mirror I saw that my lower lip

was ruined from trying to muffle my moans yesterday. Dark eyes looked back at me, glistening. A new pink blush glowed on my cheeks. It took me a few moments to freshen up, and when I stepped back into his bedroom, Jake was standing by the window.

He turned back to me and I saw how much he needed this, how he needed me. As our eyes locked, he stepped closer, his grip tightening around the shirt I was wearing, pulling it up. The black strands of my hair fell back onto my breasts. His fingers traced the dark skin around my nipple; his eyes followed the movement.

Jake wrapped his hands around my hips and pressed me into the wall, catching the brunt of the force with his palms. I barely registered the chill of the wall on my burning skin. He kissed me with such a force that we could barely breathe. I ached. My body was firmly pressed between the wall and him. I felt the need in his lips, in his hard length pressing into me.

Our eyes met for a second, both breathing hard, and Jake gently caught my wrist, and the other, and pressed them both above my head. He took a tiny step back, and I arched my back, not wanting our skin to part. I was breathless as he slid his fingers down the length of my body, excruciatingly slowly, starting from my neck, pausing on my breasts, moving down.

Then he bent to drag my panties down, his breath on my navel. Just to stand up again. His lips were inches from mine when he gingerly rubbed his fingers between my legs. He watched as my lips parted, my eyes half closing as my head tilted back.

My skin crackled with anticipation, as I stood in front of him, naked. As his finger went inside me, a tiny noise escaped my lips. He teased me with that finger, brushing the spot that burned, but not enough, keeping me on edge, the edge that I was ready to plummet from any second.

But he released my hands and went down, propping my

leg on the chair, his lips and tongue doing the painfully pleasant job as I was slowly slipping into the mist of pleasure. It was difficult to stand as trembling waves rocked my body, so I pressed myself harder into the wall. My fingers were lost in Jake's curls. I wanted to take a breath but could not.

My body was out of control, my mind, shut, as I moaned, my body sleek as I peaked, barely managing to stand. Jake found my lips with his and I kissed my flavor away.

I placed a hand on his chest, making my way down, hooking onto the towel he still was wearing around his hips. My eyes went down to my fingers wrapping around him, sliding up and down. And then I lowered to my knees, taking him in my mouth. I looked up as he scooped my hair in his hand, wrapping it gently around his fist. He wanted to watch me, but his eyes were closing to the sweet delirium, just to be snapped open again. His breathing became ragged. "Stop, Emily, I can't ..."

And I was on my back on his bed, as he slipped a condom on. He paused, finding my gaze as he plunged inside. A tremble went through my body and a raw sound scraped at my throat. He filled me in places I never knew existed. I felt him everywhere. We were moving, a tangle of limbs, lips forming uneven kisses between moans that pushed through me. His hands were on my bouncing breasts, lightly trapping my nipples, tugging. My fingernails scraped his back as I arched. Wanting to be even closer, my legs wrapped around him.

Jake caught my hand, and guided it between my legs, softly pressing and rubbing it on my clit. *Oh god*. We moved together as our fingers added the pressure that I was not sure my body could hold. I was shattering, deep rolling waves rocking my body as I was coming, drowning in the light. And as a final cry reverberated through me, my limbs went slack. Jake fell on top of me, shaking.

Our skin was sticky, pressed into each other, as we slowly kissed.

I didn't know that it could be like that. I'd never had the chance to wake, never had a person to respond to in such a way. But I was waking up then, to the deep ocean eyes that looked into mine.

Chapter Ten

Our walks resumed. I enjoyed our hours of talking, of learning more about Jake, just to get lost in the sheets afterward, mostly in my dorm room.

As my room was the last of the usually deserted wing, and my neighbor was practically living with her boyfriend, there were no people around to hear how I could not control myself.

With Jake, I learned what my body wanted, what it responded to.

As hard as Jake and Alice tried to be solitary figures, they always shone during our Friday bar nights. It was not only how they looked, both with their otherworldly attractiveness, but how attention and energy collected around them, and with Jake, I was pulled into that spotlight.

And I started shining too. It was easy when Jake's hand was draped around my shoulders.

"I've always told you that you are a diamond," Miranda

said, her voice slurring on the edge after her third tequila shot. "But you were in the dark, now Jake is the light, and look how you're glistening."

"To the diamonds," I said, clinking her glass and downing the fourth shot.

After that shot, my vision blurred, the music becoming three-dimensional in my head. It was the last Friday before Thanksgiving, before everyone went home to their families, a painful reminder that I had no place to go.

Jake suggested that he and Alice would stay with me, and that we could have a traditional dinner with turkey and movies. I protested, saying that his parents were waiting for them, but he insisted, reminding me that I was not alone anymore.

But as I watched people talking about their plans to go back home, how they complained about long commutes and needing to see parents and grandparents, I wanted to scream. They all had it, while I had never had it in the first place. Thanksgiving with my Dad always consisted of takeouts and a string of Star Wars movies. And it was my heaven, and then he was gone. A pain sliced my chest as I once again remembered his face, my Dad, who was never equipped to be a parent but managed to make it work, for me.

The fifth shot did it, it dulled the pain, it dimmed everything.

"Whoa, we need to take you home," said Alice, who appeared by my side just as the room was tilting dangerously to the horizontal.

A blink.

I was standing.

A blink.

We were out.

A blink.

I was in the backseat of the Beetle. Jake was driving, and my head was cradled in Alice's lap.

"I miss him so much," I whispered. "And everyone is bitching about how they *have* to go home, how they *must* visit their parents. They're idiots. They don't know what they have."

A gentle touch moved my hair away from my face, running down my cheek, Alice. I looked up at her, my muscles barely obeying.

"I'm sorry," she said, barely audible. She looked at me, her eyes kind.

She tucked my hair behind my ear, grazing my neck as I closed my eyes and leaned into her touch.

The car slowed to a stop, tugging me back to reality. Jake turned to us from the driver's seat and watched Alice's hand lost in my hair. He looked up at her and smiled, hopeful. And I was out.

I opened my eyes to blinding sunlight, the glare burning my retinas. I was in Jake's bed, wearing my underwear and his shirt. The previous evening was a blurring story of people, diamonds, sadness, and a warm touch. I groaned as I tilted to the side, the alcohol still thrumming through my veins, the walls spinning.

The door frame creaked and the mattress sagged slightly.

"How are you feeling?" Alice asked.

It took a lot of effort to turn my gaze to her. Her blonde locks cascaded down a blue sweater, white leggings hugged her hips, and those eyes watched me carefully.

"You're beautiful," I said simply, my mind and my lips out of sync.

Alice laughed, the sound warming something deep inside me. "Still dizzy," she said, standing up. "I'll be right back."

I managed to sit up when she disappeared down the stairs. The room was breaking into a kaleidoscope of parts … the sun, the walls, the sheets, gray eyes.

She was back with a glass of sparkling liquid.

"It should help," she said and placed a glass in my hand, our fingers grazing. "Drink it."

I did. The fizzy sour water bit my tongue. It felt good.

"Sorry for yesterday, I shouldn't have had so much to drink," I said.

"It's okay. You were sad and alcohol is famous for numbing sadness," Alice said.

I nodded, taking a few last gulps of the liquid. In the end, it turned syrupy in my mouth. The room started rotating slower, finally taking its usual position.

"Better?" she asked.

"Yes. Where's Jake?"

"He's out for groceries, he wanted to get there early because before Thanksgiving it would all be swept clear in hours. He's planning something magnificent for the day, you know," Alice said.

"You guys should have gone home, to your family."

"We wanted to stay here with you," Alice said and walked to the door.

"We?"

She froze on the threshold, her fingers on the doorframe. Alice turned back and there was something unreadable in her eyes as she studied me.

"Yes, we."

And she was gone.

I stood up; the concoction Alice had given me worked immediately. The acrid taste in my mouth from tequila still lingering, I shuffled to the shower. There was a shelf with my stuff in the bathroom. My towel, toothbrush, face cream, and makeup. I was taking up space in this small house and only then realized that Alice could have been hostile or against me, a woman who spent so much time in her space, in her house. But all Alice ever showed me was kindness, fun, and acceptance.

The mint toothpaste finally dulled the taste of the previous night. And when I climbed into the hot shower, I remembered the soft touch of Alice's fingers on my face. I brushed my cheeks as they warmed slightly.

On Thanksgiving morning I promised myself I wouldn't sulk. I would be cheerful for the people who stayed for me, who made an effort. We decided to dress up for the day. I picked out my most festive outfit, a black dress that reached my mid-calves and had long sleeves that kept me wonderfully warm even in the freezing weather, light gray tights scattered with sparkling glitter, and dark leather boots. A silver moon pendant glistened in the light as I used a curling iron, following the guidance of a YouTube tutorial. The faded smokey eyes I had been practicing complimented my nose ring. I knew there was something wrong with me when even my most festive outfit was all dark, but it had glitter. Glitter made everything festive.

Jake whistled when he saw me.

"You look hot," he said.

The kiss inside his car deepened just a notch, his hand going up my thigh.

"Yes, okay, turkey, food, Thanksgiving," he said, breaking the kiss. "I need to concentrate on those things."

I chuckled as he drove us to their house. A warm glow spilled from its windows when we rounded the corner. The gloomy gray day outside the car only highlighted how warm and cozy it should be inside.

And it was. When the door opened, the sweet smell of oranges and cinnamon wrapped around me. The walls shone with fairy lights, turning the light inside into a mysterious one. And there was a fairy coming down the stairs, right for us. Alice was wearing a white wrap dress. It brushed the floor as she rushed down the stairs and I prayed she wouldn't trip. The pleats of the dress made it billow festively as she hopped onto the last step. Her blonde hair was in an updo. Crystal freckles were scattered on her cheeks.

She paused on the lowest step, her eyes widening just a little when she saw me. Her fingers tightened on the rail she was holding.

We were yin and yang. She was all white, I was all black, connected by glitter.

Alice walked closer to me, and I smiled, hugging her. She smelled of vanilla and something tropical, and I felt how her heart fluttered against me, just for a second, before I let go.

"Hi," she sighed.

"Do I have to wear something fancy?" Jake groaned.

"Yes," Alice and I said in unison.

"Let me finish with the food and I'll change," he said, going into the kitchen.

"It feels weird to be so made up," I gestured to my face.

"It suits you," Alice said, blushing. "Not that it's bad when you are without makeup or have straight hair. God, I have to stop talking." She shook her head. "Do you want a drink?"

"Yeah, thanks."

She turned on her heels and strode to the kitchen. Her hands were slightly shaking when she opened the fridge to pull out the bottle of white wine.

I was standing just outside the kitchen when the oven caught my eye.

"Are you going to feed an army?" I exclaimed.

Jake followed my gaze and laughed. "It's Thanksgiving, we need to be stuffed with turkey," he said.

"And pies," Alice said, pointing to a countertop where three full-size pies were sitting.

"Wow, you really love cooking."

He just smirked in reply, a bowl of salad in his hands.

We sat in the living room, the space filled with the warm glow of fairy lights and candles. Alice's easel was pushed back to the window, her latest still art composition moved into the corner, as the painting was half-finished. Jake didn't change into a tuxedo, but into light pants and a gray shirt. We made a peculiar company. Just the three of us, all nicely dressed, glasses of white wine in our hands, the table covered with food, and the light jazz music playing in the background.

"To a new tradition," I said and raised the glass.

"Hear, hear," Jake said, and the room filled with laughter.

The food melted on my tongue and the wine painted my cheeks pink. I was so thankful to be there, thankful for both of them.

"I have news to share," Alice said, rubbing the back of her neck as a smile tugged at her lips.

She looked at both of us. "I signed up for a freelance platform just a couple of weeks ago, and no one was interested in hiring a person with zero experience and a clean, fresh profile. So, I was losing any hope with all my applications going unanswered," she scrunched her nose in displeasure before continuing.

"Then a company with a vague job description replied, they asked me to show more of my work, then conducted an interview, and they liked my style. That company turned out to be one of the biggest game development companies in the world. They gave me a test task, and a few hours after I completed it, the job offer came," Alice said, her voice excited, beaming.

"They hired me part-time 'til I finish university, and if everything goes well, they can offer me a full position afterward. The main thing, the job is remote, the office being in Silicon Valley."

Jake stood up and drew Alice into a huge bear embrace. "I'm so happy for you," he said, squeezing her.

He put her down and she looked at me, beaming.

"You deserve it, Alice. Your art is so intricate and beautiful," I said, and this time she wrapped her hands around me, and I pressed her a bit tighter against myself. "Well done."

"My job is to create characters, secondary at first, but who knows ..." she said.

The three of us were standing, and one more glass of wine was downed for the artist.

We ate until we couldn't anymore. They told me weird stories from their Eastern Europe trip, and I laughed when they explained open train cars, where, when you walk down the aisle, you need to dodge smelly feet dangling from the hanging beds. They told me about bars with young people who spoke English and farms where no one knew a word of it. They talked about galleries, about the streets, the old crooked buildings, and the new twenty-story high neighborhoods where people lived packed on top of each other, how they grumbled about their gray streets, while their eyes burned.

The lights dimmed, the candles flickered as we moved to the couch. I dropped my head into Jake's lap and my feet were inches from Alice's thigh. And we watched Star Wars, and I was so warm inside, not from the food, the wine, and not from the light that hugged me, but from the two people who sat by my side.

Chapter Eleven

"I have to leave for Christmas," Jake said.

We were walking through the park, the wind blowing under my jacket. He had been nervous from the moment he met me there, the usual cup of coffee in his hand and one for me in the other.

"Yes, sure. I get it. You need to spend it with your family," I said.

"Alice is staying."

I looked at him, trying to hide my smile.

"Why?"

"She wants to get ready for her job which starts in January. She wants to practice as much as possible, and at home, there would be too many distractions, too many relatives and guests."

"Oh, okay," I said. "That's good. I'm happy she's staying."

Jake turned to me, his eyes searching my face, pausing on my smile.

"She'd be happy to hear that, and I'm sure she won't spend all the time on her laptop. You could hang out. You can stay in my bedroom if you want, so both of you won't be lonely on Christmas."

"Yeah, I'm just going to move into your house," I said and laughed. "Thanks, Jake, but I have a place to live. And anyway I heard that Miranda and Brian are staying, so we won't be lonely."

"Good, I just ..." he said and paused looking straight in front of him, a curly lock falling in his eye, "I want you to get to know each other."

"Sure, I want that too," I said.

And I really wanted it. Alice was an enigma to me, her beauty pulling me in, her movements flowy, her mind sharp, her demeanor kind and lively. But she was always reserved as if she was hiding something.

I wanted to know her secret.

Jake left two weeks after our walk in the park. He stopped by my dorm to say goodbye. Our kiss lingered on my lips long after his car hid from the view.

Back in my room, I looked around. In less than half a year I would be moving out. Moving where? Where would I work? How would I live?

When Jake was around I didn't have time to worry about it, my mind was in another place, in a warm cocoon of his presence. But now that he was away, the old anxiety crept in. The feeling was quickly swept away by the ping of my phone.

Do you want to go to the movies tonight?

Alice.

Sure.

We met in front of a movie theater, the old rumbling building just a few steps from the campus. The winter wind shook its walls as if it wanted to rip the building out and carry it away. But it was surprisingly warm inside, old lamps creating flickering shadows on the walls. We bought two buckets of popcorn and sat in an almost deserted hall—many students were already away for Christmas. The movie was a black and white romantic comedy.

In the middle of the movie, there was a squeaking sound from the back row—a girl sighing lightly. I turned to Alice, my eyes wide, cheeks turning crimson.

"Are they having sex right there? With us here?" I whispered.

Alice nodded, stifling the giggle when the girl moaned again. Either the couple hadn't seen us or they didn't care. There was no one but us and them in the hall so they didn't have much of an audience. Her cries became more insistent and then she was suddenly silent.

We turned back to the screen and I tried hard to concentrate on the movie. But there was something hot in those noises, so close. A familiar tingle woke up in the pit of my stomach. A few minutes later another set of noises started——the wet sound of lips, the grunts of the man. This time the girl was working on him.

"Oh, god, I can see the porn movie in my head," Alice whispered.

"Let's get out of here?" I asked.

She nodded and grabbed my hand, pulling us up, and all but dashing toward the exit. The couple didn't even notice us.

"It was peculiarly disturbing and hot, better than any porn in its realness, but kind of inappropriate," Alice said, laughing.

"The girl sounded satisfied though," I said.

"Yeah," Alice said and I found her watching me, embarrassed. I looked away.

"What do you want to do next?" I asked.

"Do you want to watch something in color and less, em, hot at the house? My car is just around the corner."

"Sounds good," I said.

That was the first time I was in the car while Alice was driving, and as soon as she pushed the gas pedal I remembered what Jake had told me about how she drove. Mad, fast, exhilarating.

"Do you want ice cream? We could make a detour, drive around a little," she asked.

I agreed, and in a few moments, the town was behind us. As Alice pulled onto the highway she flicked on the radio—a Nirvana song played. I turned to look at her. Her skin was glowing from the dashboard light as she sang quietly, her voice mixing with Kurt's. That was another side of Alice—free, open, relaxed. As the small car revved under my seat, going just a few miles above the speed limit, I couldn't stop watching her.

She looked at me and back to the dark road, a small smile revealing her dimples.

We drove to a tiny ice cream shop that was open 24/7 just a few exits down. It was decorated in Christmas lights, the cashier in a Santa hat looking jolly as she scooped ice cream. Alice stopped in the empty parking lot, facing the slow street.

"Aren't you sad that you didn't go home for Christmas?" I asked.

"Not really. Mom and Dad decided to invite over uncles and aunts and my cousins, and they already have kids. I'm not good with kids. I would have hidden in my room the entire time," she said and licked the chocolate ice cream that threatened to drip down her fingers.

"What do you mean? About being not good with kids?"

"I don't really like that age, when they're all whining and grabby and loud. I just don't feel comfortable," she said. "Jake's good with them, though."

I shrugged. "I think I'm closer to your views," I said.

Her eyebrow shot up.

"Eat your ice cream, the car heat melts it faster than global warming," she said.

We ended up watching the Bridget Jones movies on their huge red sofa, steaming tea cups in our hands. The wind sang outside, wrestling with the trees and throwing branches at the walls and windows of their little house.

"Do you want to stay or should I drop you at your dorm?" Alice asked, taking the cups to the sink.

"I'll stay," I said. Alice nodded, turning away to the kitchen, but I saw it, the smile.

There was a knock at the door. It dragged me out of sleep, my dream already fading away.

"Yes?" My voice cracked.

Alice opened the door to Jake's room. Her white kimono was wrapped around her and her sleeping shorts revealed the milky white skin of long legs that ended in bare feet. She strolled into the room as soon as she'd made eye contact with me.

"Look outside," she said, as she stopped by the window, a huge grin on her face.

I peeled off the warm quilt and stood up, groaning. I was not an easy riser. The ice-cold floor sent a shock up my spine.

"It's freezing, how are you walking around barefoot?" I asked as I hurried to pull my socks on.

Everything was white outside. During the night, the wind had brought snow. It covered everything in a fine white blanket. The perfect scenery for the day before Christmas.

"Do you want to go for a walk?" Alice asked.

I grinned.

It was not just a walk. We fell in the snow, we made snow angels, we even made a creepy snowman. My feet were soaking in a matter of minutes, but I didn't care. Just before we headed home we had a rather fierce snowball fight with the neighborhood teenagers.

We won—almost.

Back in the house, Alice strode directly to the kitchen, saying that we need something hot immediately.

I started peeling off my wet clothes by the front door, goosebumps covering my thighs and arms as I stood in my underwear, a slushy pile of fabric on the floor by my side.

"Can I take a shower first?" I asked Alice when she appeared from the kitchen.

Her eyes darted to my black bra, down my stomach, slid down my legs.

"Sure," Alice said, her voice hitching, as she looked away. Her cheeks were pink from the exertion outside, or the cold, or something else.

"I'll be fast," I said as I went up the stairs.

After a few minutes of scorching hot water warming my skin, I turned off the shower. Alice knocked on the door, saying that she left me dry clothes just outside.

I wrapped myself in a towel and opened the door. A familiar sweater, leggings, and fluffy socks were neatly folded on the floor.

As fast as possible I put them on, diving into the smell of vanilla. I left the bathroom, shouting, "Next!"

"There's tea ready downstairs," Alice said, opening the door to her room. "I'll be right back."

Downstairs, I wrapped my fingers around the cup and took a sip, the black tea with a faint smell of bergamot warmed me from the inside. I took a chair and moved it to the big window in the living room and propped my chin on my knee. I closed my eyes and sighed. I felt a bit tired, but warm, cared for, not alone.

Alice soon joined me, pulling her own chair up. Her huge

gray eyes studied me and I noted the long strands of wet hair sticking to her back.

"How come you don't have a boyfriend?" I asked.

She looked outside, smiling. "First, I'm a terribly difficult person to be with," she said.

"I don't think you're right about that," I said. She wasn't difficult. She was a free spirit, in every way.

"Oh, I am. And second," she took a deep breath and turned to me, worry running across her features.

"Second?" My heart picked up the speed as I asked.

"Second is that I like women, Emily. I'm gay," she said.

It made perfect sense——why she never responded to any of the flirting from guys at the bar, why she never gave them a second glance.

"You are going to make some girl so happy someday," I said and she exhaled as if she was afraid of my reaction.

"The first point still stands," she laughed.

"You're not difficult," I said again, smiling at her.

She just shook her head and looked back outside. The creepy snowman watched us from the front yard. For all the fun we had had making it, the result was terrifying.

"God, he's ugly," Alice said looking at it, the same moment my stomach growled.

"We're going to starve while Jake is away," I said.

"Nah, he took care of us. The freezer is stuffed with his lasagnas and casseroles. We just need to heat them. He made a point of writing the oven manual guide and asked us not to burn down the house."

"Sounds like him," I said.

In half an hour the steaming lasagna was in front of us. Skipping the plates, we armed ourselves with two forks and polished off the dish. The icy weather and excitement had left us ravenous.

Chapter Twelve

Miranda invited everyone who stayed in town to Christmas dinner at their house. We had planned to do Secret Santa so I stood outside with a big bag of presents. Feathery snow circled around me as I waited for Alice to pick me up.

Her Beetle was visible from a massive distance as it crawled along—its sunshine yellow exterior contrasting with the snowy roads. She stopped right at my side and threw open her door. She put on her white beanie, her long hair flowing in waves from under it. She was wearing an enormous white coat and gray UGGs, her hands hidden in fluffy mittens. Alice circled around the car and threw her arms around me.

"Happy Holidays," she said, all smiles, the dimples playing at her cheeks.

I laughed. "Hey."

She opened the trunk and it was full of presents, all packed in colorful wrapping paper. I placed my bags beside them.

Inside, an old Metallica song was playing quietly—as quietly as Metallica can be anyway. The smell of chocolate hit my nostrils as she closed the door and took off the mittens.

Two cups were placed in a holder and a small bag of Hershey's Kisses sat on a dashboard.

She took the cups and put one in my hands.

"Today's a big day: the hot chocolate day," Alice said, in an official tone. She was radiant.

We clinked our cups together, or bumped them together at least. The plastic made no sound and Alice whispered, "Clink," before she took a sip from hers. I did the same. The sweet taste of hot chocolate filled my mouth. It was sprinkled with spices—cinnamon and vanilla. Alice took the Hershey's from the dashboard and popped two of the chocolates into her mouth.

She dropped the bag in my lap.

"Enjoy," she said and winked at me.

Another Metallica song was starting up in the speakers. I cranked up the volume as Alice shifted into drive. She was already bobbing her head to the rhythm, tapping on the wheel, and when the lyrics started she opened her mouth and sang *Whiskey in the Jar* along with the front man.

This was the strangest start of a Christmas I had ever had. A girl in white with deep gray eyes, who sang by my side to the guitar riffs, in a car that smelled like a candy store I visited as a kid. Alice turned to me when she stopped at the traffic lights, and I smiled back at her, opening my mouth to sing, because I knew every word of this song, every pause and change, remembering as my Dad bellowed it. A memory of him squeezing my shoulder, smiling too, and singing washed over me. As we sang along, I felt him. He was right by my side.

There were fifteen people crammed into Miranda and Brian's house. It was difficult to find a place not only to sit but to stand.

Christmas songs played from a portable speaker the size of an old boombox. I snapped a picture of the room and a selfie of me and Alice and sent them to Jake. He sent one of him back, a selfie with a long table of smiling faces in the background.

"It seems that everyone who could have gone to my parents showed up," Alice said, looking at the picture.

"You have a big family," I said, counting at least thirteen people in the photo.

"These are only those who live within a five-mile radius of my parents," she said, shaking her head. "And there are kids at a different table."

Alice made her way to the punch bowl, taking two red plastic cups and filling them up. She gave them to me to hold.

"I need to use the restroom," she said and disappeared down the hall.

Miranda held a cup in her hands as she spoke to her sister, Mary, who lived two hours away. Mary was wearing black jeans with leather boots, a cream tank top, and a leather jacket to match the boots. Her lips were blood red, the auburn of her hair darker than Miranda's. I had only met her a few times. She was a few years older than us and worked in public relations at a famous music label. She drove a classic Ford pickup—red and shiny and perfectly kept—which I was sure was parked in the single garage, pushing Brian's old Hyundai into the snow outside.

Miranda told me that Mary had had a three-year relationship with a woman who she met in university, but that the woman left her for a man and they were happily married with a baby on the way. It broke Mary's heart, and from that time she swore off the relationships, skipping from girl to girl. Being in the music industry, there was an endless supply of willing candidates who wanted to get a taste of Mary's full lips.

But although her love life was screwed by the broken heart,

she had a kind soul and was easygoing, making it simple to be around her.

I reached Miranda and threw an arm around her shoulders.

"The house is charming," I said. "I see Brian won you over on that deer."

Miranda complained for days that Brian wanted to place a big shining deer into the hall for the party, saying it would make it fun to watch drunk people stumbling around it.

"Oh, don't remind him," Miranda said, looking at Brian who was standing in a group of guys on the other side of the room. "Do you remember Mary?"

"Yes, hi," I said and she shook my hand.

"Who is that beautiful creature who came with you?" Mary asked, her eyes on Alice, who had appeared from the hallway, scanning the room.

"It's Alice, my boyfriend's sister," I said, waving at her.

When Alice saw me, she smiled a little and made her way through the crowd. Almost everyone in the room had met Alice earlier and it was fun to see how the men still followed her every movement, but I finally knew why she wasn't paying attention to them.

But it was different with Mary, she watched Alice's every step until she reached us, her deep green eyes flashing with something I struggled to recognize. I watched closely when Miranda introduced them, and I saw how Mary's eyes widened when Alice was close, how her gaze slid down her body, pausing on her chest, her hips, and looking back up. I noticed how when they shook hands, Mary grazed her thumb over Alice's wrist, finally making Alice aware of the femme fatale in front of her. Just for a second, their eyes met and Alice looked at me, moving to my side and hooking her elbow through mine.

I wanted to step between Alice and Mary's smoldering

gaze. I wanted to shield Alice, even though I knew Mary—and she was not in the habit of hurting people. She was all about fun, and if Alice wanted to have some fun ... My mind trailed to a closed bedroom door, red lips trailing Alice's collarbone, moving down. I shook my head and took a few gulps of punch, which was spiked with an elephant's dose of alcohol. It made my eyes water.

It was not my place to think about what happened in Alice's bedroom, or with whom she shared it. But as I tried to wash away those thoughts, warm fingers wrapped around my own.

"Slow down, tiger," Alice said, looking at me. "I tried this potion, and it's a killer. Miranda, do you want us all crawling in half an hour?"

"Oh, I want to see some fun," Miranda laughed. "And some dark sides of people," she whispered.

"Evil," I said, noticing how my cup was half empty already, and how the room swayed a little.

"Let's play Secret Santa while everyone can stand," Miranda said, loudly.

A few days ago Miranda sent everyone a link to Secret Santa online and a guy I had met a few times before was my giftee. I asked Jake for a few suggestions, and he sent me a list of ten items. I chose cold beer coats and a travel poker set.

It was difficult to guess, people shooting names at random, but it was fun, and it was a good way to finally be reminded of some names I always forgot.

I got a beautiful canvas with a Van Gogh Starry night paint by numbers from Miranda. Alice got a pink leather planner for the next year from a shy girl I had met a few times before. Brian got a box of Christmas briefs from Mary.

When it was all over and everyone was gazing at, trying on, or playing with their new toys, I found Alice and offered to drop our gifts at the car.

"I'm afraid that some drunk might step on my new hobby in a few hours," I said.

She gave me the car keys and I ventured out to find my jacket. I walked the few minutes to her car. There were so many guests at the house that the yellow Beetle stood farther than I remembered. The snow had picked up and it was covered in a fine coat of white already.

I dropped the presents on the back seat and made my way back to the brightly lit house. When I stepped closer I heard cheers and whoops, and when I stepped inside I noticed that someone had hung mistletoe in the hall and that two people were standing under it. I didn't want to register how my heart sank when I saw who it was.

Alice and Mary.

People circled them, clapping. Alice was relaxed when she moved to kiss Mary's cheek, but a few inches before she could reach her cheek, Mary slid her fingers under Alice's chin, turning her face and landing her lips on Alice's. Alice's muscles tensed. Her fists curled. And I watched Mary's hand encircling Alice's waist. I wanted to rush to them, but before I got a chance to take a step forward, it was over. Mary was smiling, the crowd was roaring, and Alice stood there with her fists still clenched, red on her lips.

Mary made it look sexy, she made everything look sexy. And she laughed away, joining the spirited and drunken group.

There was no denying the pain in my chest when their lips met and, even as Alice was surprised, I saw how her lips parted, inviting the kiss.

I took a step back, and Alice found my eyes. They widened when she saw me, a thousand emotions written on my ashen face. She was my friend, why was my body reacting to her being kissed with such violence? I wanted to hurt Mary, I wanted to shield Alice. I wanted her all to myself, to be her *only* friend. And I felt nauseated by all these thoughts. She deserved happiness. She deserved fun. Mary could give her fun. My stomach clenched at that thought, and I bolted upstairs to the bathroom, closing the door behind me and turning the lock with a thunderous click.

I pressed my fingers to my flaming cheeks, trying to calm the fire of the unwelcome feeling. I hated myself so much in that moment. As I looked in the mirror, the dark waves of my hair framing my dark eyes, my nose ring glistening in the bathroom light, I realized I knew the name of what I was feeling. With burning clarity, I realized that I was jealous. Jealous of Mary's lips pressed into Alice's, her hand around the slim waist of my friend. And I had no reason to feel that way. I was with her brother, Jake. Oh, Jake. I missed him, I needed him, but he was not the one who could help me untangle my feelings. No one could.

I dropped my head into my hands as someone rattled the handle, an urgent banging on the door.

I glanced at myself again and exited the bathroom, getting an accusatory look from one of Brian's pals.

I walked downstairs slowly, finding Miranda in a group of girls crowded on the sofa. Alice was sitting on a big pillow on the floor, Mary's knee almost touching hers as she sat in a lotus pose by Alice's side.

I felt Alice studying me, her eyes following my movements. I looked briefly at her. Her face was stricken with worry, but something new blossomed there, something light and warm.

I smiled weakly and turned my gaze to Miranda.

They were discussing a new series on a streaming service. It seemed lately that everyone was talking about it. I turned and made my way to the punch bowl, pouring myself a generous amount.

Someone bumped me from behind, and as I turned I

heard Brian apologizing, grabbing the scoop I had been holding a second ago.

"Hey," he said, his voice so unusually stretched. "Where's Jake?"

"He's back home with his family."

"Shame," he said and took a huge gulp of the orange liquid. His eyes turned back to the girls sitting on the floor. "I see Mary found herself a friend for Christmas night. That kiss was hot. And I don't mean anything when I say that you need to hide your feelings better. I was standing across from you when they kissed, I saw how your face changed."

I turned to him, my eyes going wide.

"What?"

"Nothing," he said just as Alec appeared by his side. He just winked at me and disappeared down the hall.

The party was not going as I had planned. People around me were getting drunker by the second thanks to the concoction Miranda had cooked up. My own horizon had started to tilt a few hours before. I talked to people, drawn to conversations I didn't care about. At some point, the music turned loud. Bodies swayed, the house vibrating. I looked around and couldn't find a familiar face. Miranda, Alice, Mary, Brian, they had all disappeared.

I went upstairs and found Miranda and Brian kissing loudly by their bedroom door, his hand under her sweater. Their bodies were so close, pressed into each other. And in a second they disappeared into the bedroom.

I used the bathroom and went downstairs. The bass boomed through the house and felt heavy on my chest. I realized I wanted to flee all of it. I tried to find Alice, asking people if anyone had seen her.

"She's outside with Mary," someone replied.

Of course.

I found my jacket in the pile and yanked it free. It was only fifteen minutes by foot to my dorm, so I bundled myself up in my coat and crossed through the mayhem. I stopped with my hand on the door handle, looking outside. Alice was sitting on the porch with Mary, a thin cigarette pressed to Mary's blood lips. Her eyes were on Alice, while Alice looked away, across the street. I jerked my hand away and looked back. Even if I used the back entrance, they would see me crossing the snow-covered lawn.

Mary moved closer and her hand covered Alice's. My heart sank. And I was too drunk to register that feeling or make any sense of it.

I turned away and crossed through the house, pushing the back door open. Somebody turned the volume down and it revealed a soft murmur of voices.

Once outside I looked around, grabbing the banister, my world tilting. Damn, there was no way out, only through the front of the house.

I pulled my hood up and stepped onto the fresh snow. No one had been out there that day. The snowflakes drifted around in a slow dance as I stopped, swaying. Why did I drink so much?

One foot in front of another, and I'd be home soon.

Of course, they saw me.

"Emily?" I heard Alice's voice.

I turned to face them.

"Hey, I ..." I mumbled, my voice slurring, "I'm going home. Bye. You two have a great night."

Mary laughed lightly while Alice stood up and crossed the lawn, finding my shoulder and tilting me back upright.

"God, you're drunk."

"Nah, I'm fine," I said. "Go have some fun."

"I'm going to take you home."

I shook my head. "I can take care of myself."

"Can you?" She asked as her face swayed in front of me.

Alice turned to Mary. "We're leaving." Mary nodded. "Uhm, thanks for the talk."

"Sure," Mary said and butted her cigarette in a red cup in her hand.

Alice wrapped her hand around my waist and we walked slowly down the street, her hand steadying me.

"You still have her lipstick on your lips," I said.

"Does it bother you?"

"No," I said and she looked at me, her brow curved upward. "Yes. I don't know. You didn't want that kiss, I saw how you tensed."

"It was just a kiss, under stupid mistletoe."

"You could have had so much more tonight with her."

"I know."

We walked slowly, the yellow Beetle peeped out from under the snow. "I'm sorry," I said.

"For what?"

"That you have to leave now, because of me. You can go back, you know."

Alice stopped and turned to me. The light from the decorations on the house played on her cheeks. "I don't want to go back, okay? I don't need it, I don't want her."

"Who do you want?" I asked.

She just shook her head, looking away into the night.

"There are snowflakes on your lashes," I whispered and swayed again, my hand landing on the Beetle's hood in the snow, stinging.

"What the hell did Miranda put in that punch?" Alice said, opening the door for me and holding my head while I fell into the passenger seat.

Sitting in the cold car should have cleared my mind a little, but as soon as we were moving and the heater started sending waves of hot air around, my eyelids suddenly became very heavy. The world dimmed.

"Emily, you have to wake up," a voice said. I opened my eyes and slowly looked around. The car was parked in front of my dorm. "You need to show me the way. Where are your keys?"

"Here," I said and pointed to my pocket.

Alice nodded and turned off the engine. Cold air rushed into the car when she opened her door. She thankfully closed it behind her. She crossed quickly to my side and opened the door for me, the icy air blasting me again.

"Come on, Emily," she said and lowered herself to me.

Surprisingly, the short ride sobered me just an inch, and I stood up, her hands holding mine. I marched to the entrance and opened the door, Alice right behind me. We managed to climb the four flights of stairs uneventfully, and in a few moments, I was in my room.

She looked around, taking in the fairy lights, the monochrome decorative pillows on my bed. Luckily my room was not a mess as it often was. Her eyes lingered on the photo of my Dad I had on the table, and then on the one on my shelf where we were laughing together.

I sat on my bed, almost missing it, and bent over to untie my shoes. My jacket fell to the floor from my weight on the bed. God, it was difficult to control my movements.

"Do you want to undress?" Alice asked as my head finally connected with my pillow.

"No," I murmured. "You know, the room is tilting like I'm on a ship."

"You're not." She laughed.

"You have a beautiful laugh," I said, turning to the left, slowly drifting away.

Alice sighed from far away, and in a few moments, she draped a duvet around me.

Even as the world was tilting, as I lay down behind my closed lids, I saw bright spots dancing in an intricate pattern.

Warmth spread inside my chest and I felt that I was cared for in a way I hadn't felt for a long time.

"Merry Christmas," she said quietly.

I wanted to say it back, thank her, thank her for being with me but the sleep dragged me into its depths.

Chapter Thirteen

I cracked open my eyes; the bright light that sliced at my retinas made me groan. I covered my face with my hands, rubbing my eyes and my forehead. Every cell of my body screamed *water*, and my limbs were so reluctant to move. But I turned and looked around, against the better judgment of my aching body.

I was alone. The sun filled my room with light, and as I propped myself up on my elbow and looked outside, I saw that the world was covered in a thick layer of white. It glittered so vividly under the morning light.

Something colorful caught my eye as I turned away from the window. A small pile of boxes lay a few feet from my bed, each one wrapped in sparkling paper.

Alice must have dropped them there while I was out in my slumber. I groaned again as I remembered the details of the previous night. How immaturely I had reacted to her being kissed, how inappropriate it was for me to question her while we walked back to the car. And how indescribably relieved I was that she hadn't stayed there when I left.

I grabbed my phone. It was ten in the morning. There were already a few texts from Miranda. Had she slept at all that night?

Merry Christmas!!! Where did you disappear to last night? Brian says he's hoping you didn't make a mess, but he won't give me details. I hate when you two have secrets (mad emoji), but you know I'll find out (ROFL emoji)

I groaned and typed a message to Brian: *I know where you live and who you love, stay quiet about your ideas, which are invalid by the way, or I'll find you. Merry Christmas, xoxo*

His reply came seconds later. *Yeah, totally invalid (winking emoji)*

Brian was drunk and imagined things yesterday. Hope you had a good time, cough, hot time. Saw you two by the bedroom. Remind me to ignore you next time when you complain about your fifty-year relationship. I texted Miranda.

Miranda replied instantly. *I don't know what you're talking about (blushing emoji)*

Right. I typed back. *You two are hotter than any porn movie (heart emoji) Merry Christmas!*

I scrolled down my contacts list and tapped on Jake's name, selecting the video icon.

He picked up after the third ring. Jake was smiling, his eyes fixed on the screen, his curly hair falling down his forehead. The image sent a jolt of longing through my heart. I missed him.

"Merry Christmas!" he said as a group of kids rushed around behind him, fighting with lightsabers.

"Hey, Merry Christmas," I replied. "I see you're teaching young Jedi."

"Oh, yes, I've been doing it since seven this morning. Alice texted me that you had had a rough night, something about Miranda trying to poison everyone she invited."

I grunted. "God, I'm feeling awful. I'm not sure I would

have got home safely if Alice didn't drive me. I wanted to go by foot, and even though it's close I'm afraid you'd find my frozen body when spring came. And look," I said and switched the camera to show the pile of presents.

"The big blue one is from me," he said.

"Thank you, Jake. It truly means a lot that you two are close to me."

He nodded, his smile warming my heart.

"I miss you," I said quietly.

"I miss you too," he said, his eyes looking deep into mine, breaking through the miles between us.

The perfect moment was interrupted as a lightsaber was jammed into his side and a girl with bushy blonde hair demanded for Jake to give up his powers.

"Hey, Olivia, meet my friend. Her name is Emily," he said and the girl's face appeared next to Jake's.

I waved. "Hi!"

"Is she your girlfriend?" Olivia asked.

"Yes," he said.

"She's pretty," she said.

"I'm not," I laughed. "I had a late night."

Her eyes sparked. "Did you see Santa?"

"You can't tell anyone, but actually I did!" I whispered excitedly. "There's no chimney in the place I live now, so he used a window to bring me presents. Look!" And I switched the camera again to show the colorful pile. "And just as I came home at night, I saw his red pants swinging down the window."

Olivia's eyes were the size of saucers, and she yelled: "Tom, Emily saw Santa tonight!"

And she disappeared from the screen.

Jake laughed. "It's time for you to open those presents. Merry Christmas, Emily."

After he disconnected I slid to the floor, tugging my blanket with me and wrapping it around my shoulders.

I took the blue one first, under the paper was a cream-colored sleeping gown. The silk flowed under my fingertips. So delicate.

There was a tea set from Alice, with small bags of leaves of different kinds: Tieguanyin, Oolong, Earl Grey, White tea. The golden paper revealed a dreamcatcher with white feathers. A note was attached to it: *Handmade by me* and a smiley face. Alice.

To a slim box wrapped in silver paper was pinned a note saying: *From both of us. Merry Christmas!*

As I slowly tore the paper it revealed the newest e-reader. The one I'd been saving for. A soft sob escaped my lips. I looked around at all the presents, chosen with care, for me. A light similar to the one shining outside shone within me. And I thanked anyone, real or divine, who brought those two people into my life.

I recorded a video saying thank you and sent it to Jake. I stood up, made my bed, took a shower, and dressed warmly, grabbing a bag with presents I had prepared. I marched outside, new purpose singing within me. I had to make Alice understand what they meant to me.

The prickling cold kissed my cheeks once I was outside. The sun glinted on the white sheets of untouched snow. I closed my eyes for a second and listened to the quiet morning on campus. So many students went away for holidays, and those few who stayed were still huddled inside. I gripped the railing because no one had cleaned the stairs from the night before, my boots sinking in the white powder.

It took five minutes walking on a deserted road to be out of the campus. The Corner was open, it was open every day of the year, making it not only a nice place to buy coffee but a convenient one. I joined the queue, and when I reached the counter I ordered two cups of coffee with croissants to go. Bundling the bag they gave me in a scarf to try and keep the contents warm, I walked outside and headed east.

There, someone had cleared the streets, and as I walked through the residential areas, people shouted Merry Christmas to me. I watched happy families behind windows in every state of celebration. Couples bundled in front of TVs, groggy dog walkers yawned, kids showed off presents to the neighbors. I stopped in front of a small house with a yellow car, warm light kindled in the windows. As always, slow sweet jazz music played inside. The buzzer chimed and a shadow loomed behind the door, and when it opened I saw Alice, who smiled at me softly.

"Merry Christmas," I said.

"Come on in."

As I stepped through the threshold a sweet chocolate smell hit my nose, and a second after the door closed behind me, Alice wrapped her arms around me.

"Merry Christmas," she murmured and let go of me. She and Jake had that peculiar habit of hugging me. "How are you feeling after last night?"

"Better than one would think I should be, actually," I said as I unwrapped my scarf from the paper bag. "I hope it's still lukewarm, the idea was to bring hot coffee."

Alice took the bag and opened it, the luscious croissant smell wafting from the bag.

"It's still warm, perfect," Alice said and walked to the kitchen.

A small Christmas tree stood in the corner of the living room. It had so many ornaments its branches sagged under the weight. I kneeled in front of it and carefully added a few boxes to the small pile with Jake's name on it. And a few to the right, Alice's name on them.

I turned around and noticed how she stood and watched

me, leaning on the counter.

"Are you my Santa today?" she asked.

I nodded, smiling.

"Let's drink coffee first, while it's warm," she said.

And I joined her on the sofa where she had the croissants placed on two plates.

"Thank you for the presents. They were perfect, honestly. You don't know how much that effort means to me," I said and she smiled. "And I'm sorry for last night, I didn't mean to drink so much. It's just …" that I couldn't stomach the idea of you being kissed by Mary, I wanted to say, but I didn't, my voice trailing away. "Thank you for taking me home."

Alice patted my knee. "It's okay. By the time we left not many people could stand on their own."

Mary could, I almost blurted out, but I bit my tongue on time. What did I want to hear? Alice already told me that she was not interested in her.

"I called Jake this morning," I said changing the subject. "He's been jabbed with lightsabers the whole morning."

"Yes, he's a saint with kids, and he's genuinely happy with them, you know. He's like that with family. He feels natural at these family gatherings."

I nodded as Alice studied my face, her eyes lighting up suddenly.

"Can I open my presents?" she asked. "I opened the ones from Jake this morning. He got me a pastel set of dumbbells and a matching yoga mat. I'm going to have such glamorous workouts now," Alice said and wiggled her eyebrows.

She slid to the floor and scooted along until she sat near the tree.

"It's nothing special," I murmured as she tore at the wrapping paper.

It was a white scarf. It had been so soft when my hands connected with its fabric in the store that I immediately thought of Alice. She wrapped it around her neck, and pressed her cheek into it, closing her eyes.

The next bit of wrapping hid a vintage photobook of still art prints. Alice's eyes went wide as she leafed through the pages.

"It's so beautiful," she whispered, her eyes glued to the pages.

"I'm glad you like it."

The last one was a small blue box, and my heart hammered as she opened it. A silver pendant of the moon lay on some silky cushioning.

She stared at it for a few seconds, stroking it with her finger. Alice lifted her grey eyes to me.

"You have something similar, right?" she asked.

"Yes. Well, identical actually."

And in a blur of movement, I was embraced again, her warm body pressing into mine. "Thank you," she whispered, her breath tingled in my ear.

I tried to laugh but couldn't. Instead, I lowered my head to her shoulder, resting it there. Her hands went slack in surprise but pulled me closer after a moment.

It was just for a few short moments, then I lifted my head, whispering, "You're welcome."

She dropped her hands into her lap, moving away, but she watched me all that time.

"Emily?" she said almost inaudibly, her lips barely moving.

I stood abruptly.

"Let's go for a walk," I said, breaking the spell that wrapped us.

"Yes, sure. Give me a sec to change," she said and disappeared upstairs.

I dropped my head into my hands taking a deep breath. What was happening? My heart pounded in my chest as I went to the door, pulled on my jacket, and walked outside, into the bright winter day.

Chapter Fourteen

One of those Christmasy songs played in Alice's car as we sped down the highway the next day. We both sang along, out of tune, giggling. Alice's fingers were smudged with traces of dark paint as she drummed them on the steering wheel.

Miranda had called the day before and with a still groggy voice suggested we go to a club in a few days, just to dance. No more booze. "I need to dance it out of my system," she said.

Alice was ecstatic. She said she had nothing to wear and that we should go shopping. When she noticed my raised eyebrow she shrugged. "It's going to be fun."

I didn't want to spend money on clothes, but as Alice expertly peeled through the rows of garments, she picked out a few outfits that could potentially make me change my mind. We managed to snatch two changing rooms opposite each other.

The first outfit Alice made me try was a black leather miniskirt with a neon turtleneck. When she opened the door to her changing room, Alice was standing in a furry leopard print jacket, knee-high boots, and a slip dress.

She watched me closely as my eyes slowly slipped down her body. When I noticed she wasn't wearing a bra I paused on the faint outline of her breasts a moment longer.

"This is sexy," I said. "Maybe too sexy."

She ran her hand over her waist, her hip. I swallowed hard, my eyes glued to her palm as it glided down the fabric.

"You think so?" she asked.

"Yeah." I breathed out, making myself look away. "I think this neon color is too much for me."

I felt her gaze on my body, assessing. "You're right."

Next on my rack was a black sheer shirt and skinny jeans.

"I feel naked," I said to Alice, who stood in an oversized jean jacket, a belt hugging her waist.

This time she watched me closely, my black bra visible under the shirt. My skin prickled under her gaze as something unfamiliar flickered in her eyes.

"Yes, it leaves too little to the imagination," she said and my cheeks burned.

"Next," I said and closed the door to my changing room, as the corners of her lips went up, smirking at me.

The next was a black V-neck dress that brushed on the floor even when hung high on the hook. It had an intricate lace covering the back. When I noticed the price tag I gasped. The gown was for a ball, not a club.

As I stripped out of my jeans and shirt my hands moved to the dress. I slipped it over my head. It was definitely meant to be worn without a bra, so I pulled mine off.

I needed help. There was a small row of buttons on the back, hidden in the lace. I drew a hand across my chest and peered out, only my head sticking out of the door.

"Alice?"

She opened the door to her fitting room. Alice was wearing an outfit only she could pull off: a white midi dress that sat tight on her slim body, hugging every line, wrapping around every curve.

"If you want the attention of every man in the club on you, you should wear that," I said.

"You know I don't want that."

"I know," I said. "Please help me."

And I opened the door wider. The black fabric sat loosely around my shoulders and waist as I tried to hold the dress up. I turned around.

"I don't know what they think about when creating the dresses one can't zip without help," I said.

Alice crossed the hall and stepped into the tight space of my fitting room, closing the door behind her.

She met my eyes in the mirror as I pulled my hair over my shoulder. An unexpected tingle ran down my spine, just a few inches from her fingertips. Alice gathered the fabric, tightening it in front, forming the perfect cleavage, and fastened the first button, and the second, but before the third she paused.

I watched her in the mirror, as her eyes were drawn to my back. The lightest touch landed on the middle of my back, slowly trailing down. She was still not meeting my eye in the mirror, and I breathed out slowly, closing my eyes. All my senses focused on the spot where her warm fingertips connected with my skin.

And then she fastened the three last buttons.

"This dress is not for the club for sure," she said.

I nodded as I watched her watching me.

She shook her head lightly and opened the door, taking a step back. The dress made me feel something I hadn't felt in a long time: beautiful. I was beautiful in it. In the front, it showed just enough skin to leave anyone wondering what was hidden, and the back was like an ink painting, the threads forming a delicate pattern.

Alice moved closer and undid all the buttons down my back before she disappeared into her changing room. As I clicked my own door shut I exhaled, and closed my eyes, pressing my bare back to a cool wall.

In the end, she bought a vermillion pantsuit with a black crop top. The unease I was afraid would come between us never came.

Chapter Fifteen

I was wearing a black shirt, jeans, and a leather jacket the next evening as I walked to the club. The music pulsed even outside the building that stood isolated, circled by a parking lot.

Miranda wore a golden dress with a huge plush coat. Brian's arm wrapped around her shoulders and an image of them disappearing into the bedroom flashed in front of me. The vigor I saw between them that Christmas night was far from a stale relationship.

A few of their friends were fervently discussing something just a few steps away when Alice rounded the corner and joined us.

Despite the statements that it was time to ease up on the alcohol, each one of us held a cocktail ten minutes after we had entered the club. The drinks were cheap, a mix of low-quality alcohol with sugary juice or tonic, simple, but mind-melting. Someone new was playing the music, an unfamiliar DJ. It reverberated in my bones, making me sway.

After our first cocktails were finished, Miranda took my hand and Alice's and drew us closer to the dance floor. It was far from packed, so I felt exposed, shy. And my focus was still sharp—it was far too early to dance. Miranda, who never minded anyone or anything on the dance floor, started moving, her hands drawing intricate lines in the air.

But Alice, God how she moved, flowing. Her body pulsed to the rhythm, relaxed. She noticed me looking at her and, smiling, motioned for me to dance. I shook my head and gestured to the bar, it was definitely too early for me to dance.

I ordered water and sat on a bar stool, close to where Brian was talking to Alec. But a few moments later Alec joined the girls on the dance floor, drawing two more guys with him. And as people filled up the club, more and more crowds packed the space in the middle, limbs swaying, hips moving.

I watched Alice's graceful moves, her hair reflecting the color of the flickering lights.

"So, what are you going to do?" Brian asked, almost shouting into my ear.

"About what?"

"About you and Alice," he said, following my gaze to a dance floor. My heart skipped a beat.

"What about us?"

He turned to me.

"As I said before, you have to hide your feelings better. The moment you are alone and you think nobody is watching you, it's written all over your face."

"Brian, what are you talking about?"

"Oh, so you still haven't admitted it to yourself. There's this longing on your face, a mix of awe and want. It's romantic, Emily. You're with her brother. Isn't it kind of wrong?"

In the warm air of the club, an icy chill ran down my arms, and I shivered, hugging myself.

"There is nothing romantic between us," I said.

He snorted. "Yeah, sure. Alice is a lesbian. And on

Christmas night, Mary practically begged her to … you know, but every time Alice removed her hand, stood aside, her eyes always looking for you."

"You're imagining things," I said.

"Okay, keep telling yourself that," he said, lifting his hands in defeat. "But if you don't stop swooning soon, everyone will notice. And just wait for the tornado of Miranda. And Emily, Jake is happy with you, honestly happy."

"I'd never hurt him," I said.

"Not intentionally, no. But—"

The panting body of Miranda slammed into mine, wrapping her fingers around my bottle of water, breathing hard.

"God, I'm thirsty," she said.

"Take it. I need something stronger anyway," I said looking at Brian.

I ordered a shot of tequila and downed it, locking eyes with Brian who shook his head. I lifted my gaze to the crowd and went to the opposite side, where Alice was dancing with a group of both familiar and unfamiliar faces. I closed my eyes, music flowing thunderously in me, disturbing every sense. I started moving.

The tracks changed, one mixed into another, the rhythm getting faster, the crowd getting denser. As we moved deep into the night the familiar faces disappeared, except one. Only one. My eyes were glued to her face. We moved so closely that our bodies almost touched.

Her hand found mine, squeezing lightly and releasing it, circling around my waist, moving just an inch closer to me. I lifted my right hand, catching the edge of her jacket, slipping underneath. Her crop top hid so little of her skin. I ran my fingers just above her navel and as I watched her lashes fluttering, her lips parting, I realized how deep in I was. Brian was right. It was wrong, very wrong.

"I'm sorry," I said, backing away, and bolted through the crowd. I took my jacket at the exit and pulled out the scarf I had stuck into the sleeve of it before wrapping it around my neck. I made it outside. The cold air bit my cheeks, assaulting every warm cell of my body.

There were a lot of people outside, talking, laughing, drinking.

I sat on the curb, dropping my head into my hands, my heart pounding.

"We need to talk," Alice said, coming up behind me. She shivered as she pulled on her coat. "Please."

I nodded and stood up, moving away from the club into a dark alley between two buildings. As shadows enveloped us, I turned to her.

"So, you see it now, don't you?" she said.

I nodded. "I can't fight it, I can't fight you, Alice."

"Then don't. You probably don't remember the moment we met, but I remember it with crystal clarity." Her voice hitched. "For me, it was the moment that tore my life in two, one part before you and one after. And then you started dating Jake, and I was so deeply happy for you two. But the more time we started spending together, the more I understood how ..." she breathed in sharply, "how drawn I was to you."

"Alice, I—" I started to say, but she went on.

"You saw how I fought it. You were so divinely beautiful in that dress on Thanksgiving, it was like you were taunting me. I can't stop looking at you. My eyes find yours in every room. You've seen that. And this last week when Jake went away you were constantly by my side, every day Emily." She inhaled sharply, struggling to catch her breath in the torrents of emotion.

"Do you remember the day we spent in the snow? And how you dropped all your clothes on the floor, standing in your lacy underwear by the door. I wanted to touch you so badly, run my fingers over your arms, legs, stomach. I fought it. Do you remember?"

I nodded. I remembered the look on her face very well. Hunger.

"You were a friend, all this time, a good friend. But you slipped," she said.

"How?" I asked, my voice shaking.

"Mary." She laughed. "I saw what that kiss under a mistletoe did to you. All evening I saw how you tried to grapple with feelings that surfaced after she kissed me."

Anger surged in me at the reminder and I all but spat, "I hated it. I hated how she acted so familiar with you, always touching you. And then the two of you were talking so comfortably outside."

"We were talking about you."

"What?" I breathed.

"She asked me how it felt to have a crush on my brother's girlfriend. She did suggest I have consolation sex with her though."

My fingers flexed into a tight fist. Alice saw it.

"Of course I refused. How could I not? When all my thoughts were glued to one person, who got dead drunk, by the way, after seeing me getting kissed by another girl."

"I didn't get drunk because of you," I said.

"Liar," she whispered, softly.

And she was right. I remembered every time she looked at me with that longing, only now seeing it for what it was. I pressed my back to the wall of the alley. The bricks icy cold against me.

"You should have kept it to yourself," I lashed.

"I did, it was you who didn't."

She stepped closer to me, and lifted her hand to my face, catching a strand of my hair. Alice smiled. And it was the smile

I loved, kind and loving. She drew her fingertips over my brow, my cheek, and I hated how my eyes closed just for a second, imagining how it would feel to kiss her. But it would never happen. I couldn't hurt Jake that way. And I knew that if I touched her lips with mine I wouldn't be able to stop. I knew it would hurt her, him, me.

I opened my eyes and saw her watching me. She placed a hand on the wall behind me, taking one step closer. I could feel her sweet breath on my face. And it felt so right, while it was so wrong.

"I can't, Alice," I said, and stepped to the side.

A soft sob escaped my lips when I saw the pain on her face. I knew I had hurt her, but there was no other way.

"I'm sorry, but I can't," I said as I turned around and walked away.

"Emily." A whisper, a plea. I didn't look back.

I gave a wide berth to the crowd standing by the club, avoiding eye contact with everyone. I looked down all the way to my dormitory. When the building loomed around the corner I sniffed, only then noticing the hot tears that ran down my cheeks, turning to damp cold when they reached my scarf.

The building was quiet, my steps echoing on the staircase. Inside my room, I peeled off my clothes dropping everything to the floor. I was cold, shaking when I lifted the blanket and dove under it. My body curled into a tight ball as I sobbed, muffling the sound with my pillow. I hated myself for falling in love with both brother and sister. I knew how wrong it was. I thought relationships were supposed to be easy, light. That was not what I was dealt.

Sometime in the night, I drifted to sleep. I was grateful there were no dreams.

Chapter Sixteen

My phone chimed, dragging me back to reality. I turned and pressed a hand to my chest—it hurt as though someone had punched me. Ah, right. It was me with my stupid decisions.

I unlocked the phone, catching my reflection on the screen. Puffy red eyes, swollen cheeks.

And in that message, I got what I deserved.

I'm back. We need to talk. Please come to our house at noon. Jake.

To be there he must have driven back from his parents' during the night. I assumed Alice had called him, and told him what? The truth?

I pressed my fingertips to my eyelids. I stopped breathing. A truck drove past outside. I heard distant laughter, my heartbeat. In a few hours, I would lose the person who mattered so much to me. He made me so happy, I loved being in his presence, in his arms. So I betrayed his trust. I fell for his sister as if loving him was not enough. But it was enough, and I didn't know how my heart could love two people at the same time. Was it a sin, greed, lust?

I took a deep breath. My mind said that it was wrong, but my heart sang a quiet song when I imagined being with them.

I squeezed a blanket to my face, inhaling the smell of fresh linen. It didn't matter anyway, what my brain knew, what my heart sang about. It all would end in a few hours. The tears came again, slow, burning.

~

I stood in front of their house. Fresh snow covered its roof again, its garden. The crooked snowman stared at me accusingly.

The small yellow car was blocked by Jake's old Toyota.

I smiled at it as if greeting an old friend and walked up the stairs.

There was no music inside the house this time as Alice opened the door for me. I met her eyes for a second and dropped my gaze to the floor. She looked pale.

I crossed the hall and went into the living room and sat on the edge of the armchair. On the table stood a bowl of freshly made cookies, a steaming pot of tea, and three cups. I looked at it, and with a slicing pain realized it was the last time I'd be sitting there.

Alice sat on the far end of the sofa, the deep gray eyes I knew so well on me. I couldn't bring myself to look at her, still looking at the cups.

There was shuffling upstairs, then steps as someone came down the stairs. Jake. I lifted my eyes to him, and my heart cracked as a slow tear ran down my face.

"Emily," he whispered and rushed to me.

But Alice caught his hand and shook her head, motioning for him to sit by her side. He did.

I swiped the tear away, looking back at the cups.

"Alice told me what happened last night, and I rushed back," Jake said.

I nodded again. "I'm so sorry," I whispered. "You both appeared in my life and in the span of a few weeks you became the two people I was closest to on Earth. I didn't think my heart could be mended after my dad died, but the two of you brought light into my life, you cared about me, and I was so happy. It was so uncomplicated at the beginning, right? But yesterday I realized that my heart was capable of loving not one person, but two."

Alice inhaled sharply, and Jake closed his hand around hers.

"You two are so close, and you trusted me and took me in. And I betrayed you. Jake, I fell for your sister when you went away. You can think I'm sick, and maybe I am, but Alice ... God, I almost kissed her yesterday. And you both need to know it, it was one of the most difficult things I've done in my life, walking away, leaving you standing there, alone," I stifled a sob and wiped away the now streaming tears.

Jake squeezed Alice's hand tighter.

"There must be something so deeply wrong with me, and you have the right to be mad at me. Please be mad at me, not at Alice. I can't be the one to get between you, no one can. You two are the most beautiful people, inside and out, and I'm so grateful for the time I've had with you. And I'm sorry for messing it up," I said quietly, as new hot tears pooled in my eyes.

"I'm sorry for loving you both," and I looked down, as the tears ran down my cheeks.

This time Alice stood up to walk to me, Jake pulling her down to the sofa.

"I knew Alice's feelings for you, I knew them from the start, there are no secrets between us," Jake said and I looked at him, he leaned closer to me, placing his elbows on his knees.

"That's why I left for Christmas, so you two could be together, just to see what this time held, and it unfolded the truth," he said.

"You knew?" I asked slowly.

"Of course."

"Why did you ..." my voice trailed off, "why?"

This time Alice said. "Because we both fell in love with you, and Jake saw flickers in you that hinted that it was reciprocal. I didn't think you were interested in me at all, nothing beyond a friend. And the most important thing for me was for both of you to be happy, but then Christmas happened."

"What are you saying?" I asked.

My thoughts were still a liquid mass in my head, as I tried to untangle that Jake knew that Alice was attracted to me, how he saw that I was attracted to her, long before I realized it.

"We have an offer for you," Jake said. Alice's hand gripped the edge of the table, knuckles white. "Would you have us, both?"

"What?" I cried.

"Not simultaneously," Alice said, "God, this sounds like a weird mess. What Jake means is that you might be interested in ... dating both of us."

"What?" I asked again, my head could not process what my ears were hearing.

And finally, I looked closely at both of them, something shimmering on both faces, hope.

"You want me to date both of you?" I asked, slowly. "Like kiss both of you, sleep with both of you?"

"Not at the same time! We'd have rules, days spent separately. In no way would Alice and I ..." Jake said and looked at Alice, both of them having horrified expressions. "I can't even say it."

"Interact intimately," Alice said and shuddered. "It would be like two separate relationships for you."

"Yes, we know it sounds unconventional, untraditional."

"Do you think I'm polyamorous?" I asked, standing up.

"You did say that you loved us both," Alice whispered, almost inaudible.

I looked around the room, the room which conjured warm memories. Two people who looked at me, who weren't moving, not breathing.

"You're crazy!" I said as their faces crumpled. "I need to think, alone."

I rushed out of the living room, grabbing my jacket and stumbling out of the front door, banging it on my way out. I stopped on the porch and exhaled. The slow snow was dancing around me, in contrast to the thoughts which sped in my mind.

Alice and Jake offered one solution to our situation, to the place the three of us were in. In the place I had never ever thought I could be in. I took a few steps and lowered my trembling fingers onto the rail, in the snow.

How could it work? From the mechanics of it to the feelings. Would it not be a mess? It would. And even more than usual relationships, twice more than usual relationships.

I went down the steps, into the front yard, and looked up. The white of the sky offered no solution, no answers to the questions I had. I closed my eyes and felt the little snowflakes landing on my cheeks. I smiled to myself and walked back to the house.

Standing at the front door I looked at the two parked cars, and back to the door, and jabbed the buzzer, the chime sounding inside.

Alice opened the door, Jake standing a few feet away. They looked at me, the two people I cared about most in the world.

"I agree," I said.

Time stopped as I awaited their reaction.

Alice clasped her hand to her lips, her eyes wide, as Jake smiled. Two arms wrapped around me, a sweet vanilla smell covered me. My fingers got lost in the silkiness of blonde hair, as I pressed her body into mine. As I looked back at Jake, whose expression was radiant, he beamed at me.

"Now let's drink that tea," he said.

As all of us wandered back to the living room, Alice sat closer to me this time.

"Are you sure? We don't want to force you, or make it uncomfortable," she said.

"It's crazy, but it's one possible decision where all of us could be happy. Couldn't we?"

They both nodded and Jake poured us cups of tea, Alice turned the music back on a portable speaker.

"How will it work? How ..." my voice trailed off.

There were a million questions buzzing in my head, but I didn't know where to start.

"I guess we'll figure it out on the way," Alice said, a small smile playing on her lips.

Jake gulped his tea and stood up.

"Well, I gotta go," he said, and only then did I notice his backpack leaning against the sofa. "You girls have a lot of catching up to do." And he winked.

"Where are you going?" I asked and also stood up.

"Back to our parents, I'll be back after the New Year."

He crossed the room and placed his hands on my cheeks, locking his eyes on mine. I heard Alice picking up the cups and going into the kitchen.

"God, I missed you," he whispered and lowered his lips to mine.

Just an hour before I had thought I was never going to be kissed or touched by him ever again. But things were like before, but even more relaxed, more open. A new level of trust opened before us.

"I see you missed me too," he laughed, a throaty sound so close to my ear as he ran his fingers through my hair.

"I don't want you to go," I said.

"We'll have all the time in the world once I'm back, but now, you and Alice need to figure things out between you two."

I nodded.

"I'm nervous," I whispered.

"It's Alice, she'd never hurt you. Just talk to her," Jake said.

"How can you be so calm about it?"

"Why shouldn't I? I trust both of you."

"Will it work?" I asked and my breath hitched. "What if it doesn't work? I can't lose you two. I—" A wave of nauseating panic loomed in the back of my mind, making me shudder.

"Shh." A warm hand drew me into him, my nose landing in the crook of his neck.

"We'll make it work. We're not the first, and I'm sure we're far from the last to even try. I've read multiple stories of polyamorous relationships."

"Of course you did the research," I chuckled.

"They work, Emily. You're trying to overthink it. Just do what your heart tells you."

It told me to trust. I nodded.

He lifted my face, gently rubbing his thumb over my lower lip. I closed my eyes. Jake slowly kissed me again, then his arms fell back, releasing me.

Alice was standing in the kitchen, her hands in bubbles of soap, washing the cups. The situation was so natural, as if nothing had changed.

Jake picked up his backpack and went to the door. Alice joined me in the corridor.

"Have fun!" he said, his hand on the handle.

Alice laughed, the sound making me warm inside. She hugged him, and Jake was gone. A few moments later the car backed out of the driveway and rumbled away. I watched it out of the window, looking everywhere but at Alice.

"Let's talk, shall we?" she asked and gestured to the sofa.

I sat back in the armchair and noticed how she sat further away than before.

"I'm not going to make any moves on you if that's what you are worried about," she said. "All this talk before, it was not to force you into something you don't want. It's just for if you ever, and I mean ever, even if it's somewhere in the distant future, would like to be the one I kiss under a mistletoe, you would know that it's okay and that Jake is okay with that. He imagined us living as a family, and I honestly have no idea how it may work. But I'm willing to give it a try. If you don't, I'd understand and would be completely fine with it. I know it all sounds crazy. The most important thing I need you to know, Emily, the most important of all, I hope we can stay friends."

I sighed and looked at her. She was so nervous, wriggling her fingers in her lap, trying to be brave.

"I guess I want more than that."

Her eyes widened.

"I've just never had a girlfriend before," I said. "And I don't know how, well, I do know how, but ... that's embarrassing, sorry."

"You don't need to worry about it, you don't even need to think about it. I'm here for you when you're ready. Just wave or something."

And I burst out laughing, Alice giggled on the sofa, finally relaxing.

I looked outside. Snowflakes swirled around the backyard.

"Do you want to go for a walk?" I asked.

"I'd love to."

As we slowly walked through their neighborhood, stopping to explore the little community library boxes, it was as it was before, easy. It was easy with Alice right from the beginning—the creature of light and laughter who wanted to be my friend.

Chapter Seventeen

T he next day I suggested we drive to a trail to get out for a
bit. The website said that the path was cleared of snow.
Alice packed a thermos of tea and sandwiches. A yellow car
honked at the foot of my dorm. A hot cocoa was waiting for
me in the car.

"That's for now, tea is for later," Alice said, as she drove
out of the campus.

The clear blue sky stretched in front of us as we turned
onto the highway, the silvery clouds of the previous day gone,
the white of snow from the trees blinding. An old AC/DC
song played as Alice murmured the words.

"What do you want to do for New Year's Eve?" she asked.
"Do you want to go to a party or something? I'm sure
Miranda would have a ton of ideas."

"Can we stay at home? Just you and me?"

"Oh, wow. Okay, sure. Don't worry, I'm going to behave,"
Alice said.

"Maybe you don't need to."

She turned her head to me and looked back to the road
quickly.

"Noted."

As we stood under an old pine tree looking up at all the green hidden in heavy heaps of white, making the branches sag, Alice cleared her throat.

"How was it growing up with a dad only? Have you ever missed a mother figure?" she asked.

I scratched my nose, my fluffy gloves tickling the skin.

"Not really. When I was little, I could only see what mothers do in regards to other children, and Dad did exactly those things. He cared for me, he clothed me, he brought me to the school, he kissed me goodbye. I think he watched mothers more closely than I did. That's why he always insisted on dropping me off in the mornings. For me, it was like kids had two fathers, not a mom and dad. And so rarely did their dads participate in kids' lives, you know, it's always mothers who do everything. And when I grew older, many of those families that had two parents, divorced, fathers going into new families, and I still had my Dad."

Alice nodded. "I like your logic."

"Oh, logic, Dad's favorite word," I said and smiled at the sky as we slowly continued down the rocky path.

"But in my teenage years, I started wondering how it would feel to have a mother, to talk to her, to be held by tender hands, to smell the perfume on her neck that stood as a unique marker of her. I was an easy teenager. Dad joked I stepped into the shoes of a middle-aged woman right after my tenth birthday. We were not huge talkers and, when I imagined mother, I thought she would be babbly, with a booming laugh. I don't know why I thought like this, my real Mom, as Dad told me stories about her, was a quiet and determined person with huge dreams and goals. Dad joked that if she still was alive, we would have lived in a mansion and would be millionaires by my teenage years."

"Are you like her?" Alice asked.

"Oh, no, I'm a carbon copy of my Dad. He used to joke that Mom would be the sole entrepreneur in our family, making all the money, while he would stay at home with me. That she would come up with a startup that would change the world. She would have done it, but she just didn't have time. And you know what is that stupidest thing?" I asked, my voice trembling.

Alice shook her head.

"I can't even miss the person I never met. I can't relate to the image of a determined young woman who had a clear view of the life before her, who knew what she wanted to do, because I don't. I'm like my Dad, he never wanted much, but he had a job he loved. A job that was like a hobby to him. And I simply don't know what to do with my life, I have no idea what happens after university ends. And I envy both of you, how you and Jake know what you want, and have a vision of a career."

I started taking fast shallow breaths, fear gripping the inside of my chest and lungs. Alice stopped in front of me, tugging off her huge mittens, and hiding them in a pocket. She pressed her palms to my cheeks, and I noticed how warm they were. Her eyes were level with mine.

"You're fine," she whispered.

"I'm scared of my future, of the moment I need to be an adult, to take care of my own life," I said.

"You already are an adult and you just don't see how independent you already are. You are scared about money, not life alone. You are the person who is perfectly comfortable alone, aren't you?"

I slowly nodded.

"Just like your Dad was, right?"

I nodded again.

"And now you have me and Jake, but let's forget this for a moment. All you need after university is financial stability, to have an income, and you'll be fine. Right?"

Again, I nodded, her palms still on my cheeks.

"And with enough money, you would relax, and have time to find what you actually enjoy, a hobby, and maybe, a glimpse of the path you want to lead."

"But what if I don't find that financial stability? What if no one wants to hire me?" I asked.

"Your Dad took care of this already," Alice said. "He insisted on you taking a Computer Science degree, and this only would be enough for you to have a job."

"I'm not even good at it!"

"Nobody says that you'd have to work at NASA," Alice said and I snorted. "You could work on an application that helps elderly people, for example, or an app about still life art."

"Or an app about books," I said.

And I could see it, why did it never cross my mind? That I could combine my degree and the thing I love: books.

Alice smiled at me, revealing her dimples. I could just tilt my head and our faces would be only inches away from each other, but she dropped her warm hands and went for her mittens. The cold rushed back to my skin.

"But anyway, you don't need to worry about any of this, Jake and I will make so much money that you won't have to work at all," she said.

And I snorted. "I don't see myself as a housewife," I said, a snicker escaping my lips.

"Yeah, me neither actually."

Alice took a few steps and stopped, turning back to me.

"Maybe you don't need to wait until the end of education to start searching for a job."

"What do you mean?" I asked.

"You can go freelance now, when we are still in university. There are so many companies hiring remote workers now, you would see what the market needs right away, sitting on your bed, no offices, no suits, no live interviews."

"Really?" I asked, my thoughts rushing as fast as a train. "I guess I could do that. I could try at least."

"I'll help you to set up a profile on a freelancing website. Your profile is already fifty percent of success, the other thirty is the number of applications you send, ten is your skills, and the last ten is luck."

"Yes, okay," I said and laughed. The brick pressing on my chest eased just a little.

Back in the car, as it was slowly warming up inside, I peeled off my gloves and with ice-cold hands picked up a cup of tea and took a sip. The thermos had kept it hot, very hot, and I closed my eyes as the warmth slowly bloomed inside. The walk had taken longer than we anticipated, and by the last mile, I had been slowly turning into an ice cube.

"Drink more," Alice ordered.

And I did. During the last fifteen minutes, she had ushered me to get back to the car faster, saying that my lips were turning blue.

Alice took a sip from her cup and placed it on the dashboard, turning to me. She wrapped her fingers around my hands, trapping them around my warm cup.

"God, your hands are icy."

I watched our hands together, how her warm skin sheltered mine. Alice moved her thumb over my knuckles, slowly, a warm touch, and then she intertwined her fingers with mine. It was a new feeling for me, something that seared in my core. I moved my eyes from our hands to her face. She was watching me closely.

Her deep gray eyes focused on me, and just for a second, they slipped to my lips, making me inhale sharply. I put my cup alongside hers and placed my trembling fingers to her cheek. Alice was still looking at me, her pupils huge, as she closed her eyes and leaned into the touch. I slowly touched her brow, nose, and her lower lip. It was silky under my fingertips.

She opened her mouth just a little, and I felt her warm breath on my fingers.

I wanted to catch it with my lips.

But I didn't.

I dropped my hand and picked up my cup again. Alice smiled and turned back to the wheel.

She took a deep breath and dragged her hand through her hair.

"Let's go home," she said.

"Yes."

In five minutes, she was chatting about making a profile, telling me all the important points, but all I could think about was how I wanted to press my lips to hers, how I thought they would taste. I could almost taste the vanilla on my tongue, and my body responded to that fantasy, a sudden tingle in my stomach, how my bra suddenly felt a bit small, there was not enough air in the car, making me breathe heavily. I turned and looked at her, her relaxed hands on the steering wheel, eyes on the road, long strands of hair brushing against her jacket.

"It's important to fill in the skills section with keywords that would help potential employers find you, so you might—"

"I want to kiss you," I said.

The car veered just a little on the empty road. She didn't say anything.

"I'm sorry I didn't kiss you before," I added.

Her fingers squeezed the steering wheel harder. Still, she didn't reply, the car was silent.

"Do you mean it?" Alice finally asked.

"Yes," I whispered.

She moved her hand and switched on the blinker, the car slowing. It was a small road, still lost in the mountains, no cars around. The icy gravel crunched under the wheels as the car jerked to a stop. Alice switched it to park and opened the door. She crossed in front of the car and opened my door. She stretched her hand out to me. It was shaking slightly. I took it without hesitation, and in a second I was standing by her side, my hand still in hers.

"Emily, I've wanted to kiss you from the first moment I saw you. I wanted to—"

I didn't let her finish. I stepped closer and wrapped my hands around the nape of her neck. I finally touched those lips with mine. And they were softer than I could have ever imagined, they were sweeter and lighter. Alice gasped and draped her hands around my waist, pulling me closer, so there was almost no space between us. And she invited me in, as my tongue touched the tip of hers.

A passing car honked at us as my fingers got lost in her long blonde hair. With a sudden jolt, I realized how much more of her I wanted.

I wanted it all.

Alice pressed me into the closed passenger door, her fingers sliding down my jaw, my neck, and further, moving between the flaps of my jacket. She slowed as she moved past my collarbone, lower, when her fingers wrapped around my breast, over the damned sweater, bra, preventing me from truly feeling her fingers on me. But when she squeezed just a little, I moaned all the same.

"We need to get home," she whispered into the corner of my lips.

And of course, she was right. Even though it was freezing outside, I wanted to peel off every item of clothing I had on me, just to feel her skin on mine.

She slowed, her teeth scraping my upper lip. Alice pressed her forehead to mine, and closed her eyes, breathing heavily.

"Just so you know, I imagined this moment so many times, when I was with you, when I was alone, but the reality … God, the reality, is so much sweeter."

She took a step back, and smiled at me, her lips raw after I had crashed into them.

"Let's go home," she said again, but this time she meant more, much more.

When she returned to her seat, she looked back at me. Her cheeks were rosy, lips swollen, eyes glinting from the light of a dashboard.

I rested my head on the headrest and found her hand with mine.

"Will you be my girlfriend?" I asked.

She giggled as I smiled.

"Yes. Yes!"

Alice moved closer to kiss me but the safety belt stopped her. I closed the space between us, placing my hand to her jaw, pressing my lips to hers. Suddenly I was very hot. A set of fireworks went off inside my head. I was kissing a woman. I was being kissed back, so passionately, so tenderly. I never wanted it to stop.

"I'd do it the whole day, but who knew it was so uncomfortable to kiss in a small car?" Alice said, chuckling.

"You're right," I said as I noticed how both of us were bent at a strange angle. "Let's go home."

Chapter Eighteen

I didn't realize at first how much I needed Alice. She was a friend suddenly turning into much more. I wanted to kiss her every moment I was in her presence, and even more when I was away from her. Every time she was in the room with me I needed to touch her, so our hands became permanently intertwined.

I didn't compare it to how I felt with Jake. It was different. They were different.

When we made it back from the trail I almost undressed her on the spot, but she asked me to wait.

"Why?" I asked, my hand still on her sweater. I could feel the heat of her skin just inches from my fingertips. I slowly rubbed my finger below her navel and she trembled in response.

"I don't want you to regret that it moves too fast. You still have time to decide if you want this, us," she said.

I found her eyes.

"I'll wait, okay, but only because you are asking me to. But you need to know, I have never, ever wanted something more than I want you now."

"You don't mean it," she said.

"I do."

And I tried to show it to her with my lips, and maybe she understood a fraction of what I was meaning, because minutes later she lay breathless on the couch, her chest heaving.

"Tea?" I asked.

We decided to spend New Year's Eve together, and I knew that night she could say whatever she wanted about how we should wait. I didn't care. My dreams were haunted by her slipping away, vanishing into thin air. And Jake would be back home soon, meaning we had only a few nights left of the house to ourselves.

And I intended to use it.

It seemed Alice was thinking the same because when she opened the door she was wearing only white fluffy socks, a big white T-shirt, and panties.

I closed the front door quickly behind me because her skin was suddenly covered in goosebumps from the cold I had brought in with me.

"This is our dress code for tonight," Alice said, her voice calm.

I shrugged off my coat.

"Let me change, then. Just one thing I need to check, should I be wearing a bra?"

Before she could reply, I cupped her breast through the fabric, gently.

"No bra," I breathed.

"Yes."

I almost ran upstairs to change. I quickly undressed, folding my clothes neatly into a pile I left on Alice's bed.

I pulled the black T-shirt I used for sleeping from my bag, unhooked my bra, and slipped the T-shirt on.

My hair was a dark mess and my almost translucent panties left so little to the imagination that, as I turned and looked in the mirror, the reflection made my cheeks hot.

The black fabric only highlighted the outline of my breasts, my nipples clearly visible, my black nail polish glinting from the light of the bed lamp. My stomach flipped for a moment before I breathed in slowly, trying to calm myself.

I looked at myself and tried to understand what a girl like Alice could want to do with me. I was simple, far from beautiful, a girl battling with low self-esteem and trust issues. But when she looked at me, I knew she didn't care about any of it. She looked directly inside, into my core, and amazingly, she liked what she saw.

My heart started beating faster. I didn't actually know how it would work, what I should do. All I knew was that I wanted to lay my hands on every inch of her, kiss her everywhere, taste her. My imagination spiraled as I pictured her between my lips, under my tongue, moving.

I grabbed the door handle and took another deep breath.

Alice was waiting for me on the couch downstairs, sweet jazz piano music was playing and, instead of a usual tea set, two flutes of bubbling champagne stood on the table.

"It's a New Year's Eve," she said, her eyes hungrily moving down my T-shirt, pausing on my breasts, widening at my panties.

She patted the couch beside her, motioning for me to sit.

My legs were slightly shaking when I stepped closer and sat down by her side.

"You're so beautiful," I whispered, and tucked her hair behind her ear, kissing the skin under her cheekbone.

"Have you ever had sex with a woman?" Alice asked, quietly.

"You know I haven't," I replied, my lips so close to hers.

"Can I guide you today?" she asked, a hint of shyness in her voice.

"Of course," I replied, moving back slightly.

She picked up the glasses and gave one to me.

"I want you every day in my life next year. I want to see your face, to hold your hand, to be by your side. I want you to know that I need you. That I'm afraid of our idea even working, of a family of three, of two relationships for you. Oh, God. I hope it works, because it's a blessing if the three of us could pull it off, and even though I'm afraid, I see how pure it is. How all of us could be happy," Alice said and took a deep breath. "You are my life, Emily."

Only the sound of soft jazz could be heard while I looked at her, while I felt my heart swelling with joy and happiness, and love. All I said was:

"We would make it work. Both of you deserve so much better than me, but by some inexplicable magic you chose me, and I'll be by your side as long as you want me to be."

"Forever," Alice said.

"It's a long time."

"It's not long enough," she said, and my chest burst with the light when she leaned in to kiss me, slowly, her tongue caressing mine.

A new flame ignited inside me.

"Do you want to watch anything?" she asked.

"I want to watch you."

"Okay," Alice replied and put her champagne flute on the table. She slipped her white shirt over her head and looked at me. Her milky skin was like marble; the veins standing starkly against a background of white. Her stomach was flat, and her chest, oh my God. I stopped breathing when I looked at it. The size was perfect to fit in the palm, my palm. The darker skin around her nipples woke up some old instinct to suck on them. She breathed evenly as I watched her.

"You can touch me, if you want," she said.

Of course, I wanted to. It's all I wanted at that moment.

My fingers were trembling when I cupped her breast, my thumb scraping the silky skin of her nipple. I rubbed a little, and she closed her eyes for a moment, just to open them back and find mine. There was something sexy about my black nails on her white skin.

"Let me lie down," she said.

And before I could reply she lowered her head into my lap, lying down, her hair spilling on my bare legs. Alice lay at my side, open, my hand could reach any part of her, easily.

I slowly rubbed the skin under her breast, the tender part, before trapping the nipple between my fingers. She was breathing faster.

"I need you to touch me, Emily, because I'm burning," she rasped and took my hand in hers, our fingers intertwining in a familiar pattern before she lowered my hand into her panties. She *was* burning. "Touch me like you touch yourself, please."

I brushed my fingers against the warmth of her. She was so wet my finger easily slid inside. She moaned and arched her back. I knew what she was asking. I pulled out my hand and dragged the soft cotton of her panties down. She slid it down her legs, revealing herself to me. She was completely naked, her legs spread. My fingers were wet as I touched her breast again, slowly trailing down, down to where she needed me.

My fingers drew a slow circle.

And then faster, and faster. Alice touched her breasts, squeezing a little as she responded to my touch, rocking, as she whimpered like a kitten while I touched her, whimpers growing into cries as she was coming.

"A little slower, please," she sighed. And when I found the right pattern, she locked her eyes with mine, and as I stroked her she came with a violent shudder, a loud cry escaping her. My fingers were wet with her juices and I had an urge to lick them.

"Are you sure you've never touched another woman?" Alice said, her voice coming out in a rasp. "Because that was ..."

"I practiced on myself," I replied and blushed.

"Later, I want to see it," she purred. "Now it's my turn."

And she lifted herself and found my lips, my reply hungrier, my teeth scraping her tongue. She grabbed the bottom of my shirt, tugging it up.

My breasts were bigger, messier than hers, everything about me was messier. But she paused and just watched me.

"I could only dream about this moment. You're gorgeous, Emily, you must know it."

When she touched my breast, the shock of want tugged at the bottom of my belly. Alice lowered me to the sofa, a soft leather sticking to my back. She kissed me for a moment before going down, her teeth scraping my collarbone, her soft lips wrapping around my nipple, as her hands rubbed my breasts. The sweet need built with each passing moment. She knew when I needed it most and rubbed her fingers over my panties, finally. A moan escaped my lips.

She slowly tugged down my underwear, moving my legs apart, lowering her face between them. Alice pressed her cheek to my inner thigh and painfully slowly dragged the finger up and down.

"You're so beautiful," she whispered as she slid her finger inside me and moved it.

My hips rolled in reply.

Alice brushed her lips over me, her tongue soft, but pressing into the place I yearned for it the most. I was dissolving in a moment, each cell of my body pulsing. She licked me, fingered me, as I was losing it. I guided her head just a little, her silky hair between my fingers. Soft sobs became moans, as she was moving faster, as I was climaxing under her tongue. I cried as it hit. Hard.

I was breathing heavily as she kissed me down there for the last time, licking her lips.

After a moment she guided my lips to hers. I tasted myself on her, and the thought was maddening, sensual.

"I want to do the same, to you," I whispered.

She nodded and stood up, draping a leg around me, going up 'til she was hovering over my chest.

"Is this okay?" she asked.

Instead of replying I lifted her hips higher, so she was on the level of my mouth. Slowly, I licked her.

"Oh, God," she whimpered.

Alice was sweet, sweeter than anything I had tasted before. She melted under my tongue as she rubbed herself into my face. She rode me, a new experience, so deliciously pleasurable. My fingernails dug into the soft flesh of her bottom, wrapping her around me, tugging her even closer.

She came, panting, almost tumbling on top of me, hot liquid spreading on my lips. She clambered off my face, her lithe limbs shaking, and was soon kissing it away, slowly.

I wrapped my hands around her body, as she pressed closer, our skin connected everywhere. I lifted my phone from the table to check the time.

"Happy New Year," I said, joyfully.

She giggled. Somewhere between sweet delirium, when our bodies were intertwined, a new year came. I closed my eyes to imagine the year and what it would bring. I squeezed just a tiny bit more, pressing Alice into me. Her head lay in the crook of my shoulder.

"Do you want to sleep with me today? Like properly sleep, in bed?" Alice asked, propping her head up on her hand.

"Yes."

She smiled, a warmth lighting her features. She slowly circled the skin on my belly in a lazy caress.

It was new, the closeness. And I wanted to wrap that feeling in a warm blanket so it stayed forever.

That night was the first night I slept with her in her bed, falling into dreams right from her arms. In the morning she went down on me again, making me grab the sheets, and move, move under her tongue until I couldn't anymore.

Chapter Nineteen

J ake came back a few days later, and even though I was kept busy in every possible way, I had missed him. I missed our walks, our talks.

There was snow in his hair from the few minutes he was outside when he entered the house. He smiled at both of us.

"How are you doing?" he asked.

But before we could reply, he crossed the hall and lifted me a few inches, planting a kiss on my lips. For those few days, I had had other lips kissing me. These were familiar, bigger, stronger lips.

"God, I missed you, Emily," he said, and buried his face in my hair, just for a moment, his nose rubbing my neck.

He dropped the backpack and hugged Alice. "I missed you too, sis."

She laughed.

"Let's get some food. We have a lot to discuss," he said and went straight to the kitchen, washing his hands before opening the fridge, and closing it. "What did you two eat? The fridge's empty." He shook his head and opened it again. He retrieved a pack of cherry tomatoes, a cheese we had no idea existed there, and a jar of sauce. "Pasta it is."

Alice moved to prepare tea, suspiciously looking at Jake's hands as they sliced tomatoes.

"How was your trip?" I asked, hovering at the kitchen entrance, the space inside was cramped already.

"It was fast. I made only one stop; I wanted to finally get back here. Honestly, I was curious about how you two were doing."

I blushed. "We're okay."

He snorted. "Yeah, I see how you're blushing. So, I guess everything's fine?"

"Yes, Jake, we're fine," Alice said. "More than fine."

"Good."

In twenty minutes three plates of pasta were steaming on the table, and three cups stood around the teapot with Chinese symbols.

Jake turned to me and asked: "Emily, are you still comfortable with the arrangement we discussed before?"

I looked at him, his kind eyes on me, his strong hands in his lap. I looked at Alice, who crossed her hands over her chest, who held my gaze.

"Yes, but how? Should we set some kind of schedule, rules of privacy, of behavior around each other?" I asked.

"I thought that you should decide where and how you want to spend each night. If it was for example, and I mean *only,* for example, three days with Alice, three days with me, one at your dorm, each week, it would turn into a nightmarish schedule," Jake said.

"It's like a kid of divorced parents, going on a schedule from parent to parent," Alice said and shuddered. "Yeah, you should choose where you want to spend your day and night, with whom, if anyone."

"That's a lot of pressure," I said and laughed nervously.

"How do I balance evenly? What if one of you needs me, and I am with another?"

"We'll just call," Alice said. "We need to have maximum transparency here."

I noticed a small impression on her face, of anguish. It was there and gone in a second.

"Also, we're talking about private moments here. Most of the time you could spend with the two of us. Like before, we spent the time together anyway," Jake said.

"What about being in public?" I asked.

"You are Jake's girlfriend," Alice said. "At least 'til we work it out between us."

I nodded. "What about signs of affection? What do you think we should show when there are three of us?"

"Let a quick kiss on the lips be the most we see of another's intimacy," Alice said.

"Everything else happens behind closed doors, or wherever, just make sure the third person has no idea."

"I agree, but it would be difficult to manage this in this house, the walls are paper-thin," I said and looked at both of them. I almost giggled when I imagined this conversation from the outside. I was discussing having sex with two of them, separately, in such a business-like way that we should all be wearing suits and have contracts ready to sign.

"Well, we'd have to be creative. I guess, use your dorm room. And anyway it's only 'til the end of university, then I'm going to move out and we could have separate places of our own," Jake said, "'til then, it's a private matter between the couples. Right?"

We nodded.

"No sounds though," Alice said to Jake. "If I hear you grunting like you did with that girl before, I'll kill you."

"Mmm, girl before?" I asked.

"At a previous uni I brought a girl to the house we were renting. Alice almost kicked me out the next morning."

"I woke up to the girl talking dirty in the room next to mine, and the squeak of a bed. And he managed to grunt in the end. I never want to hear it again," Alice said, disgusted.

"That was embarrassing but true. That girl loved to talk." Jake laughed as Alice put her hands to her ears and shook her head. "What else should we discuss?"

"Protection," said Alice.

"I'm on the pill," I said. They nodded.

"Also, Emily, it's up to you to check how frequently you want to be with us, I mean, that's embarrassing, so there aren't times when it's one after another, I mean ..." Alice grunted.

"I got it," I said hastily. "What about jealousy?"

"I'm happy as long as you two are happy," Jake said and it was true. It was easy for him, transparent.

"It'll be fine," Alice said.

The awkward silence filled the room.

"Let's eat?" Jake asked and lifted a fork. Alice poured three cups of tea, avoiding looking at me.

I honestly could not imagine how it could work. How this double dating could be a thing for me. Could I want them both equally? How could I possibly divide myself between them? How could I be the manager of the time? I wanted somebody to take care of my actions. I wanted somebody to decide with whom I should spend that day, that night, the next night.

My head was buzzing when a warm touch brought me back. Alice. She wrapped her fingers around mine.

"We'll figure it out," she said.

"Yes."

Chapter Twenty

It was awkward at first. When Jake was away I forgot how it was to be with him. It had been replaced by time with Alice. With Jake, it was easy, uncomplicated. He easily accepted the first night I wanted to spend alone at my dorm, where I had gone only a couple of times for fresh clothes during the previous week.

Was it too early to fall into his arms after the time with Alice? Alice. I kept thinking about her. I dreamt about her marble skin, her eyes, her smile. That night in my dream, she was wearing a white silky dress. We were on the beach, she was further away from me than I wanted. She kept walking, turning to look at me, smiling sadly, and walking further. I ran after her, but she always stayed the same distance away. I couldn't reach her. I woke up panting, the feeling of loss running in my veins.

Classes started again after the holidays and my job resumed. I had much less free time.

One evening, I was working on the assignment I needed to turn in a few days later. A slow fall of snow circled behind the window as I tried to focus my attention on the screen, when my phone started ringing. Miranda.

"Hey," I said.

"Hi, I'm outside of your dorm. Can I come in?" she asked, her voice unusually quiet.

"Yes, sure. Come on in."

In a few minutes, she knocked, and when I opened the door I froze. Miranda's eyes were red. Dark makeup was smudged around her eyes as huge tears rolled down her cheeks. She sniffed, a wet shaking sound, and I rushed to her, wrapping my arms around her, shielding her in a cocoon.

"What happened?" I whispered as she trembled in my hands.

She sighed but didn't say anything. I pulled her inside, closing the door behind us.

Miranda sat on the edge of my bed and dropped her head in her hands. I sat next to her and slowly rubbed her back.

"Brian doesn't want to be with me anymore," she said quietly.

"What?" I almost yelped. Out of all the things that could have happened that was the last I would have thought. "Tell me what happened, Miranda."

"We had this huge fight. It started stupidly: I asked him to fix a table for a week, he kept forgetting and I kept reminding. Today he was upset because one of his professors keeps bullying him and I didn't notice that he was upset," Miranda said and sniffed again, "and I told him angrily about the table, asked him, '*How difficult can it be to fix it?*'. And he thought that I was saying that he's stupid like his professor that keeps humiliating him always says. He went all quiet when I fumed and then he said, '*Fix it yourself*'. But I was beyond angry by that point. You know when you can't stop?"

She turned to me, tears still rolling, I nodded.

"I made a mistake. I hit where it hurt him most in that

moment. I said that maybe the professor was right. Maybe he secretly agreed with the professor, since he kept allowing himself to be treated like that. You should have seen his face." Miranda's voice shattered. "I didn't mean it. I was just so angry. And he stood up and walked slowly to me. He said *'If I'm so pathetic, from now on you can do everything by yourself,'* and he turned and left."

Miranda inhaled sharply. "It's my mistake. I didn't mean to be cruel. It was like a violent ball rolled inside me and I could not stop it. He meant it, Emily. He's going to leave me."

I laced my arm around her shoulders and slowly rocked us as she cried. "The ones we love the most are the ones who hurt us the most, they know where to hit. He didn't mean it," I said.

"He did, you should have seen his disappointment," she whispered. "I tried to call him, but he turned off his phone. I texted him that I'm sorry, so, so sorry. I asked him not to leave me."

She fumbled in her bag and pulled out her phone. "The battery is dead," Miranda said, looking at the dark screen. "He didn't reply."

I looked at the charging port of her phone, it was different from my iPhone.

"I'm so sorry," I said quietly. "It's a fight, not a breakup, Miranda. You'll laugh at it in a few days."

"But why did he say what he said?"

"Because he was angry too, and it was a way to get back at you. Did you mean to hurt him?" I asked.

She looked up at me, her hair was pushed up into a ponytail, eyes brimming with tears, red spots on her cheeks. She shook her head. "No."

"And he didn't mean it. I know Brian, he didn't."

"But sometimes I'm so angry at him, sometimes I want to claw his eyes out, or mine, whatever. Sometimes he drives me mad, and I know I infuriate him occasionally, and I'm working on myself. I'm trying to be calm, but sometimes the bomb hits and we clash so hard ..."

"That's what living together means," I said, smiling. "It can't be nice and sorted forever. We all have feelings, bad and good days, and fighting is a part of life. There is no happy couple in the world who never had a disagreement."

"Do you fight with Jake?" Miranda asked.

I shook my head. "It's too early for us, I guess, and we don't live together."

"Right," Miranda whispered.

She was calmer, her breathing even. I stood up and went to the tiny bathroom, retrieving makeup remover with cotton pads. When I returned to her, she was watching her dead brick of a phone. I soaked the pad with lavender-smelling remover and gently rubbed the black stains from her cheeks.

"Thank you," she whispered.

"Tea?" I asked.

She nodded, staring down at her empty hands.

I put an electric kettle on and poured green tea leaves from the set Alice had given me for Christmas into a glass teapot. I looked back at Miranda's drooping shoulders and fished my phone from my pocket.

She's with me, at my dorm. I texted Brian.

I barely had time to turn off the sound as the message pinged back. *Coming*

Miranda watched as leaves opened in the teapot when she finally emerged from her dark place.

"I didn't know you liked tea," she said.

"It's a gift from Alice," I explained.

Miranda didn't know about our intricate scheme, and it was not the time to tell her about it. She swirled the tea in her cup and took a sip. A slow tear was running down her cheek again.

I found her hand and squeezed it.

"Everything will be fine," I said, and it hurt me to see her barely nodding.

A loud knock interrupted the silence. I rushed to open the door. Brian was breathing fast, his jacket unzipped, worried eyes scanned the room and he almost ran to Miranda when he spotted her on my bed. Before she could say anything he made his way inside, dropped to his knees in front of her, and cradled her cheeks in his hands, kissing her gently.

"I'm sorry," she said quickly, her mouth inches from him.

"I didn't mean what I said, I won't allow you to be by yourself," Brian said, as his hands wrapped around her, as he ran his fingers over her body as if checking that she was alright.

Miranda kissed him, and her hands were restless too as she pressed him close. "I'm sorry," she whispered between kisses.

I turned away as my eyes watered. Even in such a perfectly matched couple as Miranda and Brian, there were blunders. There were always blunders in relationships. As I tried to give them some privacy, I kept wondering, what would be our blunders, in our triangle?

Alice and Jake were both silent for a couple of days, waiting for my move. I invited Jake for our usual walk in the park. We met under our usual lamp post, we drank our usual coffee, and he told me about his parents.

"They missed Alice so much. I had to lie and say that she was working. But they would understand. I hope one day you will meet them."

He truly believed that our trio could work.

"Tell me about them," I asked.

He looked at me, one eyebrow raised.

"They are strong together, and they do everything as one.

The balance has been worked out over the years of marriage. They are faithful as far as I'm aware, even though they had their fair share of arguing when we were younger," he said.

"What did they argue about?"

"Nothing major really, I guess it was the point that it comes to in each marriage, even the strongest, when the other person starts to irritate you by simply existing. My dad had a difficult midlife crisis. For months he was angry at us, at Mom. And then, fed up with walking on tiptoes around him, she just exploded, which turned our house into a minefield for weeks. But it worked. They worked it out."

My mind wandered to Miranda and Brian, who were trying to build their relationship with honesty, who were almost always together, not without the small fights along the way. But they were working on it.

"Are you proud of them?" I asked.

"I love them. I'm proud of how they deal with all troubles now. How gracefully they move together. They set a good example, you know."

I nodded, still thinking that a lasting relationship needed constant work.

"Emily?" he asked and stopped. The soft light from a lamppost shone in his eyes and his hair stuck out of his hat. "Can I kiss you?"

"Yeah, sure, why are you asking?" I mumbled.

He stepped closer and gently lifted my face up. He drew the line of my upper lip with his finger, the touch making my heart race. Slowly, he erased inch after inch between us, and his lips touched mine. It was like a question, tender probing. His fingers slowly went to my neck, as I responded to his touch. Jake let out a shuddering breath when it clicked in me, when I clung to him, opening my lips to his, letting his tongue graze mine.

"Stay with me tonight," I whispered.

He did.

Back in the dorm Jake slowly undressed me, covering every inch of exposed skin in kisses, gently rubbing the skin between my legs. When he was inside, we moved slowly, as if it were a dance, the wall of pleasure mounting as I was under him, peaking.

He wrapped his hands around me, and I pressed my back to his stomach as we lay together afterward. Jake's breathing became calmer, slower. But I was looking at the opposite wall, barely allowing myself to think.

Something was wrong. It was different this time. Even as my body responded to the familiar touch, my mind was not there. And as I lay there, my heart was thundering in my chest, hoping that Jake was asleep.

After spending my time with Alice, after loving our days together, after the tenderness of our nights, I wanted to be with her. As an icy feeling spread inside me I understood one thing. It was awkward because the person who kissed me was not the person I craved. I needed Alice.

I was surrounded by books. My job in the bookstore brought in so little money, it mostly didn't make any sense to even turn up anymore. But I did what I loved. I loved sorting the books, the smell of a new copy when I flipped through it. For just a couple of hours a few days a week I organized shelves and bestsellers lists. There was even a rainbow section my manager let me organize by color.

That job made me forget about the daily life of an adult, that soon, so soon, I would need to find a real job, and stop playing around.

It made me calm, reminded me of the library I used to visit as a kid. The first time, I clutched Dad's hand as he walked me into a well-lit local library. I remembered how I dropped his hand when we reached the kids' section. So many books were stacked on the shelves that they were like mountains, hovering above me. It was my personal heaven. It still was, but I hadn't set foot in the library of my hometown for years.

My little job was a replacement for that library.

I checked the watch on my phone and moved to straighten the shelf at the front of the shop. It was still littered with Christmas glitter. As hard as I tried to wipe it away, the sparkling pieces of plastic clung to the floor, shelves, books, and my pants.

Something yellow glistened outside. A familiar yellow car was parking in front of the shop. I watched Alice maneuvering into the tight space with a master-like precision. But right after she shifted to park, she froze for a moment, looking at her hands on the wheel. She wasn't moving, and then suddenly she dropped her head into her hands, rubbing her temples. Something troubled her. I wanted to run to her, to ask why, what was the reason she looked so worried. Because watching her like that hurt.

I turned around and went to find Jill, my manager, and owner of the shop.

"Can I leave early today, please?" I asked.

She checked the time on an ancient-looking round clock mounted on the back wall. It was ten minutes 'til the end of my shift.

"Sure, it's not like I pay you for all the hours you stay here late," she said.

True.

"Love you, Jill," I said as I hurried to collect my backpack and coat from the back office.

I rushed outside at the same moment Alice was climbing out of the car. Soft white snow was falling as I walked around the car. It danced in the air around Alice's face and she had to blink some snowflakes out of her eyelashes. Her eyes widened in surprise when she finally saw me. She didn't have time to say anything, because I draped my arms around her and found her lips with mine. Those lips I missed, lips I loved.

"Hi," I whispered.

"Hey," she was smiling. "Do you want to go for a ride with me?"

"I'd love to."

Alice beamed. Inside the car, our usual cups of cocoa stood in a holder. A small bag of marshmallows and candies was placed on the dashboard. Both Jake and Alice made a point of keeping me warm, always bringing some kind of hot drink.

It smelled perfect inside, sweet.

"I'm sorry I came, I'm not sure with all these new rules if I can see you whenever I want," she said. She put rules in air quotes.

"Don't say it like that. There are no rules, no schedules. This idea of me deciding when and who to see is draining. I don't want to decide. I just want to be a girlfriend. To whom her girlfriend makes surprises like showing up after her work," I smiled. "I'm happy you're here."

I made a move to kiss her, but it was impossible in the cramped car with steaming cups between us. So I gently stroked her cheek, her silky skin under my fingertips.

"I missed you. Having you all to myself for a few days was..." she said, her throat bobbing. "And now I can't even know if I can see you. It's difficult. I'm not like Jake. I'm not that open."

I knew that all along. She used to say that she was difficult in a relationship, but when there were only two of us, it was simple, like breathing. But that was just a few days, a few perfect days of holidays.

"You can see me anytime. Always. We'll figure it out,

okay?" I said and wrapped my fingers around hers. Her hand was so warm against my skin. I lifted it and planted a kiss on her wrist, making her giggle. She was ticklish.

Alice held my gaze for a few long seconds, her thumb stroking my palm.

"Yes, okay, we'll figure it out."

She smiled, and every time she smiled, my heart melted. She didn't know one thing about me. That I was not like Jake either, I was like his sister.

Chapter Twenty-One

"I started working for that big company, remember the one I told you about?" Alice said.

"Sure, how is it?"

"We're starting with small tasks, but I think I'm getting the grip of it. It's so easy to communicate with them, they assigned me a manager who assists me with any problems. He said they were so impressed with my portfolio, that they think I am a perfect candidate for a specific role they need. They'll teach me everything I need to know," she said, a small smile on her lips, eyes on a road ahead.

"I'm proud of you, I really am."

"It's time to set up your profile," she said.

I was silent for a bit. "What if I fail? What if nobody hires me?"

The familiar dread of future employment dripped in my veins, pulsing.

"Remember, it's just remote work. You will see if freelance works for you, if not, at least you tried. But I think," she said and glanced sideways at me, "I think you'll love it. It suits your personality."

"Okay."

"Let's set it tonight," Alice said, her eyes sparkling. "We can do it on my laptop, I'll show you everything."

"To hell with it, let's do it," I said.

She laughed. "Drink your cocoa."

The house was dark when she turned into the driveway.

"Jake is out with Brian, should be back soon," Alice said, parking the car.

I grabbed the bag of sweets and our empty cups and climbed out of the car. I looked at the dark house and a slow smile tugged the corners of my lips. I loved that house and everything that happened inside.

Alice unlocked the door and turned on the light. I shrugged off my coat and placed it on the hanger. Her running shoes were pushed into the corner; it seemed Alice resumed running after New Year.

"Let's go to my room," she said.

Her room was cozy, with stacked bookshelves, and a huge dreamcatcher. An open notebook lay on the table, unfamiliar letters formed words in Alice's handwriting, poems. She opened her laptop and typed the password to log in. Alice picked up a neatly folded sweater from her bed.

"Do you want to change into something homey?" she asked.

I shook my head. "Let me help you change."

I lifted her hoodie and slowly circled my hands around her waist, the skin warm under my fingertips. Her lips slowly parted, as her breathing became shallower. I helped her out of the hoodie, tracing the edge of her bra. She was looking at my fingers.

I found her lips, slowly, and unfastened her bra, her breast fitting in my palm perfectly.

"Emily, I know you're trying to distract me," she said, a smile on her lips, "to avoid setting up a profile."

She was right, but it wasn't the first reason on the list. The first was that I missed her, I missed her skin on mine, our bodies tangled together, I missed kissing her ... everywhere.

"I'll be quick," I teased.

But I wanted nothing more than for it to be not quick. I needed all the time in the world to have with her.

And then I didn't have her, because the familiar rumble of Jake's Toyota sounded on the driveway. Alice sighed, stepping away from me, and fastening the bra, draping her sweater on.

She looked at me for a second, sadness written all over her face. Again, a glimpse of that anguish I saw she had in the car. She was hurting.

"I'll make it right," I whispered, looking down.

She shook her head. "There is no right way, somebody would be hurt anyway. I'm trying, Emily, I really am."

The front door opened downstairs, and a familiar cheerful voice shouted hello. Alice stepped past me and placed her hand on the door handle. She closed her eyes for a second, and took a fast breath in, smoothing her features. She opened the door and met Jake on the stairs.

"Hey, look who's here," Alice said.

When Jake's eyes met mine, his face shone with a smile. He came closer, and wrapped me in a hug, burying his face in my hair.

"We're about to set up my freelance profile," I said when he stepped back.

"I'll leave you two to it. Let me know if I can help," he said and winked at Alice on the way to his room.

Alice dragged a chair up for me and we sat in front of her laptop. She opened the website for the biggest freelance platform I knew and clicked on a profile icon. A smiling photo of her looked back at us, and sections for skills, portfolio, and information were filled in neatly.

A few hours later, and after many groans from me, a similar profile page was filled under my name. It took us more than an hour to fill in my skills section. As I claimed I had none, Alice had to collect grains of information from me, typing them in sporadically.

When it was finished, I was ready to give it a day, but Alice clicked on the *Jobs* icon and typed in a few skills from my page into the search bar. It revealed three pages of results, one catching my eye immediately.

Jake knocked on the door and wished us good night, quickly kissing my forehead, and closing the door. A shower ran a few minutes later.

But I was transfixed by the list in front of me. I could actually do what was required in these jobs. Alice sorted the list so it showed beginners' jobs first, and as I read the requirements, the tight ball of anxiety that was always in the back of my mind shook, easing just a fraction.

I looked at her, stunned.

"I can do this," I said and pointed to the job. Even though it was a beginner job, the payment per hour set made my jaw drop. "I actually know how to do this task."

"And there are only three other applicants now," Alice said.

She clicked on the Apply button and turned the laptop to me. There was a standard message asking a client to take a look at my profile.

"We can leave it as it is. You have 10 free applications per month, afterward, you need to pay for them, but they are cheap. Let's apply for a few now," she said, and before I could protest, she hit Send.

She opened the next job on the list, and the next. We used five applications in half an hour.

"You see, it's easy. Now we wait," she said and turned to me.

It was past midnight. The house was silent, but I could hear my heart beating.

"What if I could actually work like this?" I asked.

"Of course, you could. Given how much you know, and the demand on the market, you'll be fine."

She stood up and stretched her back.

"Can I sleep with you tonight?" I asked.

"There's no way I'm driving you back now."

I laughed.

"I'm going to the shower. You can browse the website more," she said, taking her silky nightgown from the shelf.

I wanted to go to the shower with her. I wanted to do everything with her, but with Jake behind the wall, it would be something we agreed not to do. The rules of appropriateness.

As the water started running, I clicked through the website. At least five jobs with requirements of my skill set appeared daily. Now I just needed to wait on replies to my applications, if I got any. I turned off the laptop and installed the app on my phone. After logging in, the familiar list of applications opened. It would always be with me.

Alice came back from the bathroom, small water droplets glistening on her neck. I stood up and smiled at her.

"I'll be right back," I said.

After a quick shower, I combed through my tangled hair, and an idea sparked in my mind. Back in her room, Alice was reading a book on the left side of her bed—the right was reserved for me. I quietly closed the door behind me and turned to her.

A damp towel was wrapped around my body. With a flick

of my wrist, it slowly dropped to my feet. Alice's hand flew to her mouth, as her eyes widened. I stood by the door, naked. I wanted her to see me.

"Come here," she whispered.

And I did. I crawled under the covers, her fingers tracing the skin on my hips, my belly, my shoulders.

She kissed me deeply, a strong want building inside me. In a moment I slipped Alice's nightgown over her head. It quietly landed on the floor. I rubbed the silk of her panties, and she trembled.

"You need to be quiet," I whispered in her ear.

Alice turned and pressed her back into my breasts, that way I had easy access to the parts of her I wanted most.

She quickly slipped out of her underwear and parted her legs. My fingers slid like warm butter as she moved under my touch. Quiet gasps escaped her. I put a palm over her lips, her body rubbing against mine. She came fast.

Alice turned and faced me. She was still breathing hard. I brushed my hand over my lips and licked my fingertips.

"You can't do things like this, you just tease me. There are rules," she said, her eyes on my lips.

"To hell with rules, Alice."

She propped herself up on her elbows and looked at me. I loved the angle her shoulders took, her neck straight, how I could see just an inch of dark skin around her nipples.

"I need you to be quiet," she whispered. "I know how vocal you are, promise me to be quiet."

"I promise," I said, as she gently drew a finger over my breast.

She opened the covers, dropping them to the side. The chilly air touched my skin.

Alice kissed me slowly.

"Remember that you promised," she whispered.

And she went down on me, tenderly, growing faster. I held

on dearly to my promise, clasping a hand over my lips, the other lost in the silk of Alice's hair. God, she knew what she was doing, and she knew what I liked. Because losing myself to her was the most beautiful thing I ever did. And I lost it, muffling my moans in the covers.

Alice put a hand to my racing heart, and slowly touched my lips. In her hands, I drifted away.

Chapter Twenty-Two

In the morning the text from Miranda came.

Haven't seen you in a while, I know that you've been busy since Jake came back. Come to the bar in the evening!

With classes back, my work, and relationships with two people, I didn't have any time to see Miranda. She didn't know about our arrangement, and it hurt me to keep secrets from her. We agreed to wait until we ourselves were comfortable before saying anything to anyone.

For Jake it was easy, he was glad to share me with Alice. For Alice, the charade proved to be difficult. And me, I was on the verge of discovering something I didn't yet want to see.

But before all that, the three of us agreed to go to the bar on Friday night.

The familiar setting of a sticky door, loud music, and the usual faces made me cringe. I quickly realized that I wanted to be somewhere quiet, lost between the sheets. But I could not even take Alice's hand, because Jake's arm was draped around my shoulders.

Miranda squealed when she saw me, sloshing her beer

when she rose from the table to greet me. Her positivity was infectious, and I smiled at her.

"Okay?" I asked her and looked at Brian.

She nodded, beaming.

I realized how long it had been since we had last talked, really talked, and damned with the rules, I wanted to discuss everything with her. I needed to talk about the knot of feelings I couldn't untangle by myself.

She greeted Alice and winked at Jake.

"You could have brought her earlier," Miranda said, sitting back. "So how are you two lovebirds doing?"

"I'm going for drinks," Alice interrupted, standing up.

"I'll help," Jake said and they disappeared into the crowd.

"We're fine," I said. Miranda was smiling, but Brian's brow shot up in question. "No, really everything is okay."

Miranda looked from me to Brian and back. "Are you two hiding something?"

"No," we said simultaneously.

"Both of you are awful liars," she said. "I'll talk to you at home," she said to Brian and he groaned.

Jake and Alice came back. Jake put a glass of beer in front of me and sat by my side, Alice on his other side. He draped his arm over my shoulders, a familiar gesture that made me uncomfortable this time.

"Thanks," I muttered.

Miranda told us how she and Brian had gone to Canada to visit her parents for a few days, and how amazingly well it went, not turning into a disaster even though Brian made a few cringy jokes. Thankfully, her dad shared the same weird kind of humor, and while Miranda and her mom rolled their eyes, Brian cracked with laughter with her dad.

I could not imagine a similar story for me. How could it be explained to their parents that their kids shared one girlfriend? There would not be bonding laughter, but tombstone silence.

"Anyway, Brian and I are going on a short couples retreat. It's a weekend event organized by some yogi on how to expand your horizon," Miranda said, leaning in so only the three of us could hear.

"It sounds shady," Brian said.

"No, it's not," Miranda retorted. "There will be yoga for couples and talking about how to build a healthy relationship."

"We already have a healthy one," Brian groaned.

"There's always room for improvement. So would you two like to come? It should be fun. I can send you the details. It's in the woods. In the pictures, the cabins get lost in the trees and snow."

I looked at Alice, her gaze lowered to her hands, fingers wrapped around untouched beer. She didn't look back.

"It sounds ... magical," Jake said.

"Yeah, but we're going to pass. Thanks, Miranda," I said. Alice still didn't move.

"Okay, but just think about it. Just the two of you in the cabin, creating a new bond," Miranda said.

Brian looked fast at Alice and back at me. He clasped a hand over Miranda's.

"Don't push them."

She nodded.

"So how was Canada in winter?" I asked. "Did you see a bear?"

"Actually we did," Brian said, happy to change the topic.

Alice finally moved, she put a hand on Jake's shoulder, muttering something in his ear. She didn't look at me.

"I'm going home, guys," she said and stood up. "I'm not feeling well. It was nice seeing you."

She smiled and waved to everyone. Not meeting my eyes, she left the table to a murmur of goodbyes.

Brian tried to fill the pause, telling us how confusing the metric system in Canada was. It took me a few moments to realize that something was wrong, that my chest ached for the person who had just left.

"Excuse me," I said, standing up. "I'll be right back."

And I ran after her. Strangers kept bumping into me when I pushed through. Outside, the cool air hit my thin sweater. I shivered. My jacket was draped inside on a chair.

I knew where she parked, so I ran there. Alice was standing by her car, her head bowed, a hand on the yellow roof.

"How are you?" I asked, and she lifted her eyes to mine finally. There were tears staining her cheeks.

"Oh, God, where is your jacket? You'll freeze!" she exclaimed.

"I'm okay," I said. "What's happening?"

She walked to me and looked around.

"Please go inside, we'll talk later. You'll catch a cold."

A guy walked past us, a familiar face. He greeted us, his eyes going down to our hands entwined. Alice quickly dropped my hands.

"I'll come back to you tonight," I said.

"It's Jake's turn," she whispered.

"Damn, Alice. There are no turns, no rules. I want to be with you."

She shook her head. "Please go back inside."

Alice shifted, opened a car door, and climbed inside. A light vapor clouded her words when she said, "I need a moment to myself."

I nodded and hugged myself. She didn't look at me as she closed the door and turned on the engine. Violent shivers ran down the length of my exposed hands and neck.

I didn't want to go back. I wanted to go with her in that

small yellow car, just to drive and drive on the highway. To hear her laugh, to hear her sing to one of the old rock songs. But all I got was a flicker of taillight.

Jake was standing outside, my jacket in his hands. He draped it over my shoulders and I instantly felt warmer.

"She went for a drive," I said.

"It's difficult for her."

"What is?" I asked.

"Us."

I nodded.

"I thought it would make her happy, I really did," he said and rubbed his cheek. "You know, she's never been in love before."

I jerked my head in his direction. Love.

"Neither have I," he said quietly. "And of course, fate would twist us to love one person. But we are different ..."

"What should I do?" I whispered.

"Listen to your heart," he said and looked around. Groups of people smoked outside, glasses in their hands, a peal of booming laughter echoed around, a heated discussion—a quarrel—happened to our left. But the air between us was silent.

"Let's go inside," Jake said and I nodded.

I was not ready to face the decisions I needed to make. So once inside I walked straight to the bar and downed a tequila shot. And two more.

Finally, with the sharpness of reality blurring, the pain in the chest eased. I knew it was temporary. But it helped in that moment.

I returned to the table where Jake was talking to Brian. And Miranda eyed me, her arm draped over the back of my chair. I slammed down, mumbling apologies.

"You're a mess, Emily."

"I am."

She looked at Brian. "I'm sorry," she whispered so only I could hear. "I had no idea ..."

"What are you talking about?" I slurred.

"About you and Alice, does Jake know?"

I snorted. "It's complicated."

"Talk to me," she said, worry woven into her features.

"Later, okay? I still need to think about a lot. I need to listen to my heart."

The rush of the bar was so loud. The music pulsed in my head. Glasses clinked at the next table. Laughter rang in my ears. I looked at Jake, and he smiled at me. Not his usual smile, not open, but sad.

"What does it say? Your heart, I mean," Miranda said.

It was easy and was always there. I knew what it had kept whispering all this time, finally raising its voice so I could hear it. It screamed over the noise.

I smiled back at Jake.

Chapter Twenty-Three

"Where do you want to spend tonight?" Jake asked once we were back in his car. Finally, my head had cleared after the tequila. I had known the answer all along.

"Your house."

He nodded and turned on the engine. He drank only half a glass of beer that night, but his movements were slow.

"We never had a chance to get that car of yours. I bet she's a beauty," Jake said. It sounded like goodbye. "I'm just ... I'm sorry, Emily. You need to know that I only wanted what's best for all of us, but I see it's not working. You were always different, you changed us. And Alice, she was always lost in her world, as though she tried to hide there, hide her emotions. But with you, she's out finally. And she hurts. It breaks my heart to see her hurting."

I looked at him.

"It would be much simpler if I didn't love you," he said quietly and turned on the engine.

I covered his hand with mine on the wheel, but my silence screamed more than any of my words. He nodded and drove us back to their house. The stillness was crushing between us.

The house was dark when we reached it, though the yellow car was parked outside in its usual spot.

Jake stopped on the porch and turned to me. He hugged me. I remembered how I had felt those first times when he had enveloped his hands around me. Safe, cherished, cared for. I still had all of those things.

He kissed my forehead and went inside, heading straight up the stairs. He didn't turn back when he quietly closed the door to his room, leaving me outside at the top of the stairs.

I went to the bathroom and ran the hottest shower I could handle. The blazing water seared my skin.

Back on the landing, I watched Jake's door for a few seconds. I spun around and went through another door.

Alice's back was turned to the door, so I quietly climbed under the covers and pressed myself to her.

"You came," she whispered, her voice rasping.

"I promised."

She sniffed lightly.

"That was so embarrassing," Alice said. "I was sitting there, and listening to how you were referred to as a couple, lovebirds. And I know we agreed to keep us a secret, but I could not imagine it changing. I pictured Miranda asking how the three of us were doing, if we wanted to go to a couples retreat. Oh, wait, we are not a couple. I felt invisible there. Like you and I don't exist. And I know how immature I was, how it's stupid to want that appreciation from outsiders. The most important thing is how we both feel about each other."

She turned to me and I saw her red-rimmed eyes, cheeks wet with tears. "I saw how we could never be a couple in the open. We would never be able to hold hands in public freely because someone we know could see us. You know, I wanted to be able to be your girlfriend, to be able to hug and kiss you in front of anyone. To be referred to as a couple."

I slowly traced my fingertips over her cheeks, catching her tears.

"I'm sorry, I know that I'm whining, and needy. And the main thing is that I can be with you, but tonight I just saw what we won't have, and damn, I can't stop crying. And do you know what is the most awful thing about all this? I envy Jake. I envy how easily he can drop an arm over your shoulders, run fingers over your wrist, simply be close."

"Do you wish you never met me?" I asked, almost inaudibly.

Alice froze and looked at me.

"No, don't you dare think like that!" Alice said, sitting up. "I need you to know one thing," she whispered and pressed her fingers to my chin, "you are the most wonderful thing that happened in my life, you woke me up, I feel ... I feel you here." Alice slid her hand to her chest. "I just wish it all was simpler. I wish for you and Jake to be happy."

"You two are the most selfless people in the whole world," I said.

She snorted. "Jake is, I'm most definitely not."

Alice dropped back to her pillow, her face inches from mine.

"I'm sorry about tonight," I said.

"Come here," she said softly and snuggled me into her arms. Alice smelled of vanilla as I rubbed my nose on her neck. I traced the skin on her back, our legs entwined. I never wanted her to cry again, and as I tried to shield her from the outside world I pressed my body closer. She was so warm, so soft, her breathing calm. We lay there in silence, slowly drifting to sleep.

I heard a whisper. "I love you, Emily."

But I was dreaming already.

~

I opened my eyes. Alice was breathing lightly by my side. A soft light poured from the window in her room. It was minutes past sunrise. I quietly stood up and put my clothes on. Alice was a deep sleeper, even a cannon fire wouldn't wake her before her usual wake-up time. I gazed at her blonde hair as it spilled onto the pillow, how her features were so serene—eyes closed, lips slightly parted.

I took a piece of paper from her printer and found a pen. The three words I wrote made me smile. It was simple, and complicated at the same time. But what I felt toward the woman sleeping in that bed had been right in front of me the whole time. Jake realized it before I did.

I put the paper on the pillow and quietly left the room.

I love you.

Outside the house, I looked back at it. The fresh layer of snow gave it the look of a gingerbread house covered in soft powdered sugar. As I stood there my heart sang for the feeling I had finally accepted, naming it to myself and to her gave it clarity. But my heart also broke for the pain I would need to inflict on another person. Another heart I was about to break. I turned and slowly went back to my dormitory.

I didn't know that it was all irrelevant, the feelings I felt didn't matter a bit. As I walked down the street I didn't know one thing: I would never see one of them again.

Chapter Twenty-Four

As I reached my dorm room I had a clear understanding of what I wanted to do. I wanted to talk to Alice, to say that I'd fallen in love with her and that I wanted to be her girlfriend, in all possible ways. But before that, I needed to talk to Jake, to confess everything, to tell him that it was not working. That our trio was doomed from the beginning, that I was not a polyamorous person. And what actually happened was that I fell in love with his sister while dating him. How I actually betrayed him and his trust.

I was not sure they would accept me. Alice might reject me so as not to hurt her brother. How could it work out? Alice and I lived happily ever after with a hurting Jake by our side? No.

This time I'd let them decide. I would spill everything that was on my mind and in my heart and hope for the best. No more schedules, rules, dividing. My heart couldn't accept what my mind agreed to. The truth finally surfaced, I loved her.

I picked up my phone and dialed Jake's number, the call going to voicemail. I left a message asking him to call me back as soon as possible.

Then I waited. I called back a few more times, and when it was impossible to stay inside anymore, I went to the park. I stood in a usual queue at The Corner, ordering a latte, and slowly walked down the path. I tried to see the beauty around me, the trees dressed in white, the clear blue sky, the sun playing on white patches of snow a million shades of gold.

I could not understand why he was ignoring me. Even though he might have known what I wanted to talk about, as far as I knew him, he always was up to a dialogue. Especially when it concerned Alice. Finally, as my fingers started going numb, and the sun hid behind the trees, I called Alice.

Same. The call went to voicemail. A crippling feeling of worry scratched at me. I shook my head, thinking that I might as well get used to being alone again. Even though I loved Alice, it didn't mean that she would want to be with me. The bond between brother and sister was much stronger and more important than any girlfriend. But I hoped they could talk to me at least, even if it was for the last time.

A feeling of panic was rising fast as I slammed my fingers into my phone screen calling them both again and again.

I stopped and looked up. The sky to the left was turning purple, my favorite time of the day. Long shadows covered me while the sky up above me turned into a brightly lit canvas.

The phone vibrated in my hand. I smiled, finally one of them was calling me back. I didn't look at the caller id when I picked up the phone.

"Emily? Emily, where are you?"

It was Miranda. Her voice was rushed, worried.

"I'm at the park. Sorry, now isn't the best time, I'm waiting for a call," I said.

"Oh. I need to see you, when could you be at the exit of the park?" she said, her voice shaking.

"In fifteen minutes. Is everything alright? How's Brian?" I asked. I'd never heard her voice so trembling.

"He's fine. I'll meet you there in fifteen minutes."

Before I could say anything, she hung up. That was weird, but Miranda needed me. I hurried my steps to reach the exit. I would explain everything to her and go to Jake and Alice's house. If they kept ignoring me, it was time for drastic action. I *must* talk to them.

I stopped under the sign saying that the park had a circular trail, its length, and flora and fauna details. Miranda still had a few minutes. I was trying to read the information about the endemic bushes that grew only in this part of the country when I heard her voice.

"I'm so sorry," Miranda said as I turned around.

She was breathing hard as though she was running. She was. But what stunned me most was the expression of pure shock on her face.

"Oh God, what happened?" I asked, rushing to her.

"Emily, Jake is dead," she said.

I stopped in my tracks. I noticed how the gravel crunched under my boots. I knew where my heart was, and in that moment I felt it falling. Somewhere deep.

"What?"

"This morning he drove to the farmers market outside the city. It was a head-on collision. A teenager was texting when he hit an ice patch. He didn't make it. Jake died instantly." Her voice was wet and trembling, but the words didn't make any sense to me.

"Miranda, it's cruel to joke like this," I said calmly.

She reached me, slowly. Her eyes were on me. Miranda shook her head, as her fingers covered her mouth.

Something punched me in the gut as I bent in two. Suddenly I wanted to vomit, but only a low gurgling sound escaped me. I could not understand what was happening to my body, because clearly, it was not true. A misunderstanding. My mind was calm, as my body started shaking.

"No, I saw him yesterday. I need to talk to him," I said and started walking in the direction of their house. "I just need a few words with Jake."

Miranda rushed to my side, walking with me.

"Emily, he's not there."

"It's Saturday, he went to the farmers market, as you said. He should be back home now," I said, quickening my steps.

"Jake died."

I turned to her and screamed.

"Shut your mouth, Miranda. Shut your damn mouth! Stop lying to me."

It was as though I had slapped her, hard. But she shook her head and looked at me.

"I'm so sorry." She sobbed.

I stood there, a wind slowly rocking the tops of the trees as a feeling of understanding crept in. My mind was catching up with my body.

"Alice," I breathed. And I ran, I ran as hard as I ever had in my life. The snow, the ice, the roads, the cars honking, it all blurred around me, as one thought pulsed inside me. I needed to get to Alice.

But I was too late. The house stood dark, with no cars parked in their usual spots.

I ran up the porch and jammed my finger into the buzzer. It blared inside, but it was the only response I got.

"Please, open, please, please," I muttered. But there was no reply.

I pressed my forehead to the door, and it was so, so cold. My fingers rattled the door handle, locked.

I went down the steps and looked around. The house stared back blankly. I fished my phone out of my pocket, but my hands were trembling so violently that I dropped it.

Thankfully it landed in the snow, just inches from concrete that would have been the end of it.

I picked it up and called Jake.

"Oh, God, pick up, pick up, please pick up," I cried, the last two words turning into a shout as his cheerful voice asked to leave a message.

And it hit.

I fell to my knees, pressed my forehead to the dirty patch of stone, and shut my eyes. It didn't help to stop the liquid pouring out of them. This could not be happening.

Miranda was confused. Somebody had tricked her, and as trusting as she was, she believed.

"Emily, you have to stand up," she said, tugging me up.

She had run behind me all the way, but I was faster, getting there first.

"How do you know? Who told you?" I asked, my voice clearing, steadying. I would get to the core of this trick.

"Jenny, she volunteers at the hospital," Miranda whispered.

"Oh, Jenny. She doesn't even know Jake well. How many times has she seen him? Twice?" I tried to laugh, it turned to a choke.

"She saw the body."

I stood, stunned, watching her. Body. I turned to the side, clutching a fistful of my jacket not far from where my heart was. Everything stung, everything burned, and I retched. My mind went blank as I watched the meager food I had eaten that day leaving my body. *Alice would be furious*, I thought.

Alice. I coughed one last time. I must find her.

I started walking.

"Where are you going?" Miranda asked, following me.

"Hospital."

"It's out of the city," she said.

"I need to get there. Alice is there."

"Let Brian drive you," she said.

"I'll walk."

And I walked. But Miranda was by my side, calling Brian, whispering something urgently into the phone. We walked what felt like hours, days, years. My brain was on pause, as tears ran down my face, as snot froze on my burning skin.

A car stopped in front of me. It was familiar. Miranda rushed to the door and opened it for me.

"Get in," she ordered.

Brian looked at me from the driver's seat. He didn't say anything as his red-rimmed eyes followed my moves. I climbed inside and gripped the door.

I watched the cars passing by. It seemed that we crawled on the highway, and I wanted to scream. I closed my eyes and heard Jake laughing, his eyes crackling. I felt his hands on my shoulders. I felt loved, and even though I fell in love with his sister, Jake was first. Jake was the one who brought me back to life with his light, who brought joy, who stood by my side.

And they said there was no light anymore.

I lowered my head between my knees—the brace position on airplanes—but that posture wouldn't save me from this crashing and burning. I rocked back and forth, attempting to soothe myself. That morning I had been ready to break up with him, and he knew it. Encompassing guilt squeezed my lungs, my stomach, as I tried to take a breath, no air coming in.

Miranda turned to me from the passenger seat. She squeezed my shoulder and pressed a palm to my back, grounding me.

"Shhh," she murmured as I rocked.

The car came to a stop. A spring released in me as I jumped from the car, and I was running again. Miranda screamed my name.

But I ran on, sliding doors, people making a way for me, their eyes widening, the blinding light of the hospital reception sliced my retinas.

"I need to see Jake, Jacob O'Neal," I said to a woman in blue scrubs.

Her expression didn't change as she typed in the name on the computer. She looked up at me, her expression blank.

"Are you family?" she asked.

"Girlfriend."

"Please contact the family," the woman said.

"I can't!" I cried.

"I'm sorry, there is nothing I can help you with," she said.

"What?"

"All information regarding the person can be disclosed to close family members only," she said in a dull drill.

Miranda placed a firm grip on my shoulders. "Let's go," she said quietly.

I saw the look she gave to the woman when she pulled me away from the counter, of pure hatred.

"I'm not family," I whispered as Miranda let me outside.

I stopped right at the doors.

"I'll wait for Alice here, she must be somewhere in the building," I said. "She must be."

Miranda nodded and took me by my arm and led me to the waiting area. We sat there. I looked at the door. Alice might be going in, or out, any minute. I couldn't look away so as not to miss her. Every time the door opened my heart leaped, and every time it was someone else.

Miranda sat by my side, silent. Sometime later Brian joined us. We waited, and waited, and waited. I didn't look at the clock when we first sat down, but sometime later I noticed how its hands sped and dragged, counting seconds, minutes, and hours. I was afraid to blink, afraid that Alice would float past me like a gust of wind and disappear inside the hospital.

Someone was touching my face, I turned to see Miranda brushing my forehead with a wet wipe. There was dirt on it when she pulled it away. I vaguely remembered how I had pressed my face into the concrete outside the house. But I could not look away from the door. Any minute. She'd be there.

She never came.

Chapter Twenty-Five

Five days later I was sitting in Miranda's living room. It was quiet, except for drops of melting snow hitting the ground outside. The drip, drip, drip did little to ground me.

I didn't remember a lot from the previous five days. My memory didn't store information anymore. Everything hurt. My limbs were heavy. A dull static ache hissed inside my chest. My throat still burned. When I asked Miranda why it was so sore, she said it was from my screams. I didn't remember any screams, but apparently, I lost it when Miranda and Brian took me away from the hospital after hours of waiting. Miranda said we sat there for ten hours.

Doctors gave me a sedative shot. I opened my eyes in their house, and there, I spent all those days. Somewhere during this time Miranda took me to Jake and Alice's house, it was dark. There was a funeral, but I was heavily sedated. The casket was closed, and I spent the entire time looking down at my feet. Alice was not there, but a lot of people were. And I didn't know many of them.

I met their parents. Jake took many facial expressions from his dad, while Alice was a copy of her mom. Of course, they didn't know me. When Miranda said I was Jake's girlfriend, they just nodded. I think they were sedated like me because nothing but naked grief was in their features. I asked where Alice was.

"Gone," her mother said.

All I remembered from the funeral was the sky. Gray, heavy, rolling sky. Then nothing.

Only pain. I welcomed it as an old friend. I was familiar with it. I'd lost a person before. I knew how it worked. And I was so worried about Alice, because she didn't know.

A few days later I asked Brian to drive me to my dorm room. Miranda protested, she wanted me to stay, she said it was too early for me to be alone. I hoped Alice was not alone.

I hugged Miranda and said that I was okay. It was the second time she was saving me.

My room was tidy when I came back, Miranda had taken care of it. I spent hours sitting on my bed and watching the dreamcatcher that hung above it, white feathers unmoving.

I missed Jake, his light laugh. From our first dates I felt his presence, always close, and now I knew I was alone. He was there for such a short time, but he was there. His care was like a warm blanket. He wasn't there anymore, only a chilling cold gripped my body.

I knew how to cope, my mind remembered all the books and articles I read about it for months after my dad died, when I finally was ready to move on.

One night I found myself standing under the lamp post in the park, the one Jake always met me at. I stood there and watched the trees. It was dark and quiet, and no one was around. I didn't know I had it in me, but a gurgling wet sound pressed my chest. I was not whimpering, no, I was choking. I was choking on my grief—the miserable feeling of missing them both so much I could not breathe.

I took my phone from my pocket. The screen was covered

in a tiny web, the bottom cover cracked. It was from the days I didn't remember. Miranda said I threw the phone at the wall after one of the times I had called Alice.

It showed three AM. With familiar movements, I scrolled down to Alice's number and dialed. It went to voicemail. I stopped leaving messages some time ago. I was sure she was not listening to them.

I sat down on the bench and pressed my fingers to my eyes. They were wet, and all I saw were dark spots.

"Where are you?" I asked out loud.

Only the wind replied. She could be somewhere in Eastern Europe for all I knew. She could be anywhere. But all I hoped for her was that she was not alone, that there was someone to ease the pain.

Slowly I returned to my dorm room. That night I dreamt of Jake. He was laughing, and by his side was my dad, they were both smiling. It was a bit easier in the morning, just a little bit.

I stood by Miranda's front door. A doormat cheerfully said that I was finally home. I wasn't.

She opened the door, surprise changing to worry in a second.

"Emily, come in," she said, opening the door wider.

I went inside; it was warm. The big illuminated deer stood turned off in the hall. They put it there after the Christmas party. Brian peered from the living room and waved at me. He didn't know how to behave around me, like I was a crystal ball ready to turn into a bomb at any moment. He had seen the worst of me when I had screamed and clawed at them in the hospital. It took three male nurses to calm me down, Miranda said. I listened to it as if it was a story of someone else.

I wanted to tell him that I was still just Emily, sad, shattered, but still the girl he knew.

I cleared my throat. No sound came out.

Miranda took my hand. "It's ok," she said, as I watched our hands together.

"Could you ..." my voice trailed off, as the tears came back again. They always returned those days. When I thought there was nothing more to shed, no liquid, they came. They came in the most inappropriate place: in shops, in lectures, where I made myself go again, for the old promise I had made to my dad. But mostly, they came at night, smearing my pillow with stains.

I wiped them quickly as I noticed Bryan looking away.

"I'm sorry," I murmured.

Miranda nodded, squeezing my hand lightly.

"Could you please drive me to their parents' house?" I asked quickly.

"Emily," Miranda started to protest.

"Yes, okay," Brian said. Miranda turned to him, her brows raised.

I took a shaky breath, as more tears blurred my vision. "Thank you."

Somewhere deep in my mind, I thought about how uncomfortable I made Brian, with all my crying, and grief.

"I'll go," I said and turned to the door, dropping Miranda's hand.

But before I could even take a step, Brian came up to me— I was slow those days. He did the unexpected, he put his arms around me, wrapping me tightly in an embrace. My body shook with sobs as I cried into his shirt.

"I miss them so much," I said. "So, so much."

"I know," he said, his hand on the back of my head. "I'm sorry."

When he released me, I looked at Miranda. Silent tears ran down her cheeks.

"God, this is so unfair," she said angrily, her hands going to fists. "Jake was full of life, he should have lived! How could it happen?"

"Death happens." I said the phrase I had read in one of the books a year after my father died.

"Stay here tonight?" Miranda asked.

I looked at her and then at Brian, who nodded. I was so weak, I had no strength anymore to fight, to protest.

I glanced up. I was standing on the place where during what felt like ages ago, the mistletoe had hung. I remembered those red lips kissing Alice. I remembered figuring out what I felt toward her. The time we had afterward was such a short, short time.

Miranda and I sat on a battered leather sofa in front of their massive TV; Brian sat in his armchair, which he called Chandler's and Joey's chair copy. They turned on some random show, and as it played I knew none of us was really paying any attention.

I watched as Brian tried to hide his eyes with his hand, giving up some time later, and just wiping the tears from time to time. They grew closer when Jake had moved into town, spending a few times a week together discussing God knows what. Brian lost a friend.

And I lost them both. In my wildest dreams—before Jake disappeared from the world—I imagined him letting me go, imagined him happy for me and Alice, him and I staying friends. How it would have been in reality, I didn't know. Probably not so amicable and light. But they would have known the truth. And I hated that the night before he died, he figured everything out. I hated that I didn't have a chance to even speak to him. But what would I say? Sorry, we have to break up, I love your sister.

It was all so messed up before he drove to the market that morning. I had made it messy. All I had left was a scorched emptiness, the land of my heart where two people I loved used to be. I loved them both, but differently.

"You know," Brian said and turned to me, interrupting the spiral of my thoughts, "he was happy with you, you need to know that. He loved you."

I nodded. "I was about to break up with him," I said quietly.

They didn't ask why. By then Miranda and Brian had figured it out.

"I love his sister," I said to the silence and turned back to the screen.

Chapter Twenty-Six

I sat in the back seat, watching the familiar highway twisting up ahead. Alice loved to drive that road, just drive, for hours on end. And I loved when she took me with her, sweet treats for us on the dashboard, rock music playing in the background. I could almost hear her voice as she sang out of tune.

This time Brian was driving. It was a different car, a different smell, different people. We were driving to the one place I thought Alice should be. Her parent's house.

I pushed my sneakers off and pulled my feet up to the seat. The snow was melting, gray patches showed the dirt. A lead sky seemed to crush the earth.

"You know, the three of us were a couple for some time," I said.

Miranda's hand stilled as she was brushing a lock from her forehead. She turned to me.

"They were brother and sister, even though Jake was adopted," she said slowly. "Didn't you think it was a bit gross?"

"Did the three of you sleep together?" Brian asked, old humor in his voice. Hilarious.

"God, no," I said, disgusted. "They would never do that. It was separate. I was his girlfriend and hers, they never crossed over. Jake believed that I was polyamorous, that I could divide time between them, to create two separate relationships."

"It didn't work, did it?" Miranda asked.

"No." I shook my head. "I was just falling in love with Alice while dating him. He believed we could make it. Alice struggled from the start but agreed to try because Jake loved me. And I just couldn't, you know. I couldn't."

"He just didn't want to lose you," Brian said.

"But ... but that sharing concept was sick," Miranda turned to me.

I looked out of the window. I remembered three of us dressed fancily, sitting at the table, happy.

"You know, it wasn't. There were never any disgusting moments between the three of us, I just couldn't navigate it. I always ended up in her room, in her arms. Subconsciously delaying the moment I would need to break his heart. And I think I broke everything in the end," I said.

"Did Alice love you back?" Miranda asked.

Before I could reply, Brian said: "She did."

I pressed my trembling fingers to my lips as I looked out of the window. "She did," I replied.

The drive took hours, the daylight was already fading when we reached the small suburban city. The houses were bigger there, freshly painted, mostly new cars stood in the driveways. When we stopped I looked around, my eyes going wide.

"This is it," Brian said, checking the address.

We stood by a huge two-story house, a circular driveway leading to its door. It had a garage on the right, closed, a black BMW crossover was parked by the garage door.

"Wow," Miranda whispered. "Are they rich?"

I didn't know, I didn't know a lot about their family.

Brian looked through the window of the house. "The family always had money, it seems they did well with investing."

I spent only a moment imagining Alice and Jake in that house, which slightly resembled a palace. One thought pumped through my mind: there was no yellow car. It's in the garage, it must be.

With trembling fingers I opened the door, stepped out of the warmth of the car, and stopped, looking around, my hand on the car roof. The lawns would be lush green in just a few months. The immaculate neighborhood of the upper class. I could imagine Jake and Alice there, sheltered from the outside world. I could imagine the library inside where Alice devoured books written by poets in foreign languages. I could imagine Jake there on Christmas, the house easily accommodating his vast family, children running around, unpacking their pricey gifts.

I took a deep breath and walked down the driveway. My heart was beating so fast I could not hear my thoughts. She must be there.

I stopped in front of the door and looked back, Miranda gave a thumbs up from the car. The door was painted midnight blue, a rich color, with a silver knocker in the shape of a delicate hand placed in the middle. My hand went to use it, but I stopped in time, only tracing its outline with my fingers.

There was a modern-looking buzzer with a camera on my right. I pressed the button.

Nothing happened for minutes, even though I knew someone was inside, there was a light in the windows.

I pressed again and hugged my torso. I looked around, the tight darkness was lowering itself.

The door opened and a thin ashen face looked back at me.

"Hi," I said. "I—"

"I know who you are," the woman said kindly. Even though her face was streaked with grief, I saw how lively it could have been just weeks before.

"I'm so sorry for your loss," I whispered. She shook her head, a jerking motion.

Alice looked just like her and I knew I was staring. The woman touched my wrist for a moment.

"And I'm sorry for yours."

I nodded, looking down. I could not break down in front of their mom.

"Is Alice here?" I asked.

"No, sorry, sweetheart."

I rubbed my jacket near my heart, because it burned. "Where ..." I stopped, taking a shaking breath, the dreadful tears pooling again. "Where can I find her?"

There was a movement behind the woman and the door opened wider. A man was looking at me, their dad.

"Please," I whispered, catching my hand on the door frame. "I need to see her."

"She's gone," the man said.

"Where?"

"She travels, hops from place to place. She asked not to look for her," he said.

I looked up at him, he was tall, like Jake was. "How can I reach her? Please."

The woman shifted and caught a single tear running down her cheek with her thumb.

"Emily," she said quietly. "Alice doesn't want to be found."

A slow understanding was creeping under my skin. "She doesn't want to see me. She ..." I looked into the woman's eyes as mine clouded, "she doesn't need me."

The woman nodded, as fat tears ran down her cheeks.

"I see," I said and sniffed. "Please tell Alice the next time she contacts you that I love her."

"God, I'm so sorry," the woman said and turned around, disappearing inside, her back hunched.

The man walked closer to the door.

"I think it's best for you to forget her," he said.

"How can I?"

He took a deep breath and looked down, bracing himself.

"Please don't come here again," he said and started closing the door. Just before it clicked shut he whispered: "I'm sorry."

Midnight blue was in front of me again.

I sobbed, my palm spreading over the door, the cold smooth surface. I lowered my head, another sob escaping, and I covered my mouth with a shaking hand. I looked at the ground, my tears disappearing in the doormat.

Alice didn't need me. Cruel burning words flashed in my mind. I was slowly going down, my knees were weak. But before I could touch the ground, strong hands caught me. Brian and Miranda stood by my side, their faces dark.

"Let's go," he whispered and pulled me up.

I stood up, despite my legs turning into a heavy concrete. But I made one step, and another, walking away from that door. In the middle of the driveway, I turned around and looked at the house. The windows on the ground floor were lit, the shapes of windows upstairs hid in the dark. But I stopped and watched one particular window, because there, between the curtains and my tears I noticed movement, a flash of something light, like... like blonde hair. Was it my pained imagination?

"Alice," I whispered, my hand going up.

Nothing but a blank window looked back at me. In that moment my heart cracked in two, finally breaking like crystal glass on ice.

Miranda hugged my shoulders and turned me back to the car. Inside I lay down on the back seat, like a rag doll, my body going limp. We drove into the dark as I quietly broke down.

Part Two

Chapter Twenty-Seven

Seven Years Later

What am I doing here? I thought sitting in an elegant restaurant, the delicate stem of a wine glass between my fingers.

My profile on the dating app said that I loved wine, when in reality I would much prefer a simple sweet cocktail with an umbrella on top. But that was a small lie on the list of truths. My profile boasted that I loved driving and was proud of my 1969 Ford Mustang Boss 429. That was the car my Dad had left me. It sat covered at the house I had rented out for years, and that car was my most helpful remedy when I finally woke up from the dark, murky place I found myself in during my early twenties. After Jake and Alice.

I had just hit thirty. I had thought something would change in my daily life, some fundamental shift in me turning a year older. I'd be wiser, stronger, happier.

None of that happened.

I still was me. My happiest moments were behind the wheel of the Mustang, alone.

As soon as I started making money I poured all of it into the car restoration. And it became my most striking and exotic feature, my car. I was sure many men invited me on dates just to see the Mustang.

Yes, only men. That feature was set as the default on the profile when I first filled it in.

Straight. I left it as it was.

After that decision, I spent many mornings waking up in strangers' beds, their arms draped over my body. I felt nothing. Even though my profile said I wanted a steady relationship as time went on, a few handsome candidates noted that I rejected anything that turned remotely serious. Maybe I should have changed my profile afterward. Or deleted it altogether.

My phone held a few numbers of guys who would gladly spend the night with me. In the mornings we would dress silently and drive to our fancy jobs. Easy, comfortable.

This was the last chance, I promised myself. The last chance to find a real partner. I scratched my nose, considering whether I actually needed one. Thank God I lived in the twenty-first century. Thank God for the internet, and all the benefits it brought.

My dread over finding a job after university looked laughable in hindsight. But during that time I was afraid I would not wake up in the morning because my heart would stop during the night. It hurt like hell that year. Of course it would. My dad had died, then Jake, then those moving curtains—ignoring me. They brought a final blow. Alice was there, in that house. I knew it. And during the first nights, after everything happened, I thought that having a dagger pierce my heart would have felt like a soft caress compared to what I felt at the time.

I tried not to think of that time anymore. I didn't want to look past that fog that covered the memories and pain.

"Emily?"

I looked up at the man standing next to my table. He was much taller than I had imagined, and the photo on his profile didn't show the sparkling gentleness of his eyes. That was the first feature I noticed.

"I'm so sorry for being late, there was an accident on the road which stopped the traffic dead for half an hour. I wanted to get here first," he said, shaking my hand lightly and sitting across from me. His hand was big and smooth.

"Showing up first isn't always a good idea, it doesn't let you run away if needed," I said.

"Have you ever done it? Run away from a date?"

I thought for a second. "Sure, when the photo on their profile doesn't match the reality. One time a man used a photo of his brother, he later confessed to me in a message. And one clever guy photoshopped a photo of him twenty years ago. Those times I didn't get there first so I could escape. A few times I wasn't so lucky and cursed my punctuality afterward."

"Have you been on a lot of dates from the app?" The man asked.

"Yes," I said and sipped my wine. "But you will be the last."

He raised an eyebrow.

"Hm, sounds like a lame punchline, right?" I laughed. "I decided that it's time to end this dating app thing. Either way, if it works today or not, I'm deleting the app."

He leaned back and ran his hand through his short blond hair.

"Let's make it work," he said.

"That was a great punchline," I said and smiled as he bowed his head in a mock appreciation.

I had stopped having long discussions on the app before

meeting the person after a few tremendous failures. When I realized that spending so much time typing messages was time and energy-draining, just to have to flee the date as soon as possible, I changed how I went about things. Now my strategy evolved and I was sure to meet in person as fast as possible.

But with Arthur, who sat across from me in that moment, it was different. His profile picture looked too good to be true, which had become a warning sign. But after a few pleasantries, I suggested we meet. By the time I decided we should meet though, he had left for a business trip to Japan, so I had been ready to say goodbye to the pretty image. He had somehow managed to keep me intrigued despite the great distance separating us. He actually sent me daily updates from Japan and as hard as I had tried not to spend too much time on my phone, Arthur roped me in by talking about one thing I actually cared about a lot. Books.

He was an avid reader, and his reading list was almost identical to mine. It was actually pleasant when I lazed around in the evening and discussed evolutionary trends from the latest non-fiction hit he read on the plane, which I had devoured two weeks before him.

All I had to do was wait for his weird side to reveal itself, because the man in front of me was too good to be true.

He had a deep voice, which sounded like the pleasant rumble of faraway thunder. With a heavy British accent, his vowels rolled in unfamiliar ways. He didn't dress fancy, simple jeans and a crisp white shirt. Arthur definitely worked out, because even in the dim light of the restaurant I could see his well-formed biceps. A typical macho man who spent hours in the gym and lived with his mom, that could be true of him. I would find out. But so far he was smart and sharp as a razor, at least in his messages, and when I saw him scratching his chin, short stubble covering it, a watch showed everything I needed to know.

He was rich.

It was always like that in the Valley, difficult to judge someone on their image. A person who was dressed in comfortable worn shoes and old jeans could own millions in stocks. And a shiny exterior often covered nothing but a desperate man in search of his sponsor, be it a woman or man. I met all kinds, and was tired of all of them, wishing to be alone from the second any of them opened their mouth.

Life had made me hard, cold, and calculating. The belief in beauty and warmth had died on the driveway of a suburban town years ago. All that was left was divided in exactly three ways: my job, Miranda and Brian, and my car.

"So, what's your story with the dating app?" I asked, leaning back. "Please don't tell me any soul mate search stories."

He laughed, and it was a pleasant sound. The sound suited him—matched his exterior.

"Anyone still do that?" he asked.

I nodded. "Some actually believe they can find love on a dating app."

"And you don't?"

"I haven't been searching for it, so I've mostly found what I needed. You're good at dodging questions," I said.

"Sorry, it's part of my job." He smiled. "Anyway, I haven't had a lot of dates, not many proved to be interesting to text with. My strategy is the opposite of yours. I enjoy texting people and getting to know them first before a date. If a woman sticks with the texts, and only a few did, it usually proves to be a good match for a few dates."

"You set traps in text," I said.

He lifted his brow. "These were not traps, more like challenges. You did well by the way."

"I'm honored," I said mockingly. "So, is that how you get your entertainment?"

"Yeah, it is actually. Does it come across as rude?"

I thought about it for a moment. "They are just texts," I said. "And if you want to make your own game by building levels and seeing if the player reaches the end, that's fine I guess. As long as you don't abuse anyone."

"Never," he said, looking directly at me. "Right, so I play games with real people on my phone when I travel, and I travel a lot. What are your games?"

"My life is a game," I said.

Arthur held my gaze, his eyes were a greyish blue.

"You don't believe that," he said, smiling.

"Maybe."

It all sounded like a real-life game to me. The natural continuation of our texts, which sometimes were lengthy discussions of questions of life. It sometimes felt like our back and forth was made of clever chess moves.

A waiter appeared by our side and took our orders. I wanted a salad, while Arthur ordered a rare steak.

When the waiter disappeared, Arthur leaned in closer to me and a soft trace of cedar wood and dark spices reached me, mixed with something I hadn't smelled in a while.

"You smoke?" I asked.

"Yes."

It was such an outdated habit, costly, and so harmful. I never saw anyone smoking anymore. Yes, lots of vapes and electronic cigarettes, but no real smoking. I had forgotten what it was like when someone actually held a cigarette in their hand.

"Why?"

"I like it. But I'm giving it up in two years. I know the consequences, so I allowed myself time 'til I'm thirty-nine. Then, it must stop," he said.

I nodded.

"So, tell me what you do. I know what your interests are,

what you like, even a hint of your life views, but tell me about your daily life," Arthur said. "All your texts were abstract, philosophical, and quizzical."

I pulled my shoulders back, straightened my spine, and tucked a strand of my hair behind my ear.

"Read me," I said. "Tell me what you see."

"Wow, you are a player too."

I laughed. "Cheesy."

"I know," his eyes sparkled as he put his elbows on the table, scanning me up and down.

"Damn, you're good. You could be anyone. Neurosurgeon, teacher, waiter, hooker, CEO," he said. "You don't wear any jewelry, I can't see your purse or phone to judge. Your nails are neatly trimmed, but with no polish. Your hair shines—could be from an expensive hair salon or it could be natural. Minimal make-up, linen shirt and jeans. And the most striking feature where I should be able to read any information is the eyes, and I just can't read them. Nothing to tell me."

"Unlike your watch," I said.

He smiled. "Not a teacher if you know this kind of thing," he said and shook his wrist. "I could have borrowed it."

"You are too casual with it, not afraid to scratch," I said.

"This is proving to be the most interesting evening I've had in years," he said.

"Oh, it's just that we have one thing in common."

He raised his eyebrow.

"We are bored."

Arthur held my gaze for a long moment. It was unusual to see a reflection of myself in another person. The moment broke when the waiter brought our food.

It was one of those places where you paid a colossal sum of money for the right to be there, not for the food. And the bigger the price tag on the item, the smaller the portion would be. My salad was lost on a massive plate, while Arthur's steak was the size of a ring box.

"Did they feed the cow with gold? Why do I need glasses to actually see what I'm eating?" he asked.

I laughed. "You suggested the place."

"Yeah, a suggestion from colleagues. Next time I should read reviews."

My plate was empty in a few seconds. And not because I was a fast eater.

I leaned back. "I could kill for a pizza now," I said.

Arthur was finishing off his minuscule steak.

"Let's get out of here," he said, turning to a passing waiter and asking for the bill.

When it landed in his hands, I turned to my purse which was hanging on the back of my chair.

Arthur smiled like the Cheshire Cat.

"What?" I asked. "Let me pay my share."

He just waved his hand. "Not a teacher for sure."

Damn, the purse. I didn't spend a lot of money on clothes or accessories, but if I estimated, my purse cost the monthly salary of the waiter who rushed to take the money from Arthur. It was a gift from Miranda and Brian on my thirties birthday.

"It was a gift," I said.

He just winked at me and, it was such a boyish thing on his very adult face, I laughed.

"That's a first; you have a nice laugh," he said.

"More cheesy compliments?"

"Later," he said, standing up.

It was a warm evening outside, a soft breeze playing with my hair. I unlocked my phone and opened a taxi app.

"I know a great pizza place," I said.

"Lead the way."

The app showed an available car right around the corner

and, a few minutes later, we climbed in. It was a short ride to a plaza with closed for the night businesses. Only one sign was blinking: Mario's.

I watched Arthur closely as he stood below the sign, the red colors of it reflecting on his face. There was one plastic table and chairs outside the place.

"This is ..."

"Different?" I finished, smiling. "Let's go, it's the best pizza in the world."

I went in and Mario, an old Italian man, turned to me. He was mid-sentence saying that they were closing, but when he saw me, he smiled.

"Hello, Emily, it's great to see you," he said with a heavy accent.

"Hi, Mario."

"The usual?"

I nodded. "We'll sit outside."

"Suit yourself. You just caught me leaving." Mario looked at Arthur. "Would you like to choose a pizza from the menu?"

"I'll have the same as Emily."

Mario just laughed, a deep rolling sound, and gestured for us to take a seat.

I walked outside; the crickets were boisterous there. An empty parking lot was a buffer between us and the loud road.

Arthur moved the chair back for me, and I sat. I loved that spot, and usually, I went there by myself. Just late enough to catch Mario leaving. He always served me pizza in a box, with a paper plate and a roll of napkins. My usual companion was my Mustang, which I parked right by the table.

"There was no table here a year ago, but I think Mario took pity on me eating standing with a pizza on the bonnet of my car. He put a table here a few months after I started coming," I said.

"This is an unusual place for a date," Arthur said, looking around.

"Sorry, but the place you suggested was awful. I needed to take matters into my own hands."

He laughed.

"Okay, now we are nice and settled, I am ready for an answer," Arthur said.

I looked at him, raising an eyebrow.

"Who are you, Emily?"

"That's a question I ask myself every day."

He didn't say anything, just watched me.

"I'm a product owner of a book app which recently got sold to one of the biggest software companies, and they are merging us with an existing app which didn't do well before. The merging is a coding nightmare, and now I am overseeing it."

Arthur nodded.

"I used to be a software developer, started freelancing in university, then I was invited to work in an office. And when we started developing a new set of apps, I took an active role in pitching ideas, so here I am," I said.

"Is this merging now a good thing?"

"Yes, after the merge the app would be in a default set of apps which are installed on phones from the beginning."

Arthur whistled.

The door opened and Mario appeared with two paper cups of orange liquid, ice bobbing inside. The one he placed in front of me had a pink umbrella.

"My niece from Naples said it's a big hit now," Mario said. "They mix Aperol with soda water and Prosecco. And since you're not driving today ..."

I took a sip. "It's perfect, Mario, thank you."

I had drunk Aperol Spritz before, but the mix Mario made was strong, a generous mix with much less soda water was probably a good idea. The umbrella was a perfect addition.

Mario smiled. "Are you keeping this one?"

Arthur coughed, as he was about to drink his cocktail.

"I'm not sure yet," I said.

Mario shrugged, completely ignoring Arthur.

"Emily, you need more joy in your life," Mario said, his accent strong.

"Do I look like joy?" Arthur asked.

Finally, Mario looked at him, his gaze slowly going up and down and up again. He shrugged.

"She's brought better specimens here before," Mario said and shrugged, walking away.

"I'm not sure what should insult me more, that I'm not the first one you've brought here or that they looked better," Arthur said.

"Yeah, well, Mario and I have different tastes," I said. "And I don't know what's the problem with modern men always taking girls to places that starve them."

"I think it turned out pretty well since I'm here now."

"Wait 'til you try the pizza."

On cue, Mario opened the door and placed two pizza boxes, two paper plates, and some napkins in front of us.

"Thank you, Mario."

He beamed at me and walked back inside but he stopped right in front of the door and pointed at Arthur. Mario winked and gave a thumbs up. I sighed.

Arthur opened the first box.

"Let's see your choice of pizza," he said, and after looking closely at the steaming dish in front of him, "suits you."

It was my favorite. A generous layer of red sauce on top of the dough, slices of prosciutto, baby arugula, halves of cherry tomatoes, and shredded mozzarella. I ignored the connection to the past of this particular mix.

I didn't wait for him as I peeled a slice away, a savory smell coming from it, and dug in.

"Oh, that's good," I said.

I closed my eyes as the rich flavor enveloped my senses.

Arthur took his slice, and bit a generous piece off. I watched him.

"So?"

"You're right," he said, taking another bite. "I'm silently singing odes to Mario in my head."

Mario dimmed down the light inside and brought us a bill and a huge candle, which he placed in the middle of the table.

He lit it. And when I moved for the bill, Arthur snatched it away.

I took another sip of my cocktail and watched Mario taking the money, and moments later turning off the light inside and the sign. He locked the front door, waved to us, and disappeared into the darkness. There was a sound of an engine rumbling, and he was gone.

The candle gave us just enough light to see the food.

"What about you?" I asked. "Who are you, Arthur?"

"Unlike you, I know very well who I am. It has been years since the last time I surprised myself. Or anyone did." He paused. "Hey, disclaimer, one more cheesy line is coming. Ready?"

"Fire away."

"This evening is surprising. And as I said, I don't remember the last time anything surprising happened to me," Arthur said.

"Yep, cheesy."

But it wasn't. He said it not in a way to lure me with his words, he just stated the fact. He looked around, and a warm smile painted his face as he looked up to the dark sky.

"Anyway, I'm a financial consultant. Companies hire me to optimize expenses and gain more income. I help with investment and help foreign companies open branches in the US. And much more. In simple terms: I help them grow."

I nodded, chewing on my pizza.

"I work a lot, mostly twelve or fourteen hours a day. I'm focused on making more money, but I don't spend even a small part of what I earn. I got working in the industry and found myself surrounded by everything lavish, having a house full of designer items that I bought furnished." He leaned back in his chair and rubbed the back of his neck. "But my favorite thing in all that wealth is an ancient leather chair I found at a flea market back when I was a student. I was so proud of having it. I imagined it belonged to a man who made serious things of his life. Now I think, was he like me? Achieving everything but missing something important in life."

Arthur looked up again.

"I don't remember the last time I looked at the sky," he said quietly. "I wish I believed in something otherworldly, something spiritual, but, to all the questions I have ever had, I found answers in science. I'm not even that curious anymore."

I looked up at the sky. There were no stars, the lights from the city dimming them. A helicopter zoomed by and the lights of a plane flickered in the distance.

"You can't even see the sky here," I said.

He laughed softly, his face still tilted up.

"I know a place where the sky shines in the night, where there are so many stars they are like a shimmering veil over the infinite darkness. I can take you there," I said.

"I'd love that," he whispered.

And we sat in comfortable silence, the sounds of the city just a few feet away, the sky, which was not the sky, looking down at us.

Chapter Twenty-Eight

I stirred a dark liquid in my mug as I sat in my kitchen a few hours later. One habit that crept into my life long ago was tea. Usually, I spent thirty minutes every morning on my tea. I brewed it in a small Chinese teapot and drank it in small cups. It was like a meditation. Mostly, I sat in silence and thought about the day that lay ahead.

But this time it was night, 2 AM. So I just brewed black tea directly in my mug and watched the leaves opening as they swirled in hot water.

I thought about the evening. Arthur was different from anyone I had ever met before, but he reminded me of myself. We had everything we needed, comfortable in our daily existence, but something crucial was missing.

Sitting in silence with him was the most intimate I had been with another human being in years. Just encompassing quiet understanding.

That was new. And it was not something I thought could possibly be found through a dating app.

I unlocked my phone and swiped. The blue icon of an app looked back at me. I opened it and clicked on settings. There was no hesitation when I tapped on Delete My Account. After that, I held my finger on the icon and when all the icons started shaking, I clicked on *delete* again.

It was gone for good.

The next day Arthur texted me that he had to fly to Tokyo again in the evening and asked if I was free for lunch. That's how I found myself sitting outside my office on a bench, in the shade of trees, eating an overpriced salad Arthur had brought.

"Better?" he asked and gestured to the bowl in my hands.

"Better, but still far from perfect. I have the idea that I will need to show you places where people cook food with soul."

"Does it have to be so poetic?"

"Okay, I'll show you places where people cook food that is amazingly mouth-wateringly delicious," I said.

"Great, what's the point in having this lean body if no one uses it. It's time to fatten up," he said pointing to his torso. I imagined a profoundly shaped six-pack under the shirt, but I could have been wrong.

"Poor Arthur," I said.

"Since you're off the dating app now, you can go with me on the journey of gaining a few pounds."

"Nah, I worked too hard to get to the point I am now," I said.

I watched as his gaze move down my legs, and up again.

"I can see that."

I took a forkful of leaves from my bowl. "If I'd have eaten only this and in fancy places like we were at yesterday, I would be half my size now."

"Next time I'll bring Mcdonald's," he said.

"When are you coming back?"

"In five days."

"I can drive you to the place with the stars I talked about yesterday," I suggested.

He looked at me, smiling. "I can drive us."

I snorted. "No way, we'll go my way or we won't go at all."

"What's about you and driving anyway?"

"You'll see."

Arthur had matched with me on the app after I removed any mention of the Mustang from my profile.

"Do you have friends?" I asked after a few moments of silence.

I got the feeling that these silences sometimes were more important than us talking.

"Two close ones, but they are both deep into fatherhood now, and have more topics to discuss between themselves than with me. They are ..." his voice trailed off, he cleared his throat. "They are from before, before I moved to the city, before I became who I am now."

I nodded.

"What about you?"

I smiled. "Just two of them too. Miranda and Brian. They have been a couple forever. I met them at university. They," and I took a deep breath, "they saved me many times. It started with Miranda, but when Brian helped her, he saw the other sides of me too."

Arthur was silent for a second.

"Did you notice how both of us stumbled on describing them?" he asked.

I breathed out and scratched my wrist. I did.

"They saved me too. And now I'm afraid that with their lives changing, something so fundamentally important coming, something I don't have and even not sure I want. That—"

"They won't leave you," I said. "They are the same. Deep down they are the same guys who saved you. They just need time to adjust to a new life, and maybe they need your support as much as you need theirs."

Arthur turned to me sharply.

"What?" I asked.

"You're good, Emily. You're good."

I bowed as Arthur finally smiled. That smile lit his features like a Christmas tree, and I saw how he wasn't used to smiling.

"Smiling suits you," I said. "You should do it more often."

"Not often I have a reason to," he said, and smiled wider, turning his face to the sun.

"Miranda and Brian are childfree by choice. She is an avid educator, and they even record a childfree podcast. She would be delighted to hear that you are not sure about kids. She believes that people should have kids *only* when they really want it and are ready for it financially. She is a solicitor by day."

"Are you going to talk to her about me?"

"Sure."

Arthur laughed. His phone pinged in his pocket, and he sighed.

"I have to go, Emily."

We both stood up and packed the empty containers back into a paper bag.

"Will you text me?" I asked quietly.

He stopped and looked at me. "Of course."

I nodded, looking down.

"I'll be waiting for that drive you promised," he said.

"Oh, you'll love it," I said, turning back to my office building. "Safe travels."

Out of the corner of my eye, I saw him turning toward the guest parking. He was still smiling.

Chapter Twenty-Nine

Arthur texted me as he promised. He complained about how long the queue at the airport was, he texted me from the lounge, and scoured the stores in the airport in search of a book I suggested he read on the flight. It was about the stars.

He said that the stewardess hit on him and, when I said he was delirious, he sent me a voice recording of her serving him his dinner. She was definitely hitting on him.

I giggled into my phone when he sent me a detailed review of various weird Japanese foods. And when he video chatted with me later that day, he said his hotel room smelled of pickled cabbage and it was my fault that I told him to buy that weird jello in the first place and try it back in the hotel.

But then he disappeared for hours on end, always saying that it was time to go back to reality and work.

It was a transition period in my work, we moved offices, said goodbyes to colleagues, and braced for a new environment as a team. It was difficult to leave the place that made me. But I knew that our new place was far more structured while allowing more freedom. Lots of employees worked from home or all over the world.

Arthur found it hilarious when I called him when I got back from one of the farewell parties. I stumbled home, drunk, and tripped on my kitchen rug. But I managed to brew myself tea under careful instructions from him. Then I sat there and demanded that he tell me all his secrets.

"I could tell you, but what's the point, you won't remember anything in the morning anyway. And I would want you to remember at least some of them," he said, sitting somewhere on top of a skyscraper on the terrace, smoking. "How about you tell me some of your secrets instead," he said.

I watched on my screen as he exhaled the smoke to the side and took another drag. It was a bad, bad habit. But Arthur smoked so gracefully, and it looked so old-fashioned, that I couldn't look away.

"I don't have any secrets," I said, shrugging.

"I don't believe you," he said, and took another drag.

The bleak gray sky of Tokyo was behind him, while a light wind caressed the hem of his shirt. Light eyebrows framed his big eyes and a scatter of freckles on his cheeks looked strangely youthful on a man's face. He had high cheekbones, of course he did.

Arthur smiled, and looked to the side, as if embarrassed.

"You're staring," he said.

"I'm not. Are you Irish?"

"No, British. I grew up in Worcester but managed to get into Yale."

He looked at his watch and back at me. I tried to stifle a yawn.

"You need to sleep, go to bed, Emily."

I listened to him and stood up. Suddenly a wave came at me and I swayed.

"Wow, careful there. I'm kind of looking forward to going

with you on that drive, so please don't smack your head on the bathtub, or anything," Arthur said.

I said goodnight and stumbled to my bed. He was right, I didn't have any strength, and the coordination of my brain with my limbs to go to the bathroom was lacking.

My head hit the pillow and I thought about how my eyes would sting in the morning because I hadn't taken off my makeup. But I didn't care. I was smiling.

"So, I'm driving, getting tea and I have two folding chairs in my trunk already. You bring food and blankets," I said when he called me on the day he landed. "And please, don't starve me again with salads."

He laughed. "You're lucky, I know a perfect place for sandwiches."

"I don't really believe your *perfect* when it concerns food."

"And yet, I am in charge of it, again."

"I just hope you'll get better at it," I said. "Okay, so what time do you think we should start? If you want to see the stars, it would be better later in the night. But there are breathtaking sunsets. So, if we want to see the sunset and the best stars, we would have a few hours in between to wait."

"We'll play Monopoly."

I laughed. "Okay."

He sent me a text with the location of his house, and we agreed to meet at five the next day.

But it was Friday that day. So a couple of hours later when I was grocery shopping, I texted him.

Are you resting from the flight?

A photo of a TV and Netflix logo turned up as a reply.

Do you want to go out? There's a local band playing tonight at the rooftop bar. I typed back.

You and your music, which I still might question, or a night of binge-watching…

A soft smile warmed my face as I wrote back. *And my dancing, you'd probably see my awkward robot dance tonight. And I'm sure that you're not ready for that. So stay home and watch the series.*

The three dots appeared as he typed.

Where and when should I be?

I laughed.

His next message said: *The thing is…*

There was a dramatic pause, and I didn't notice how my pulse picked up.

I am an excellent dancer myself, he ended.

The person standing next in line at the shop looked back at me as I sniggered.

We met in a few hours at the base of the office building. A neon sign pointed to the elevator which took people directly up to the bar. I was wearing a white top and black jeans, and a checkered jacket was tied around my waist. Arthur was in jeans and a long sleeve shirt. Both of us wore sneakers.

"No more than one cocktail tonight," he said. "I need you to be sober tomorrow."

"Yes, sir. As long as it has an umbrella."

The band didn't start for another half an hour, so we ordered drinks and stood by the railing, looking out on the darkening city.

"I loved the expression of the barman when you asked if he had an umbrella for the glass," I said.

Arthur looked at my plastic cup, a blue umbrella was bobbing between the ice cubes.

"Yeah, I will now always ask for an umbrella," he replied.

"Why do you like them? I remember Mario put one into the Aperol."

"They just make everything look a bit more festive."

Arthur raised an eyebrow. "Do you need more festivity in your life?" he asked.

"Sometimes, yes. Once I had a really bad day at work, and I drove straight to Mario's.

He made me promise that I wouldn't drive back home but call a taxi. I promised. We sat there 'til the night hours on the plastic chairs, sipping limoncello with umbrellas in it, while he told stories about Sicily and his younger years. Later his wife came, and we sat there 'til the morning hours, the three of us. She died a few months later."

I stopped talking and looked to the horizon. The city shimmered for as far as I could see.

"I'm sorry."

I nodded. "So yes, I need more festivities in my life."

The crowd started cheering and clapping, and a few moments later a band spilled out onto the stage. They were a beautifully diverse mix, from young to old, of different races. The band had seven members.

"What do they play?" Arthur asked.

"Covers," I said, and smiled widely as the familiar notes of It's My Life blew up the crowd. That evening there was no slow shy dancing to start off the night, everyone started jumping immediately.

And to my astonishment, Arthur took my hand and went into the boiling center, where people were packed tightly. He lifted his hands and started singing along with the crowd. I watched him for a moment, and he lightly squeezed my hand, before releasing it.

I never danced as much as I did that night.

Chapter Thirty

I stared at the map on my phone. Unsure, I glanced at the house on my right and back to my phone. That was the exact location Arthur had sent me the day before. I turned off the engine and opened my door.

It was a luxury neighborhood with lush green—not only lawns, but well—everything. Tropical palms and exotic flowers framed the driveways. It looked as though an army of gardeners worked there. Similar white houses stood farther into each plot. Floor-to-ceiling glass showed the opulence inside them.

I vaguely remembered Arthur saying that he had bought his house furnished. I looked at my phone again and turned to his house. It was in the sweet middle size compared to other houses on the street. The immaculate green lawn crushed into white walls, the curtains hid everything inside.

A Bentley stood by the house—a glossy black. I turned to the sound of kids running down the street. A girl was wearing a yellow swimsuit. Of course each house had its own pool.

I turned to the sound of steps and saw Arthur. He was holding a paper bag with an unfamiliar logo, a bag with blankets, and a Monopoly box was pressed to his side under his arm.

I marched to him. "Do you live *here*?" I asked, my voice loud, with a hint of hysterics.

He wasn't looking at me, he was looking behind me.

"Do you drive *that*?" Arthur asked, similar notes to mine coloring his voice.

"Are you Elon Musk or something?" I asked.

He huffed. "No. Stop screaming and let's go for a drive," he said, walking to my Mustang and dropping the bags. He gingerly brushed his hand over the curve of the hood. Yes, my car awoke more feelings in men than I did. "But if you want to argue here on the street we can do it, this neighborhood needs a little shake from time to time. It's just too blissful."

I shook my head and opened the trunk for him. Arthur placed the food, blankets, and the boardgame in the space I freed for him.

"This is too organized," he said and pointed into my carefully divided trunk. "It should have oiled clothes here, dirty magazines, and maybe a body."

I shot him a deadly look and shut the trunk, loudly. A flock of birds scattered from a nearby tree. I rolled my eyes and climbed into the car.

When he sat by my side, I mumbled, "Of course you live in a goddamned paradise."

I turned the key in the ignition and slowly drove on a circular road, looking at the fancy homes to my sides.

When we hit the highway, I pressed hard on an accelerator, the speed forcing us deeper into our seats. I frowned, clenching my jaw. Arthur looked at me all that time, a smug amusement on his face. He shifted in his seat and scratched his chin.

"May I know what exactly is bothering you?" he said, hardly containing his laugh.

"You are rich, like very rich. You said that you work as a financial consultant."

"I do."

I just fumed.

"You know, usually when women see where I live they turn into placid dolls, hoping to score a ring on their finger. Not that many women have seen it by the way," Arthur said, and I grunted. "But you look so angry, as if you are ready to kick me out of this car, and you won't even slow down. The Mustang is gorgeous by the way."

"Of course it's gorgeous," I said angrily.

"So, what's the matter?"

"Now I don't know how to be around you. Are you one of these rich jerks who buy girls for cash? Am I some kind of entertainment?"

I felt lied to. Because from the moment I met Arthur it was warm and meaningful, fun and open. After this, it felt as though I found out that he was the prince of the British crown with all its consequences.

He was silent. Something dark clenched in my stomach.

"No, Emily. You are not."

His voice was void of any merriment. He was looking straight ahead.

"It's just money," he said quietly.

"Money is never just money. You were born into the upper class, right?"

When he nodded I continued. "When I was younger, I was so afraid that I wouldn't be able to find a job, to make a living, that I had panic attacks. There was no one to help me, no parents to take care of me, there was no one 'til there were two people, and then I was alone again," my voice shook as Arthur watched me. "Money is never just money."

"Do you want to turn around?" he asked.

I was quiet, my heart thumping loudly.

"No."

"Thank God," he said, a smile lighting his features again.

"Just no more surprises, okay? I hate surprises," I said and looked at my smartwatch.

"We have two hours of driving, you can tell me everything. Like, if you have any weird habits or you like eating the fresh livers of elderly people."

He snorted.

I took a deep breath and said, "I'm sorry for overreacting. I'm just not ready to lose you."

"You won't."

And I wanted to believe in those words.

The usual comfortable silence covered the space between us, like a blanket.

"You're a good dancer," I said, and his laugh was so warm that I looked away from the road for a moment to glance at his face. A fuzzy feeling started blooming inside me in reply to the pleasant sound.

I parked the car at a rest stop in the middle of nowhere. The sky was still blue, but the sun hid behind the tops of the trees. We grabbed chairs, food, a thermos, blankets, and the Monopoly from the trunk and I led the way to a hidden path. The trail looked abandoned, branches catching our clothes. Arthur was silent as we wormed our way through the forest.

"How the hell do you know this place? Did you hide a body under one of these trees?" he finally asked.

"Just wait for it."

He huffed. In five more minutes, and thank God for our jeans, because the skin on my legs would have been scratched to hell, we reached the spot. I stepped to the side as soon as the trail opened to a wide clearing. It was littered with small purple flowers, and it ended with a steep drop, opening to the view of nearby hills. The hills were lush green from the swaying fir trees. A soft wind lulled the brunches, making a quiet whistling sound.

Arthur looked at me for a second, and back to the view. He dropped our things and went to the edge of clearing. He just looked at the horizon and froze for a second. His gaze roamed the treetops, and he ran a palm over his hair.

"Wow."

I smiled as I watched him, taking in the view. He turned to me and our gazes locked for a moment. I wanted to look away, but suddenly that smile that lit his face appeared, and I just couldn't.

"Right," I said in a few moments, finally catching myself.

I picked up the chairs he dropped and unfolded them a few feet before the edge. I placed the thermos to my left and took the paper bag. A delicious smell wafted from it.

Arthur reached for the bag with blankets and held them up. There were four, different colors and textures.

"There's a tag on one." I pointed.

He looked at it. "Damn, missed that one. I bought them today."

"You could have said that you didn't have blankets, I would have brought mine," I said.

"It was fun," he said. "I don't remember the last time I went to the store."

I shook my head. "And what about food?"

"I have a cook."

I groaned. "Of course you do."

Those tidbits of information about his luxurious lifestyle kept stunning me. Apparently, his parents were old money in Britain. He grew up in a mansion somewhere deep in the countryside. His young years were spent in private boarding schools and riding horses. He told me about all of it as we drove up to our lookout spot. And when he spoke about horses, I coughed, whispering "Prince." He just shook his head.

"Emily," he called, stepping closer to me. "I am still me."

I nodded. "Okay."

"Choose a blanket," he said.

I pointed to a black and white plaid one. He chose a pink one with Winnie the Pooh and sat on my right. I laughed as he wiggled on his chair, getting comfortable.

"Oh, that's good," he said.

The sun was setting slowly, coloring the light clouds into beautiful pinks and purples. I gazed at the changing colors, mesmerized.

"Tell me about your parents," I said.

"There is nothing to tell, really. They are posh, cold, British aristocrats. I spent all my childhood jumping from one nanny to another. I think I can count on one hand how many times my mom held me before I was sent to boarding school. And there I met lots of boys who were the same as me. Who were born just to continue the family name, not out of love. Can you believe that this kind of stuff is still happening in old families? Like two hundred years ago. There was no love in our families. And thank God I have an older brother, who is a mad fan of all these rules. His existence allowed me to run away to America."

"This is surreal, Arthur."

"Yeah. I know," he paused. "What about your parents?"

I told him about my dad.

"You are lucky," he said.

"What? Where do you see luck in my story?"

"Your father loved you, and that is much more than I had. I'm sorry he's not here anymore," he said.

I looked out at the last sliver of sun touching the treetops.

"I miss him every day. If he'd met you, he would never have stopped mocking your ancestry."

Arthur laughed.

"Humans are so influenced by our childhoods, at least based on yours you should believe in love," he said.

I shook my head. "I don't *do* love."

"As far as I know it doesn't work like that," he said.

I stayed silent, watching the sun hide, leaving vividly colored clouds.

"It's time to hear your secrets, Emily. People don't do love," he said and put last words in air quotes, "only after it's burned them before."

"There is nothing to talk about."

"I don't believe it."

I didn't say anything.

"I'm trading secret for a secret," Arthur said. "You asked me about my secrets when you were drunk."

I groaned. "And you said that you wanted me to remember them."

"I do, so do we have a deal?"

"Okay."

It was difficult to tell the story of Jake and Alice, my voice trailed off a couple of times, leaving silence. And it wasn't the same warm comfortable silence we usually had between us. He watched me, listening intently and waiting through every pause for me to continue. I hadn't told anyone about what had happened. No one needed to know how I had broken down years ago. In the final chapter of the story, my voice cracked.

"Shit," Arthur said when I finished.

I laughed darkly. "Yeah."

"That was messed up, to begin with," he said slowly. "But she broke your heart."

"For some time I told myself that she really loved me, but

was so hurt after Jake died—they were really close—that she couldn't face me. But in the end, I didn't get any answers. She just left me. Alone. And that's the truth of it."

Arthur stood up and went over to the edge, looked around, and turned back to me.

"Damn ... That's really not what I expected your secret to be. I'm so sorry that that happened to you," he said.

"Thank you," I said and walked up to him. "Your turn."

"Right."

The clouds still burned with the fire of the sun which was not there anymore. They burned in oranges and reds, deep purple backing them. Arthur looked up and exhaled. His fingers flexed on the sleeve of his shirt, he slowly folded it up and then did the same with the other one. He turned his wrists to me. Long scars ran along his wrists, following the line of his veins. The skin was smooth, but the scars were still visible— silvery gray.

My hands flew to his, but I stopped inches before I touched him.

"May I?"

He nodded. I ran my fingertips over the scars, slowly tracing the lines. The skin was warm, velvety, his pulse beating against my skin.

"Why?" I whispered.

"It was a stupid medical mistake, ignoring side effects. It was right before Yale, I was still at boarding school. When I came home for the holidays my loving parents took me to a doctor, regarding my knees. They made me a weak team player, they said. So, the doctor prescribed me pills, and for a short time, it eased the pain in my knees. But nobody read the long list of side effects that went with the drugs and our doctor didn't bother to enlighten us. I was slowly falling into depression. Only my mates who shared a room with me noticed the change, as I gradually fell into the darkness, taking the damn pills three times a day."

I entwined my fingers with his, and he looked at our hands, smiling.

"They saved me, those two, who are deep into fatherhood now. I was lying in my bed, slowly bleeding to death. If they had come in a few minutes later, it would have been too late. I remember Callum's panicked face when he tied his belt around my arm to slow the gushing blood, as he screamed at me to stay conscious, while he gripped my other hand. Jack ran for help. Callum said that I still had so many beautiful things to see in life. He screamed to me that I had to live. And then I blacked out."

"God," I said quietly.

"Later, the doctors worked it out. It was not me, but the pills. The drugs influenced my nervous system— neurotransmitters and all that—leading to a deep depression."

"Callum was right, you know. You still have to see so many beautiful things," I said and pointed to the now purple sky.

Arthur looked at it, but then back at my face. "Yes, very beautiful things."

"I'm glad you're here," I said.

"Me too."

I cleared my throat, releasing his hand.

"Let's drink tea," I said and returned to the chair, draping the blanket around my shoulders. After the sun finally disappeared below the horizon, it gradually became colder.

"So, now you know I'm damaged goods," Arthur said, taking the steaming cup I poured from my thermos.

"Both of us are. I was abandoned, and you wanted to abandon life," I said.

"What a shiny pair we are," he said.

I laughed.

"I don't have any more secrets to trade," I started. "But, have you ever loved?"

"Oh, it's not a secret. I'm not sure, you know? I had a strong infatuation with a girl at Yale, but she just played with me for a couple of months and dumped me for another guy. So I would not say it was love. I wanted to live after my accident, to feel the whole spectrum of feelings. So I guess I chose an unreliable girl in the first place, to feel the sweet pain of being dumped. It was not like it was for you. I recovered fast and decided that feelings were all good and well, but I was a student—it was time to have fun."

"What kind of fun?"

"A hot body to warm my lonely nights, often a new one every other night."

"Prick," I said, masking it with a cough.

"Well, I didn't ask them to fall in love with me," Arthur said.

"Smug prick," I said.

He grinned and stood up. He placed a cup down on the blanket and took out a cigarette box.

"May I?"

I waved a hand.

He lit a cigarette and picked up the cup. "And I was hungry, don't forget that I spent all my life up to that point in schools for boys. Sweat, blood, and fights are all good, but a body wrapped around my torso was much better. Also, I spun tales about my posh upbringing, which only heated the interest."

"It was a distraction," I said.

He lifted his brow, taking a long drag.

"I know because I did the same. Later, when I was out of university. I wanted to forget the pain, and someone's arms around me did the job."

He exhaled a cloud of smoke, which hid his face for a moment.

"As I said before, you are good at it," he said.

"As I said before, we're similar."

Arthur was silent.

"Who the hell smokes and drinks tea at the same time?" I asked. "People do it with coffee, but not tea."

"It adds a nice ashy taste."

But, as awful as that habit of smoking was, I could not deny that it fit him.

"Prince," I mumbled.

He laughed.

So we waited for the stars, and we talked and talked, the Monopoly laying forgotten in the grass. He told me about how he missed the British countryside and I told him about my job: how it was becoming remote and that I was glad that it finally was. He told me about Callum and Jack, and how it was difficult to stay in touch when he traveled so much. I told him about Miranda and Brian, and how they stayed in my life. Hours ticked by, and the sky, which was burning just hours ago, turned into a dark void shimmering with a scatter of diamonds.

I sat bundled in two blankets, as Arthur stood a few feet away. Only the burning point of his cigarette floated in the dark. He didn't move, his head up.

"I haven't seen the sky like this in years," he said. "I'm a bad sleeper, and I woke up a lot when I was a kid. Sitting in my dark room was boring, so I'd go outside to watch the stars. They were the same, silent, beautiful, staring back."

"They always make me feel small and insignificant. The whole of humanity is like an ant with so many worlds out there."

He turned back and sat by my side, the paper bag crunching under his feet. The sandwiches we ate an hour before were good. Arthur said that he stopped by a food truck before his flights because the food at airports was awful. The lady who made the sandwiches knew his preferences, and always added extra cheddar.

The sky was shimmering above us as we sat silently, looking up.

Chapter Thirty-One

My team was moved to a new office. There, we didn't have assigned workspaces, the employees flowed from meeting rooms to spaces where people could sit around and work. Everything in that company was shaped for remote work, making us come to the office only for important meetings. It was a new way of working, and a few of my colleagues didn't want to stay at home, so they transferred from the team to stay in the previous company that had normal working hours and traditional office setups.

But I wanted to travel, had always wanted to, so I was looking forward to getting settled there and going remote as soon as possible.

In the morning my team received an invitation to spend a week in Sri Lanka, to meet the CEO, who had spent last year working from there. He wanted to meet us all to discuss the next steps and tell us more about the company culture of remote work.

The team was ecstatic about a 'free vacation', as they called it. Sri Lanka was as good a place as any to start traveling.

I texted Arthur, and he said that it would be my turn to

review weird local food and customs for him over videos. He said that he hoped I would find a fruit that stinks my whole room, sweet revenge for that Tokyo jello.

When I called Miranda and told her about the upcoming trip, she reminded me of a party she was preparing. It was the day before my flight to Sri Lanka.

"Can I bring someone?" I asked.

"Sure, is he your new toy?"

Miranda was always excited to discuss my love life, but she had stopped taking it seriously a long time ago: after John changed from Adam to Oliver to Thomas. The long string of guys who never stayed.

"No, he's more like ..." I paused, more like who? "A friend."

"A friend? This is new. Bring him on, let's see if he can stomach my punch."

I groaned. Miranda had perfected her deadly concoction over the years. It killed faster after all those years, showing darker sides of guests, which Miranda loved to watch.

Arthur was thrilled to get to meet Brian and Miranda. So, when we stood in front of the entrance to their house, fast techno music blasting from inside, I repeated for the hundredth time not to drink more than one glass of punch. We wore bright psychedelic shirts and neon glowing bracelets and there was a streak of violet in my hair. The theme of the party was underground techno.

"At first everything will be good and civilized, then it's going to turn into hell. When it turns into hell, it's time to get away," I said. "They're notorious for their parties, so be vigilant."

A taxi stopped in their driveway and people spilled out in neon outfits. One woman was wearing pink leather pants.

"It looks like a college party," Arthur said, looking around.

"Exactly. But many people here are past their thirties, with kids, expensive cars, and money. They all love Miranda's parties because of how unruly they become. They feel young again here."

"Let's go inside," Arthur said as a party of newcomers strolled past us into the house, slamming the door carelessly.

I took a deep breath and laced my hand over the door handle. "Oh God, be ready to see the dark part of me."

Arthur grinned.

"And I'll see yours," I said and winked, opening the door.

The house was big and modern, but unlike usual, it was decorated in fluorescent posters and all the windows were covered with shades, creating a dark atmosphere. The music was loud, but not so loud that you couldn't hear the voices. Groups of people swayed, excitement in their eyes.

Miranda appeared at my side. Her long burgundy hair was curled. She wore ninja boots with a separate finger for each toe, a black one-piece jumpsuit, and tiny pink glasses that complemented the look. She threw her arms around me.

"I'm so happy to see you," she said. "This is going to be wild. Introduce me to your friend."

Miranda lowered her glasses and looked Arthur up and down. He shook her hand.

"You're lucky," she said to him.

"Why?"

"Emily becomes a barbarian at my parties," Miranda said and winked.

Brian appeared at Miranda's side. He too was wearing all black, but his lips were covered in a deep shade of pink, which complimented Miranda's glasses.

I cracked up at the sight of him, and he planted a kiss on my cheek, leaving a stain.

"You look hot, Brian," I said.

"Oh, I know."

Brian turned to Arthur and shook his hand.

"You are different," Brian said to him.

"Is that good or bad?"

"We'll see after tonight."

Brian grinned at me and winked. He lowered his face to my ear and whispered. "He's in for the long run."

It was always like that with Brian. It all started when he saw me and Alice, and continued through the years, always giving me prophecies about my new boyfriends. And unnervingly, he always guessed right.

Miranda disappeared for a moment and came back with two glasses of a deadly potion she called *The Punch*.

Arthur took a glass and lifted it up to one of the only normal lights left on in the house.

"Smoke fumes from it," he said.

"Cool, right?" Miranda said, bouncing on her feet.

Brian looked around. "Somewhere in the crowd, there's a plate of cookies spiked with something hallucinogenic. If you spot them, throw them in the trash. Okay? I swear this music makes people do crazy stuff."

More people arrived and their costumes showed the outlines of bones in fluorescent light. They pulsed to the rhythm, grotesque glowing bones moving in the crowd.

I turned back to Arthur; he was grinning.

"Ah, to hell with it and with all the control," I said and lifted my glass.

After three gulps my throat burned as if someone had slid a rusty iron wire down it. Acid bit my tongue, but in a few seconds, the pleasant taste of oranges settled in my mouth.

Arthur watched me and took a cautious sip.

He coughed, his eyes watering. But when the orange phase came he took a deep breath.

"God, Miranda, what did you put there?" he asked.

"It's a family secret," she said and winked. "Keep Emily away from the hot tub, last time she ended up there with a bunch of puritans who sat fully clothed and discussed classic literature all night."

Arthur choked but masked it with a few more gulps from his glass, making him choke even more.

"Well, tonight there are enough people to look out for me, so goodbye everyone," I said, and downed the glass.

Brian groaned, Miranda laughed and did the same. Arthur, the poor British soul, watched me and went back to his glass, taking a small sip. I waved and bowed graciously, feeling the drink pulsing in my veins. I blinked and I was dancing in the middle of the room, the light from my bracelet moving in intricate patterns in front of my nose. It was impossible to follow the rhythm of the music, so I just pulsed with all the people around me. Arthur was by my side, and his eyes were closed as he managed to nod in time with the rhythm.

He opened his eyes and looked at me. "I love this track, this is classic!"

"You listen to *this* for pleasure?"

He just grinned.

Blink. I was standing with Miranda.

"His accent is kind of sexy," she said.

Blink. I was standing by the front door with another glass in my hand.

Blink. I was going to check on the hot tub, hoping to find my literature friends there.

Blink. I was dancing again.

Blink. I was standing in a queue for the restroom, listening to the sounds of someone having sex in the guest room across the corridor.

Blink. I was outside, sitting in the grass, my bracelet light almost dead.

"It's impossible to follow you when you're on The Punch," Arthur said. "You kept running away."

He sat by my side and looked up at the sky. I did the same.

"No stars here," I whispered.

He nodded.

My memory from the previous few hours was sketchy, with a lot of blank spaces. I rubbed my forehead trying to fill them in. Blank. Only those few fragments I did remember came to mind. Arthur was close all the time, he held my hand as I tore through the house, as we danced, his cheeks turning crimson as we stood outside the restroom.

I turned to him. "Arthur?"

"Hm."

"Can I kiss you?"

His eyes went wide for a moment, but he held my gaze.

"This is the drink talking," he said, his pupils huge.

"The drink makes it easier. I'd hoped you'd kiss me under the stars," I whispered.

I needed to stop talking. I didn't want to sound pathetic.

A vicious chill ran down my arms and I realized I was cold. I stood up and hugged myself.

"Sorry," I whispered.

I turned and started walking back into the house. My senses dimmed, turned down from the alcohol and tiredness.

Warm hands grasped my shoulders, turning me, and Arthur pressed me to his chest. He put his chin on top of my head.

I lifted my face to look at him and, suddenly, my senses rushed back to me. I was in Arthur's arms. His smell enveloped me and I felt his pulse under my fingers. He was looking at me.

"I missed the perfect time for our first kiss, under the stars. I was just so afraid to ruin it. And now, you are half-conscious and I am high from the cookies I was *not* supposed to eat. But all I can think of is you. You and your perfect lips, your eyes which look into my core, you who tease and joke about me. You're so damn smart, and I'm afraid that I am just one of many of your suitors. But I want more, Emily."

"What do you want?" I asked quietly.

"I want your heart," Arthur said, as he slowly moved his fingers over my cheek.

"I told you, I buried my heart with those people I loved and who left me. I can't love anymore. I can't offer what I can't give," I said.

"Liar," he said and lowered his lips to mine.

It was so painfully slow at the beginning, his lips caressing mine, while a tight knot in my chest eased. He tasted of oranges and chocolate. And I kissed back, needing it more than air. Our tongues met, craving going wild. Suddenly his hand was on my waist, under my shirt. The feeling of skin on skin sent a powerful pulse through me. But suddenly he stopped.

"Not now, not like this. Not when we're not ourselves," Arthur said, putting his hands on my shoulders again and breathing hard.

I was pressed to his tall frame, feeling his need against my hip.

"Damn, you're romantic," I mumbled.

"Yeah, so romantic that our first kiss was under the influence."

"It just made us braver," I said. "Let's go home. Not one home. Our homes, I mean."

Arthur laughed and retrieved his phone from his back pocket.

We found Brian and Miranda dancing in the middle of the hall, elaborate movements amazingly matching the rhythm. We said goodbye, and Miranda wiggled her eyebrows at me, asking me to call her tomorrow and wishing me a good trip to Sri Lanka.

We stood on the curb, watching the house pulsing behind us for a moment. Our taxi came minutes later.

Inside, I said, "They would host these parties 'til they are in their eighties," shaking my head.

"That was ... educational," Arthur said, as he rubbed his temple.

"Wild, it's always wild," I said and kicked back my head on the headrest.

Chapter Thirty-Two

I woke up in my bed and looked at my phone. It was still early in the morning, and my flight was late that evening. I had the whole day to pack, but honestly, I didn't care an inch about the trip. I was ready to be back already.

I remembered our kiss yesterday and groaned. My alcohol-spiked brain thought it was so romantic, sensual even. In my relatively fresh brain, I guessed it was more grabby and needy than romantic and sensual. I hoped Arthur didn't feel the same. Although, Arthur was on a cookie he had snatched from that plate. So I was sure his ability to remember would have been even worse than mine.

One major advantage of Miranda's Punch was that there was no hangover, ever. Only tired limbs from excessive dancing. I decided to pretend nothing had happened. When I saw Arthur the next time I would tease him as usual. There was a big chance he'd follow my lead. But ... I liked when he kissed me. I liked being in his arms.

I'd have more time with him when I was back from that damned Sri Lanka trip. And maybe, just maybe, he'd kiss me again.

My phone pinged. Arthur.

The text said: *I NEED COFFEE. Do you? I can come over with take-out.*

I looked around. My apartment was on the tidier side this time of the week. It was a decent-size condo, with a spacious living room, a bedroom, and my library-slash-home office. White walls framed the whole space, and the patio opened to a view of the ocean. Miranda said that I had to try to live in a house. But I loved it there, and anyway, in a few months, I would pack up everything and go globetrotting.

I texted Arthur my address and ran into the bathroom. Astonishingly, I managed to remove make-up the night before when I stumbled back into the apartment. I washed my hair and stood for five minutes in front of my wardrobe deciding what to wear.

Finally, I put on an oversized black T-shirt with a heavy metal band logo and knee-length leggings. I would act as if nothing had happened, I told myself as I looked in the mirror. My still damp hair lay over my right shoulder and I looked like a teenage skater in the outfit, but I didn't care.

The doorbell rang, and my heart skipped a beat. I knew it was just Arthur, but my heart leaped all the same. The man who I enjoyed talking to, not just being wrapped up in his arms. I nodded to myself and went to open the door.

"Hey," he said. There were two cups of coffee and a box of donuts in his hands.

"Come on in."

He walked inside and looked around. He was not the first man to stand in my apartment, but he was the first I actually enjoyed seeing there.

Arthur placed the cups on the counter and cleared his throat.

"I hate that you're leaving today," he said and walked to me.

"Yeah."

He was not looking at me as though nothing had happened the day before. He was looking as though it was just the beginning.

Arthur slowly traced the skin on my neck with his fingertips.

"Where is your sharp tongue to stop me?" he asked, his eyes on mine.

"Maybe I don't want you to stop."

He grinned, and I cut the space between us by walking right into his arms, finding his lips. I acted completely at odds with what I had decided. It was so perfectly familiar and delightfully new. I scratched my nails along the base of his neck, pulling our kiss deeper.

I didn't know how much I needed it until it happened. Until his lips were pressed to mine and a burning thirst flailed down my stomach, as his fingers slowly traced the skin under my shirt. As he unhooked my bra and cupped my breast. I didn't make a sound until he gently rubbed the skin around my nipple. It quickly became hard under his fingertips. A light moan escaped me, and he stopped kissing me.

"Are you sure you want that?" he whispered into my neck, as his fingers slowly slid down the skin of my stomach.

"No, let's drink tea instead," I said, and brushed my hand over his pants.

"Tea sounds good," Arthur murmured, as his fingers lazily circled around my belly button.

"You sure?"

This time he groaned as I rubbed the length of him through his pants.

"I can offer you something slightly better than tea," I said and took off my shirt.

"Where is the bedroom?" he said, his voice gruff, eyes on my breasts.

I took his hand and led the way.

He didn't look away from me as I stopped and dragged his shirt off. Slowly scraping the fair skin of his flat abdomen, tracing the light hair running down and hiding in his pants, I took off my leggings.

I was standing only in my panties in front of him, my hair spilling over my breasts, breathing hard. Arthur cradled me in his arms as if I were made of glass, trying to rein in his craving. His lips studied every inch of me—his teeth finally scraping the base of my throat. He paused between my breasts, looking up at me, as my fingers roamed his muscled shoulders.

"I feel your heartbeat," he whispered before catching my nipple between his lips and gently tugging. His fingers slid down my ribs.

With shaking hands I unzipped his pants and wrapped my fingers around him, the shock of touch making him pause. I gently rubbed my finger over the top of him, his softest skin under my fingertips—a slow tremble running through his body.

Before I could say anything, he kissed me again and lowered his fingers between my thighs. He moved the fabric of my panties away and rubbed my most sensitive part. I was shamelessly wet.

In a moment I was lying on my back, my panties on the floor, as he widened my knees and went down on me. His rough tongue caressed the parts of me that swelled and pulsed under his touch. He devoured me as his finger went slowly in and out of me. He was hungry, as though he hadn't eaten in years, and I was oh so willing to be his meal. I was quick, arching my back and climaxing after a few sweet minutes.

He curved his eyebrow. "So fast? You're making it too easy, Emily."

"Let's see how long you'll last," I said, still breathing quickly.

When I put him in my mouth, he groaned. He gently gathered my hair as I started moving. All that time he continued to watch me, intently. He was close, but I stopped and moved to my bedside table, taking out a condom. I slipped it on and climbed on top of him.

I rode him slowly, watching the madness growing in his eyes. He roamed his fingers over my body, as I bent back, and he rubbed his thumb where I needed it. His constant rubbing made me move faster, and faster. His fingers guided my hips, as my dark hair spilled onto his white skin. A sharp spasm of pleasure seized me and I collapsed on top of him. Arthur followed me just seconds later.

We breathed hard.

"I would rather have the tea," he said, and I punched him lightly.

But he only hugged me closer.

He was happy, I could see it in his eyes as we sat on my patio overlooking cerulean water. The coffee was cold by the time we left the bedroom and returned to the kitchen. So it was tea with the donuts.

I wore a silky gray gown, while he put his clothes back on.

Arthur looked at me over the cup he held. He drank his tea with milk like a proper British man should, for me it was just a plain green. I was ravenous. Soon, chocolate from the donut stained my fingers.

"I see why you choose living here instead of a house. No house could have such a view," he said.

I nodded. "My lease is running out in a few months, you can move in," I said.

His eyes grew darker for a second. "Where are you moving?"

"It's time to follow the dream I've had for years—I want to work remotely from all over the world. When I was growing up, my Dad and I were homebodies, comfortably tucked away in our house. He didn't like to travel, and it's not like we ever had enough money anyway. Later I studied and my career moved me up in the world. Now that I have the means, and my new company encourages its employees to work remotely, it's time I sit somewhere on the white sand with a laptop on my knees."

"You know it's impossible to work like that, right? The sand ruins laptops, and don't even mention how the glare from the sun messes with your eyes," Arthur said.

"I know, I know, but I want to try to be that person in the picture I have in my mind—just for a while. The one sitting under the palm tree with a laptop. Or in a café in Paris. Or a pub in Prague."

He snorted. "It would be impossible to work there too, among the drunk tourists."

"Maybe, but I've always dreamed of trying."

And it was easy. I had a whole plan built up. But that was before I met Arthur. Not that it changed anything, not that we were something serious. No, I was a distraction from his work, and he was ... a friend. I blushed as I remembered how he tasted.

"Why do you want to travel?" he asked, his eyes looking deep into mine. "To me, it just seems like a new trend—people boasting about their travels on social media, collecting likes from envious followers. What is it for you? Freedom?"

I looked out at a seagull that circled in the sky.

"It's more to prove to myself that I can. Apart from all the places and cultures I want to see, it'll show that I'm independent enough to ... do it. And do it without help."

It was certainly not because I told the girl I loved that I had wanted it, and that it was finally time to prove that I could do it without her. During those dark hours of the night when I was wrapped around her, that soft vanilla scent caressing me, I dreamed that we would travel together, work all around the world. And when I mentioned it once, she had looked at me intently, with those huge grey eyes, knowing perfectly well that Jake would not come with us. I saw how she wanted it, how she shared my dream. It was certainly not to prove to someone I hadn't seen in years that I could do it myself.

"You're one of the most independent women I've ever met, and when I found out that you didn't have a supportive family and an array of friends to help you, it just proved the point," Arthur said and gestured around at my space. "Look at where you live, at your job, at the company and your product. You built it all yourself. That fire burning in you got you where you are now. And with only that mad couple as friends, God, you *are* the definition of independent."

I laughed. "They aren't mad."

"That's not the point. You are strong, Emily, you are strong without needing to prove anything to anyone. Please remember that."

He didn't know me that well, we were … I didn't know what we were, but he spoke to me like no one had before. He sincerely believed his words. And I wanted to believe them too. I stood up and walked to the edge of the patio, looking out on the water.

"When is your flight?" he asked.

"10 PM."

"I'll drive you to the airport. What time should I pick you up?"

I turned to him.

"Stay." My voice was quiet. "Please."

He sharply looked at me. "Of course."

Arthur stood up and in a few moments, he caught a strand

of my hair, looking deep into my eyes. He didn't say anything before he kissed me, deeply, his hands tangled in my hair.

"Come," he whispered in my ear, taking my hand and leading me back to the bedroom.

He parted my gown and slowly traced down my stomach. I didn't move as his fingers glided up to my breasts, to my collarbone, to my neck, as he slipped the gown over my shoulders. He laid me on my bed so delicately, treating me like a fragile creature. And his lips ... oh, god, his lips. They paused on my neck, as they slowly traced down. My skin burned where he kissed me.

I had a crazy urge to drag my fingers over the places he kissed, and I moved to touch the softness of my breast. Arthur paused and watched my fingers circling around the dark skin. He placed his knee between my thighs and moved up to find my lips, my tongue greedily finding his.

And then he lowered his lips to the place my fingers had been just moments ago. He bit me lightly, and a soft sound escaped my lips. I slid a little lower and ground my hips into his knee. He teased me slowly, and my need burned. He played with my ribs, my outer thighs, squeezing my hips, making me rub his leg more, and it was almost enough.

And then it wasn't. Because when he lowered his fingers and slid them over me slowly, teasingly, a loud moan escaped me.

"Oh, you could have just asked," he murmured, circling his fingers, as my hips moved to guide him.

I was too far gone, as Arthur covered every gasp with his lips. And then again, right as I was on the brink, he entered me, and it was better than anything I could hope for. All my senses came to life as I scratched his back, as I looked him in the eyes when he was above me, my fingers digging into his short hair.

We lost it. Messy, loudly, sweaty, together.

I lay in his arms, my back pressed to his chest. His fingers lightly traced my skin.

"Can I cancel Sri Lanka?" I asked. "I want to stay here."

Every word I said was so pleasantly tired. He rested his warm hand at the bottom of my stomach.

"Sleep, Emily. I'll wake you up with enough time to pack," he murmured in my ear.

I waved slowly. "Nah, I'm staying here with you."

He was silent as I drifted off to sleep. Sometime before I fell into nothingness he said quietly: "I wish you would."

I opened my eyes to the dying light outside. Something had changed. I was covered with a light blanket and my cheek was pressed into something warm and solid—it moved with each breath. His chest. An arm circled my waist. I lifted my face to him, and he looked down.

"Hey you," he said quietly.

I propped myself up on my elbow and lowered my lips to his. His reply was slow and seductive.

"Can I keep you?" I asked.

"For what?"

His hand got lost in my hair, as he gently rubbed the base of my neck.

"For this," I said and closed my eyes, leaning into his touch.

"My services are pretty expensive," he said.

"I'll take a loan."

"We could work something out," he took a deep breath and traced his lips over my chin. "It's time for you to pack."

I groaned.

And he laughed, the sound so beautifully joyful that I raised my eyebrows.

"I'm just flattered that you'd rather stay with me in bed than go to Sri Lanka. I know what I'm comparing myself to, Sri Lanka is a paradise," Arthur said.

"You are an arrogant Brit," I said, smiling. But he was right. I would gladly trade my trip to stay with him. And it was not only the sex … I pushed the thought away.

I stood up and fished my gown from the floor. But right before I tied it, I looked at Arthur. He was watching me, propped up on his elbow. I parted the gown, and he raised a brow as his eyes roamed the sliver of my skin it showed.

I stuck my tongue out before tying it. Arthur laughed. I watched his face, it was somehow different. The usual hard lines around his lips relaxed, a soft crinkle appeared around his eyes. I shook my head as I went to the bathroom, running a hot shower.

When I looked at my phone after exiting the bathroom, steam following me, I gasped. I only had two hours before I had to leave for the airport. And I was *so* not ready.

I was a tornado rushing through my apartment for the next two hours, trying to decide what I needed to pack. I only paused when I entered the bathroom while Arthur was taking a shower. I honestly had to fight the urge to drop everything and climb in with him. But I made myself open the cabinet instead, take a bottle of lotion, and march away.

He sat quietly on my patio as I threw my clothes into a yellow suitcase. Typing something into his phone, his brow creased.

And I wanted to take away that crease, whatever bothered him with his work. And that thought was disturbing. It meant I cared. And I didn't want to care. Care often turned into something more powerful. I shook my head, trying to erase the thought because it didn't help to overthink something that was not even real.

But I did go up to him and put my hand on his shoulder. He stopped typing and looked from the screen to me.

He smiled softly and squeezed my hand. As I walked inside I looked back, he was typing again, but his brow wasn't creased anymore.

Chapter Thirty-Three

His car smelled of leather—of an expensive type—as I slid inside. The interior was light brown and all the seams sewn perfectly highlighted its class. The leather-covered steering wheel stood out starkly against the dark dashboard.

"Posh," I whispered, covering it with a cough.

He just laughed.

My yellow suitcase took up most of the space in his trunk. It looked out of place among the sleek and polished interior. I watched Arthur's fingers on the steering wheel as he backed out of the parking lot. He was an easy and relaxed driver—I felt safe with him as the car sped along the highway toward the airport.

He told me about a book on painkillers he had read recently, the dynasty who created and made money producing them. He made me promise to find it at the airport.

"Can I take you out when you're back?" he asked suddenly.

"Yeah, I would love that," I replied.

Arthur smiled as he glanced at me. "Are you blushing?"

"No."

"You are totally blushing," he said. "I wish you didn't need to go anywhere. I kind of like you in my life."

I laughed. "I'll be in touch. No naked selfies though."

"Really? Damn."

A comfortable silence filled the space between us. I was smiling, and Arthur scratched his chin, covering a sideways smile.

He parked in a short-term parking lot.

"Wait here," he instructed, climbing out of the car.

I nodded and watched him circle around and open the door for me. He took my hand, and when I was out, he immediately enveloped me in his arms.

"Oh."

That was all I could whisper before he kissed me, gently pressing me into him. When he released me, I went up on tiptoes, and whispered in his ear, "Please, don't fall in love with me. Remember that is the one thing I can't give you back."

"You are a party pooper," he said, stepping back and walking to the back of the car.

"I'm serious, Arthur."

He looked up, his hand on the trunk.

"Don't worry about me, Emily. Okay?"

I nodded. He nodded back, his eyes on me.

"I'm always fine," he said.

"And the thing about me is that in the end, it's me who is always not fine."

He was grinning. "And some things don't have to end."

"Do they teach you how to speak so romantically in those boys-only British schools?" I asked.

"Come on, Emily, you're going to be late," he said and stretched out his hand. I placed mine in his, and warm fingers enclosed it.

We walked through the crowded airport and stood in the

bag drop-off line. I knew I was flying with only two of my colleagues, the other five had left early that morning.

As I watched my bag disappear on the belt a loud squeal interrupted my train of thought.

Jessica, our graphic designer, crashed into me.

"Emily, you're here," she said. Her blue curls spilled into her face. "Dave is at the back of the line," she gestured to a tall man who stood with two suitcases. A pink T-shirt with two palm trees looked perfect against his dark skin.

"Have you seen their photos already?" Jessica asked. "They just landed recently, and it's heaven," she almost sang. "I follow Anna's Instagram, and you know how she films everything. God, I'm so jealous, I can't wait to be there, on the beach, a coconut with something strong in my hand."

It was always like that with Jessica. She got excited so easily and practically about everything, sometimes it took hours for her to calm her frenzy. But unlike with her words, it only took her minutes to create art on her huge tablet. And she was a wonderful artist.

"We're sitting together, by the way. God, I'm so ready to run to duty-free to stock up on those tiny bottles of whiskey, you know. Let's wait for Dave and ..." Jessica's voice trailed off as she looked at Arthur who stood by my side. Her eyes went wide as she watched his face, looking away quickly. "Oh, you're not alone. I'll wait there," Jessica said and gestured to the start of the TSA line. She nodded and practically bolted there, looking back for a second to Arthur.

"That, my dear Emily, is the usual response I get from women. Something is so wrong with your wiring that you aren't in awe of me like they usually are," he said, and I punched him lightly in the stomach.

"You have such an inflated ego," I whispered, shaking my head, and he grinned. "And it's not you, Jessica is always terrified of unknown men, she just freezes."

"Finding a husband must be hell," Arthur said.

"She's married to her high school sweetheart actually, Jennifer. Jennifer and Jessica, the two of them are a buzzing tornado. So you've completely misjudged everything."

"Usually I'm good at reading people. But you take too much of my attention," Arthur said and took my hand. "Give me a few moments and I'll let you go to your peculiar teammates."

"Wait 'til you meet the rest," I said.

I waved to Dave, who inched forward in the queue. He dismissed my wave, looking at Arthur.

"Is everyone on your team gay?" Arthur whispered.

"We are a very diverse company. And when you were talking about women being in awe of you, did you mean the look Dave gave you?"

"Yes, actually."

And Arthur winked at Dave, making him look away suddenly. He searched vigorously in his pocket for what I'm sure was nothing in particular.

We stopped behind a burger ad, which shielded us from the bustling crowd. Arthur looked at me, and I smiled as my heart picked up speed.

"Come back to me, Emily," he said quietly, brushing a dark lock out of my eyes.

"I will," I said.

His lips were restless on mine.

Chapter Thirty-Four

I grinned all the way to Sri Lanka. That stupid smile I could not erase got me unwanted attention. When Jessica asked what had happened, I tried to make a serious face which made me giggle even more.

"I'm ready to bet my monthly salary it's tied to that handsome man," she whispered.

I just shrugged. The flight was crowded, and the three of us kept bumping elbows. The book Arthur told me about was good, but my thoughts kept wandering away.

Eventually, I closed my eyes and tried not to smile even wider. It felt good to be with Arthur, light, easy, fun. A comparison started creeping into my mind, to a brother and sister who meant the world to me before. And as much as I wanted to compare my feelings for Arthur to what I felt with them, I could not. I didn't remember how I felt before the all-consuming grief ate everything inside, before my heart cracked that day at their parent's house—the swift movement of curtains planting a final blow.

I was not smiling anymore.

I hurt for the girl who was left behind, for the boy who

didn't live, and for the girl who disappeared. I didn't want it to define me, but as much as I wanted to believe in the goodness of people, I could not anymore. Love was just too massive, too painful. And I was not ready to feel it again.

I just hoped Arthur would listen to me because he was a light I was ready to accept. I hoped I was enough fun for him —to be friends with benefits. And those benefits, god. A pulsing tightness squeezed my core as I remembered his lips between my thighs. He ate and sucked me as if I were the most delicious ice cream he had ever tasted.

I opened my eyes and looked around. Jess was sleeping, Dave watched a movie, and I was blushing vigorously again. Maybe I could take a naked selfie or two.

Jessica squealed as we stepped off the plane. The wet warmth of the air instantly clung to my skin, and I did my best to blink the feeling away as Dave put on his sunglasses.

The flight was too long, the transfer was too short, leaving us to run across the airport to catch our next flight. I hoped they managed to transfer our bags because after spending even a few seconds in the humid Sri Lankan air, I already needed to change.

I could also already feel the excruciating jet lag creeping in, and I could not understand how Arthur managed those flights so easily. It was my bedtime at home, but at our destination, the sun continued to blaze in the blueness of the sky.

I fumbled for my phone and sent Arthur a text saying how I had possibly exaggerated the beauty of travel, because all I could think about in that moment was shower and sleep.

Tomorrow you'll feel better, he replied.

A short smiling man held a sheet of paper with our names on it and greeted us when an excited Jess and a red-eyed Dave accompanied my tired self out of the airport. He gathered our three massive suitcases and rolled them to a white minibus, heavenly cool air wafting from inside.

I scooted to a window, Dave stretched his long legs on the rear row of seats, closed his eyes, and started snoring lightly within a minute. Jessica sat by the driver and spilled a million questions a minute on him. The driver, only glad to have someone to talk to, started explaining the old Sri Lanka's traditions. I looked at Dave with envy and put on my noise-canceling headphones, slow acoustic rock murmuring in my ears. I closed my eyes.

Someone was shaking my shoulder. I opened my eyes to see Jessica's face inches from mine. Small beads of perspiration gathered on her forehead.

"We're here, Emily," she said when I pulled down my headphones. "It's a paradise."

Dave was standing outside already, rubbing his eyes. Jessica jumped from the car and cried as our project manager walked out of the lobby.

Olga was a stern Ukrainian woman in her thirties, with a hard gaze, but a warm smile. She kept the goals of our project clear, and steered the ship with an iron fist, helping us secure the sale of our project.

She reached the car, patted Dave on the shoulder, gave Jessica a coconut with a bright pink concoction, and looked inside the vehicle at me.

"Half of our guys are sleeping, the other half are drinking by the ocean. No major meeting today. You'll find an invitation for tomorrow's breakfast in your rooms. It'll be with the CEO, so best be early. But for now, we're free to wander," Olga said.

"I'm wandering in the direction of the bed," I said, climbing out.

A short laugh, more like a bark, was Olga's signature

sound. She pointed in the direction of reception, and I grabbed my suitcase and rolled it along the uneven pavement made up of small white stones.

It didn't roll that well, so I ended up dragging it, an unpleasant grating sound following me as I went.

A nice woman in white typed my name into the system and gave me a key card for my room. A smiling teenager wearing a white uniform picked up my bag and asked me to follow him.

My room was not a room at all. It was a tiny bungalow hidden in the dense greenery, the sound of the ocean coming through the windows. A small backyard opened to a tiny pool, wide banana leaves sheltering it from the outside world.

I thanked the boy and shuffled to the bathroom, washing my hands and splashing water on my face. I grabbed my phone and checked the Wi-Fi reception. To my delight it was strong. Arthur picked up after the third ring. He was wearing a gray shirt, his elbow propped on a dark blue pillow.

"I have news," I blurted instead of greeting. "I think I hate traveling. How the hell do you do it all the time?"

"It was a bad flight, was it?" he asked, rubbing his eyes.

"Did I wake you?"

"It's okay, I'm glad you called," he said, his heavy accent tilting on the edges.

I smiled and looked at my screen. It *was* good to see and hear him.

"Emily?"

I cleared my throat. "Anyway, the flight was packed. And those babies. Where do they get the energy to cry non-stop? My noise-canceling headphones didn't help. There was also basically no place for my legs. It was just constant screaming and shuffling for hours."

"And you say that I'm posh," he mumbled.

"I guess you're right, I'm whining. Look."

I turned the camera and showed him the pool and my bungalow. Arthur just whistled.

"Wow, this new company spent a lot on this trip," Arthur said.

"Yeah, we're meeting the CEO tomorrow. I hope my headache will be gone by the time I need to open my mouth."

"Get some rest, Emily. You just need to sleep and stay hydrated, and that god-awful flight will feel like a dream tomorrow. You'll love Sri Lanka, just enjoy your time, okay?"

I nodded. "Thanks."

"What are you thinking?"

I shook my head. "Nothing."

His eyebrow went up, and a smirk touched the edges of his lips. "Oh, I know. You just realized that you're missing me already."

I laughed. "Thank god not everyone has such a massive ego," I said, still laughing. But he was right, I was missing him. And it was new. So new that I could not allow myself to dwell on it.

"Get some rest, Emily. You can even dream of me."

"You are impossible!" I said, but both of us were smiling. "Bye, Arthur."

He was grinning when I ended the call.

"Impossible," I murmured and unzipped my suitcase.

The shower was indeed a paradise, warm rivulets cascading down my skin. The sound of waves crashing was a low murmur against the silence when I lowered myself into my huge bed. I would explore the island in the morning, I told myself. The morning would bring even better things. But right then, I needed to sleep.

It was almost instant—my consciousness slipped from Sri Lanka to a man who was sleeping thousands of miles away, to nothingness.

Chapter Thirty-Five

I opened my eyes to the shadows of the bungalow. It was still dark, the constant sound of crashing waves murmuring outside. I picked up my phone and tried to work out how long I had slept—more than twelve hours as it turned out. Then, I checked when sunrise was. Just forty minutes away.

I slipped out of bed and slowly walked around the room, taking in the details that time. The wooden panels along the walls were well cared for, a dark blue velvet settee stood by the foot of the bed, along with a small wooden table, carved in intricate patterns.

When I stepped outside, the private pool shimmered in the low light, casting hues of green and blue onto the walls of the bungalow.

The sound of the ocean was almost teasing. So I walked back inside and dug out my swimsuit, changed, grabbed a towel, and marched outside.

The hotel premises were carefully lit, all trails adorned by strings of lights. The reception building was dimmed, and other bungalows hid among the trees. I followed the sound of waves.

When the path gave way to the beach, I slipped off my flip-flops and bore my toes into the cool sand. I stepped closer to the waves, the ocean finally licking at my feet. The water was warm, soothing. I snapped a photo and sent it to Arthur.

The beach was deserted except for one man sitting on a yoga mat. The darkness was slowly lifting, giving way to a new day, but it was still impossible to see more than the man's outline. I turned in the other direction, so as not to disturb his privacy, and stood knee-deep in the water, facing the shimmering light on the horizon.

I closed my eyes and took a deep breath. Everything about my life was finally not terrifying or coated in sadness. I was doing well in a job I loved. I had met a man, a friend.

More than a friend, my mind whispered.

But I was not ready to label anything yet. I *was* ready to travel. I was already traveling! I felt a new possibility tingling at my fingertips as I slowly started trusting life. The waves that licked my calves just proved that I had so many beautiful things in life still to encounter.

"Emily?"

I was jerked out of my blissful thoughts by the sound of an unfamiliar voice. I turned around and saw a tall man standing a few feet away on the shore. His shaved head and dark beard explained why he knew my name.

"Sorry, I didn't mean to startle you," said Benjamin Oliver, the CEO of the multimillion-dollar company that had bought our app for integration.

I walked back to the edge of the water and shook his huge hand. It was warm.

"Beautiful, isn't it?" Benjamin said. I nodded, following his gaze to the almost blinding light on the horizon.

"I come every morning to the ocean to meet the day. Sri Lanka soothes the soul, you know," he said.

"I can imagine," I said.

I had read as many articles on Benjamin as I could before we finished the sale. He was a wolf in the business world, but one day he cracked. The pressure and constant running around almost stopped his heart. So he reorganized his position in the many companies he owned, and for a few years worked remotely, managing businesses from all over the world.

"How long have you been living here?" I asked.

"Soon it'll be two years. And I don't plan to move, it's just too perfect here. Sri Lanka brought not only peace to my life, but my Muse," Benjamin said.

"Muse?"

"Yes, my fiancée. You'll get to meet her later today," he said. "I'm so glad all of you could come. I just hope this little trip will inspire your team to find the right balance between work and life. I believe that only when that balance is found, is the job done most productively."

I agreed.

"Well, enjoy your morning, and I look forward to seeing you at breakfast," Benjamin said. "Welcome to Sri Lanka."

His voice was calm, velvety, a startling difference from the one I had heard on the videos of speeches he had given. Before his heart attack, he was a shark, ready to bite; during our brief moment, he was ... relaxed.

Benjamin smiled at me, walked back to his yoga mat, rolled it up, and moved back to the hotel entrance. But right at the edge, he stopped and turned back, to the sliver of sun that appeared on the horizon. He stood there for a minute, then waved at me and disappeared between the green leaves.

Sri Lanka helped him find peace, and love as it seemed. I didn't want to run to the edge of the Earth to find all those things. Not that I was interested in love anymore. *Yeah, right,* the voice in my head sang as the sun crept up. But peace, I wanted that. I didn't want to run anymore, run for money, run for recognition, trying to be the best at what I did. I just wanted to sit in my Mustang and drive. Maybe my happiness was not abroad in beautiful scenery, but at home, just driving to see the stars. And maybe, just maybe, a smug British man could be by my side.

It was impossibly beautiful there on the beach, but all that shimmering sunrise did to me was clear my head and help me realize that maybe, I had already found everything I needed.

That was until my carefully constructed happiness and peace shattered over the hard Sri Lanka stone.

Chapter Thirty-Six

Breakfast was the perfect time to gather the team. People who were struggling with jet lag like I was had woken up hours before and those who had spent the previous day enjoying Sri Lanka could not stay out that late anyway. Whatever they'd spent the last few hours doing, that moment was the perfect time for their morning smoothie.

A wide terrace was booked for us, shaded by white sail-like drapes. A beautiful wooden table was laden with various fruits, the colors mixing in an intricate palette. As I was almost the first to arrive, I took a seat facing the ocean. Gentle waves decorated the aquamarine waters with foam. In the next few minutes, the rest of the team joined me.

Jessica looked as though she had decided against going to bed the previous night, spending the night with those who partied, and she now battled the worst hangover. It was okay, we were on a mini-vacation anyway. Olga sat by my side and was composed like always. I bet she hit the gym around the time I went to meet the sunrise. Dave was looking at the water and smiling, his hair was still damp from a morning swim. The rest were in various stages of pumped up energy and bliss.

I heard a familiar voice and within seconds Benjamin appeared with the waiter, murmuring directions. He stopped in front of the table and everyone looked up. Jessica's eyes widened as she took in the shape of our new CEO. He was tall, broad-shouldered, and his dark eyes shone under the Sri Lankan sun as he looked at each of us. Finally, a warm smile appeared from under his bushy beard.

"So nice to finally meet you all," he said. He was wearing a white linen shirt and matching pants, looking more like a health coach than the CEO of the largest technology company in the world.

He plopped onto the chair, one still vacant on his right, and slid his hand over his shaven head.

"Hope everything is fine," Benjamin said to a low murmur of agreement. "How do you like Sri Lanka so far?" he asked no one in particular.

There was a bit of silence before Dave leaned on the table and gestured around.

"This is heaven, man."

Benjamin looked at Dave and laughed. "It truly is."

And after that everyone relaxed, conversation slowly building around the table.

Some talked about what they had done the day before and some hungrily chugged smoothies, as Benjamin slowly made his way around the table shaking hands.

I was talking to Olga about the latest feature we had added to the app before merging, and how we barely had time to collect the data on it, when Benjamin turned to the entrance and his face shone with a smile.

"Here she is," he said, beaming. "Meet my Muse."

And I was falling.

My heart stopped beating, and then resumed with full force as it dropped to the cold stone floor. It ached.

She was different now, her hair shorter, stopping just

above her shoulders, but she was still so beautifully blonde. Her body was leaner, the muscles on her arms more pronounced. She was wearing a flowy white dress, which rustled on the breeze.

"Alice," I whispered.

At the same time, Benjamin kissed her, their lips connecting for a brief moment.

And right after that she turned to the table and looked directly at me. Her deep gray eyes were the same, and they bore right to my core. They widened the moment they connected with mine, and she gave the slightest nod.

A web of delicate lines formed at the corners of her lips, making her look just a little bit sad. She was still so fiercely beautiful.

My throat closed. I stood, slowly picking my shattered heart up from the floor, and excused myself, while Benjamin slowly introduced her to everyone around the table.

My knees were made of lead, and my fingers shook so hard when I tried to open the door to the restroom that I had to steady my tremble with my other hand. Finally, the handle gave way and I clicked the door shut behind me.

I stood watching the closed door, noting every crevice as my heart screamed, as my mind slowly shut. Alice.

Alice was there, right there outside.

For a minute my body forgot how to work. My lungs refused to take a breath, my balance shifted, my body slowly slid to the floor.

My heart that had sung so happily just that morning remembered the pain in a second, the pain, and before that the all-consuming love. I remembered that love when I looked at her.

God, I had loved Alice so much, so purely, so selflessly before. Before she left me. And Jake. A tremble jerked me against the door as I remembered his face. I remembered it as clearly as I had seen Alice's just moments before. The pain at the memory was razor sharp. I struggled to keep my body from shaking even more.

I gagged and scrambled to the basin, hoping that my body would be cleansed from the pain. But nothing came. Nothing but a shattering pain.

How was it possible? How was she there?

Alice. My Alice.

I looked up at the mirror. My skin was pale with a bluish tint. She was never *my* Alice, was she? Never.

I noticed in the mirror as my hand moved to my face, to cover my eyes. She knew I was here, she had looked directly at me. What did it mean?

My fingers were pressed into my eyelids.

Oh, God.

My mind kept piecing together the truth while my heart ached. The sale and merger of our app was too good to be true in the beginning. We wondered why they chose us, a small company, to acquire. It wasn't because our product was unique, it was done with meticulous care, yes, but there were much bigger and more widely known apps. We thought that they were buying us to grow and outgrow the competitors. And I was so proud of it.

But after that, remembering how Alice had just looked at me. She knew. How long had they been together? How much did she influence Benjamin? Did she ask him to look into our small company? Did she point to a particular app that would be of interest?

Finally, my fingers released my eyelids. And that same hand fumbled in the pocket of my pants, finally closing around my phone.

I unlocked it and dialed Arthur.

There was no video this time.

"Hey," he answered. "Please don't brag about how the

fruit is too fresh and the sun is too warm. I spent the whole day in a stifling office with the Japanese."

"Alice is here." It was all I could say.

"What? Who?"

There was a bit of shuffling and then it stopped.

"Bloody hell," Arthur said.

That was so British of him.

"She knew I would be here, Arthur. She knew. I saw it in her eyes. There was no surprise, as though she was ... I don't know, waiting."

"Shit," he said again. "Where are you now?"

"Bathroom. Gagging, trying to breathe, and feeling so damn manipulated."

"What do you mean?"

"I think she had a hand in our company merger. In the whole deal. You should have seen how the CEO looks and talks about her. He calls her his Muse."

Arthur snorted. "His Muse? Now that's a cliché. I guess she's the one pulling the strings then."

"What should I do, Arthur? I don't want to be here. I don't want to deal with it, with her. I don't want to poke around in the past. I was finally, finally ready to move on. I was happy."

"You were?"

"Yes," I whispered.

"I hope that was solely because of me," he said, his voice lighter.

"Partially, maybe."

He breathed out loudly. "You're not feeling well if you're agreeing with me. I was waiting for the usual retort about my smugness. And now you're saying that ... Damn, I'm so sorry. Can you get away? I can book you the next available flight home. You'll curl up under the blanket in your cozy apartment and forget about everything. Or you'll drive, drive with open windows, so the wind can blow away all your worries."

I smiled. He knew what I liked.

"Drive for sure," I said quietly. "But I can't. My team needs me. They need my help. They all worked so hard for this, and they are so proud. I can't take it from them."

He was silent for a second.

"Do you think she'll try to get you back?" Arthur asked.

I snorted. "They are engaged, the CEO and her. I have no idea what her plan is, and what all of this means."

"I guess you'll find out soon," he said quietly. Arthur cleared his throat. "Just imagine you are driving that winding road. The wind is ruffling your hair, the beast of your car is murmuring beneath you. It all will be over soon, you'll be home in just seven days."

With you, I thought and finally smiled a little.

"Thank you, Arthur," I said.

I heard as he took a drag of his cigarette and I remembered that smoky smell of him. Smoking was bad, and he said he would stop soon, but there was something meditational in the way he held the cigarette between his long fingers. Exquisite. I imagined him in that moment.

He cursed so elaborately, so Britishly, that I could not understand half of the words he said. I laughed.

"That was perfect," I said, chuckling, "you need to teach me."

"I was just explaining my view on the situation," he said.

I giggled again.

"Just call me anytime, and I mean literally any time. And if at any moment you think it's too much, I will get you a ticket back that same moment."

"Thank you, Arthur," I said again, and I meant it.

"Always," he just replied.

When I put my phone away, I looked back at the mirror.

My usual skin color had returned, my eyes were not looking as haunted, and my lips turned back to rosy instead of bluish.

I took a deep breath and stepped back out onto the terrace, where everyone had missed my departure, except the pair of stunning gray eyes, which followed my every move.

Chapter Thirty-Seven

"Emily, great, you're here," Benjamin said. "Meet Alice, my fiancée, and the reason the sun shines for me."

I nodded, avoiding looking at her at all costs. Everyone was looking at Benjamin, their eyes bright. It was like being with a celebrity, his magnetism taking hold of everyone.

"I was just telling the story about how Alice stumbled upon your app and explained the potential of it to me," he said. "As you may have heard I stepped away from operational management, but she can be persuasive. So, here we are."

I breathed out slowly. Just as I had thought, Alice was the reason we were there. A perfect blow to my ego and belief in my abilities. Bloody hell, as Arthur would've said.

"Here we are," I said and smiled weakly.

"So, I was suggesting doing a small tour through the nearby villages today," Benjamin said. "I would like to show my favorite nooks here and there, quiet and comfy places I like to work at. They built an amazing new coworking center. You'll love it," Benjamin said, scratching his beard.

I had been fascinated by him. I had downed every piece of information I could find before the trip. But right then I was just angry, so damned angry. All my fascination had gone out the window.

Benjamin kept shifting his attention around the group, perfectly blending as a friend, not as a barefoot multimillionaire—our boss.

I put on a fake smile and kept nodding along, looking everywhere but at the blonde fae with eyes like a stormy sky.

It was impossibly distracting to sit there and try to make sense of what everyone was saying.

"Are you okay?" Olga whispered to me when Benjamin was talking to our senior software developer.

"Sure, why?" I replied, my voice more like a squeak.

She looked at my hands that gripped the sides of the stool I was perched on. I was almost hovering above it, the tension in my body trying to protect me from the minefield that surrounded me. My mind was a minefield too. I couldn't escape.

Just seven more days. God, this is a disaster, I thought.

Finally, Benjamin said that we could have a few hours to ourselves, and we should meet at noon at reception for our short tour.

After counting to five in my head, I waited for someone to stand up first. It was Jessica. I followed suit, my chair scraping the floor. The sound was razor-sharp on my nerves.

I nodded to no one in particular and almost ran from the terrace, down the wide stone stairs, toward the sound of the ocean. I almost crashed into a cleaning lady, mumbling apologies and going faster, faster to the stunning blue water. And then I was on the shore, far from the hotel.

There were soft footsteps behind me, of course there were.

A voice behind me said, "Stop running, Emily."

And I stopped, spinning around.

Alice was standing there, and that time I looked at her, truly looked at her. The years that had passed since I had last seen her only made her look more dazzling. The delicate features of her face were coated in sadness, but it was still so alluring. Images of her smiling, our lips pressed to each other, her arms around me, they all crashed into me in one moment.

I cut the distance between us in a few steps.

"How could you?" I said, pointing my finger at her. "How could you?" I said more quietly this time, my finger curling into my palm as I pressed it to my mouth.

I stepped back, our eyes locked. The roar of waves crashed on my left.

"Emily—"

"Don't," I lashed out. "You made it all happen, didn't you? You are the reason we're all here, right? Why?"

"Yes." It was all she said. She watched my face.

"Why?"

"I needed to see you."

I laughed madly. "There were easier ways to see me, easier than making your husband-to-be acquire my project! And what the hell is with the husband thing, Alice?" I walked closer to her. "You are gay! You are a lesbian! Or was it all a lie? Like the rest of the meaningless relationship we had."

It was as though I had slapped her. Alice took a step back.

"Right, so here I am," I said and waved a hand along the length of my body. "Say what you needed to say, why you dragged me here. Let's get it over with."

The anger sizzled in my every word. I was so mad my body trembled.

Alice just stood silent, watching me. I shook my head and turned to the ocean.

"I worked so hard on this project. I poured my soul in it, just to be so fucking used," I said.

"Ben loved it when I showed it to him, he used it for months before making the suggestion to the board about acquiring it. I just showed it to him, he decided on everything himself. You did an amazing job. I saw your ideas in the app. I saw you," Alice said quietly stepping to my side. "I didn't make him buy it, I just showed it to him."

"He said you persuaded him."

"It's impossible to persuade that man on anything. He made his mind up himself, I just nudged him."

"Why?" I asked again.

"You always wanted to work remotely, and in Ben's company it would be possible."

I laughed. "Thank you for your help, but I would have managed myself."

I turned and started walking back to the hotel.

"I knew you would," Alice said quietly.

My feet sunk into the warm sand as I tried to breathe.

I didn't look back.

<h1 style="text-align:center">Chapter Thirty-Eight</h1>

Not only did Benjamin attract people like moths to a flame, but Alice did too. When I finally left my bungalow, wearing a simple blue dress, a straw hat, and a layer of sunscreen, I firmly decided that I would ignore Alice. There was nothing to talk about.

But when I entered the lobby, everyone was already gathered around Benjamin and Alice. Jessica was talking to her, her eyes slipping over the length of her body. Oh, Jess.

Alice turned to me, her hair hung in flowy waves, a tiny braid with a goddamned flower sat on one side of her head. She was wearing jean shorts and a white shirt that showed a cropped tank beneath it. Simple white sneakers complemented the look of the casual queen, the huge stone on her finger did not. I tried not to stare at the ring. She looked at me and smiled uncertainly. I looked away.

Everything about her made me angry. Just looking at those eyes I had drowned in before, left me enraged.

A text pinged on my phone, and when I unlocked the screen, a little smile crept onto my lips.

Thank God there is no Miranda's punch on that island. But

there is rum and jet lag which can have the same effect, so please be careful. A hot tub with talks about literature can turn into naked swimming in the sea. And it's not that I'm against swimming naked. I would very much like it. Anyway, what I wanted to say is ... Forget it. I'm just worried. How are you?

I typed back: *Already swimming naked (grinning emoji)*

Three dots appeared and disappeared again.

A white minibus stopped right by the hotel entrance, and one by one, we filed inside. I climbed right into the back, hoping to sit alone, but Dave sat beside me. Alice and Olga were in the row in front of us.

Benjamin turned from the front seat and flashed his relaxed smile at us. His eyes flicked to the phone in my hand, and he smiled wider.

"Emily, could you please snap a picture of us from the back?" he asked.

I nodded and when I turned the camera to them, he shook his hand.

"A selfie, so everyone is in," Benjamin said.

I turned my phone and tried to fit every smiling face in. One of the most insincere smiles I had ever given tugged my lips as I snapped a few shots of everyone.

"Thanks!" Everyone chimed.

I nodded and slumped back. Even Dave who hated being photographed was smiling in the photo.

I sent it to Arthur, and then to Miranda.

You're snarling. And which one is Alice? Arthur asked in a text.

The one with the flower.

Blimey. Good luck, Emily.

I snorted. Dave turned to me from the window, raised an eyebrow, and looked back. I finally looked outside as our bus rushed through the streets. It honked aggressively, dodging colorful buses with blaring music. Everything about the roads in Sri Lanka was the opposite of serene, nothing like the serenity of the hotel and everything promised to tourists. Cows lounged on the side of the road—one crossed slowly without batting an eye at all the honking and shouting. Cars and bikes easily maneuvered around it. They didn't flinch as they brushed past the big animal.

It was such a different world, and I could not look away as my phone kept vibrating in my hand. I realized that Alice being there stopped me from even looking around. I had been shielding myself behind my phone's screen. As we rushed madly through the streets, I watched rows of fish drying in the sun, with a perfect view of the ocean and palm trees behind them. Stalls with numerous fruits, bright and unusual, were dotted along the side of the road, inches away from the rushing traffic.

But my phone kept buzzing in my hand. I looked at the screen and scrolled down to the end of the longest line of curse words I had ever seen. Miranda was furious.

Why the hell is she there?!

Those few years after Jake died, I had not really been alive. Only a shell-shaped form of me existed. My heart had shattered into pieces; Miranda had picked each of them up and tried to glue them back together. It was a slow process and I had healed with her help. And when I could finally take a breath without my chest feeling crushed, Miranda had confessed that she hated Alice. She hated her for leaving me. For leaving me knowing that I had lost my dad so recently. Even with that knowledge, she had chosen to disappear. Then the wave of bitter rage came for me, and it stayed. Miranda never forgave Alice. Neither did I.

I'll explain later. I texted back to Miranda.

And switched off the phone.

Dave was glued to the window, and I was too, but a few minutes later my eyes turned to the face I had loved before.

Her soft lips moved sensually while she murmured to Olga. Olga, always business-like and all sharp edges, looked relaxed, smiling at Alice.

Alice, who always attracted looks wherever she went, had honed her soft skills, now looking more confident than ever before. As I watched her, I realized what was different. She was there, but a part of her was detached, untrusting.

I didn't know if everyone saw it, or if it was only me. Because the woman I knew was not there anymore. The same sort of polished shell I had lived in for so long was talking to Olga. But I had shed my shell years ago with the gentle help of Miranda and Brian.

But there was no one to help Alice.

And she still lived with it, with that pain, the girl I had loved before hidden somewhere deep inside. Alice noticed that I was looking at her and tilted her head a little, our gazes connecting.

My breath hitched in my chest because all I could see in her eyes was pain. She still hurt, even after those years, she was suffering. Only a smiling mask interacted with the outside world, while a soul screamed for help inside.

But I couldn't help. I didn't want to. It was not my place anymore.

Chapter Thirty-Nine

The driver took us a few villages down the shore and parked by a shack of woven palm leaves. A short smiley man made us freshly squeezed juice. Plastic cups in hand, we ventured into the local market, rows of unfamiliar fruits mixed with all types and sizes of bananas. The part of the market, which smelled so much of fish that my eyes watered, was almost empty by the time we got there.

"We'll order fresh tuna for tomorrow's dinner," Benjamin said, walking beside me.

I just nodded.

The air was so humid and, with the mix of suffocating smells of fish and fruit, I felt dizzy. The driver of our minibus greeted us outside the market and Benjamin stopped to talk with him, a moment later gesturing for us to follow.

The driver, Nirved, told us in his heavily accented English that he lived in the village, and he wanted to show us around. We walked along a path hidden in exotic greenery, the sounds of birds screaming above us. We stopped by a house and Nirved proudly opened the gate, ushering us inside.

The house was crooked, though surprisingly large

compared to the shacks dotted in the area, the second floor built upon the first in a different style and color. Nirved explained that when his son married they built the second floor for him to live there with his new family. Nirved's wife opened the front door and welcomed us inside. A younger woman was sitting by the table, her round belly making it almost impossible to fit in the narrow space between furniture.

Nirved wanted to show us every nook in the house, and we followed him through each room, barefoot. He was so proud of his mismatched furniture, colorful drapes, and gold ornaments on the walls. He pointed to an air conditioner in each room, and after Benjamin nodded approvingly, Nirved seemed to grow a few inches, his back straightening. It was a sign of luxury to have such a big house, with flat-screen TVs in each room, and air conditioners.

Alice split from the group. As much as I didn't care about her, my eyes kept returning to her face. I wanted to ignore her presence, but some kind of compass I couldn't control pointed toward her. She moved, my body moved.

And then she stepped back into the kitchen, while Nirved talked about his kids, showing us their pictures. The group was shifting, feeling uncomfortable, while Benjamin seemed genuinely interested in his family. Dave stood by the window, looking outside longingly, Olga hugged her body as though she didn't want to touch anything. Jessica looked around with saucer-sized eyes.

Finally, Nirved's wife appeared and called us outside to a table hidden in the shade of palm trees, benches around it. Everyone sat around, and I noticed how Benjamin's eyes darted to each of us. Not finding the ones he was looking for, he stood up, just to sit back when he saw Alice helping the younger woman bring cups, a ceramic kettle in her hands.

Alice sat by his side, and he pulled her closer, lightly

touching her elbow. She looked at me. Those piercing eyes caught mine. I looked away to the kettle.

A woman, the wife of Nirved's son, explained to us that she worked as a tour guide at a tea factory before her pregnancy and told us a short history of tea before pouring each of us a small cup. The cups were transparent, and the rich amber liquid glinted in the sun. And when I took a sip, my eyes closed, the savory taste hugging my tongue, tickling my senses. The flavor was deep and intense.

I opened my eyes and noticed two pairs of eyes on me, Benjamin and Alice.

"Do you like tea?" Benjamin asked.

I nodded. He didn't need to know that tea was a big part of my life, a ritual, a meditation. I would share that piece of information gladly if the roots of the fascination weren't in the woman by his side.

"Emily is a tea junkie," Jessica said helpfully. "She knows everything about it. In the previous office, she even had a personal set of boxes with different kinds of leaves, and a clay teapot stood by her laptop all the time. When everyone was running to the coffee shop Emily always drank tea."

I felt my cheeks burning, and I hoped someone would say something, not about me or tea, someone, anything. I glanced down at my cup, as every pair of eyes around the table looked at me. But only one pair bore deep.

"How far are you?" Olga asked the young woman.

And everyone looked away from me. A warm smile spread across her face, a hand going to her belly, caressing it.

"Any day now," she said.

I turned to Olga and hoped my eyes conveyed gratitude.

Finally, we stood up from the table, thanked our hosts, and walked down to the beach. The shore was wrapped up in black volcanic sand, which glistened. I took off my sandals and dug my toes into the dark powder, looking out at the sparkling water. Nirved brought three huge mats and we slumped down on them.

Dave took off his shirt and waded into the water, a smile shone on his face right before he dove under. Benjamin laughed and followed him, a few of my colleagues stripped down to their swimsuits and ran in.

Alice was smiling as she watched the group splashing in the water, and slowly untied her shirt, pulled down her shorts, and walked to the water's edge. She was wearing a black top and white bikini bottom. I watched her from behind, noting how she gathered her blonde hair into a top knot, her movements graceful. Flashes of memory lit my mind, her skin under my fingertips, under my lips.

Damn. I did not need to remember it, I did not want it. These dark memories of limbs tangled in sheets, the air between us, her fast breathing.

I dropped back to the mat and squeezed my eyes shut, rubbing my fingers over them. A shuffle by my side brought me back.

"She's kind of enigmatic, isn't she?" Olga asked.

I didn't reply.

"You knew Alice before, right?" she asked again.

I nodded with my hand still pressed to my eyes.

"It's complicated," I said.

"Everything is these days," she said. "There's a beach bar a mile down the shore, I saw it on Maps. Fancy a drink?"

"God, yes, please."

I sprang up from the mat, my knees crunching, and grabbed my sandals. Olga said to a colleague who sat with closed eyes, her face lifted to the sun, that we were going to a bar, she nodded.

The sand beneath my feet was so soft, as if silk threads wove between my toes. I watched the hem of white foam meeting the black sand as Olga walked quietly by my side.

"I wish I didn't come here," I said, finally lifting my eyes.

"I'm sorry," Olga said. "She watches you, you know."

I rubbed my forehead. "We were a couple in university, kind of."

"Does Benjamin know?"

"I don't think so."

Why was I telling her? I looked at the woman walking by my side. She was wearing white shorts and a blue shirt, dark hair cropped short, her wrist hugged by numerous bracelets. She was a vault, she never gossiped, never showed any emotion, any preference. I had always liked her quietness.

"What do you think will happen if Benjamin finds out?" she asked.

"It's not me who kept it secret in the first place."

Olga nodded. "That's why we are here, right?"

"Maybe."

"Alice doesn't seem like a bad person, she has kind eyes, and is sort of sad. Did she hurt you?" Olga asked, her green eyes watching my face.

I took a deep breath, rubbing my forehead again. "She left me."

But suddenly I was angry, so angry that I kicked the small stone with my toe and immediately regretted it.

"I don't know why we are here, what she wants, what game she's playing. Or why she dragged the whole team into her murky scheme," I said.

"Well, as far as I know, this merge brought only positive change for everyone. Finally, we can work remotely, and no one has complained about the pay rise, so don't worry about us."

"I'm sorry."

"Everyone loves it here, our app is kind of a big deal now. I thought it was pure luck, but it seems we had help ... Will you talk to Alice?"

We reached a small bend, and a string of voices and light music touched my ears.

Finally. I leaned on the counter and ordered local rum with Cola. Olga perched on a bar stool by my side and ordered the same. Not that the menu had a long list. Just three items, featuring rum and Ceylon arrack. Well, at least my plastic cup had an umbrella. I smiled.

"I guess I'd have to," I finally said, and Olga nodded as if there had been no pause.

We undressed to our swimsuits and dipped our feet into the warm water. It was easy to talk to Olga. She was an avid traveler and, with her husband who worked remotely for years, they planned to pack all they had in a storage unit and leave for Bali as soon as our project was settled.

"I just feel so much calmer there. Not in America, not back home in Ukraine. But on the waves with a surfboard, on a bike between the rice fields, swimming at the foot of the waterfall. We already found a villa to rent," she said.

I confessed that I had never really traveled and that it was my dream, but as I was saying it, I was not sure it really was so important to me after all.

Olga watched me closely. "Often it's not about the place you go to, but about the person who shares those moments with you."

I nodded and turned to the water.

The peace and quiet didn't last, because not long after we finished our drinks a group of familiar faces joined us. All of them sitting by the water's edge, watching the sun going down, the sky painted with a honeyed hue of orange and pink.

Olga stood up, and walked into the water, watching the sun, and dove under. When she emerged she chuckled.

"Come," she said to no one in particular.

And I watched as our team, people who were the best at their jobs, stood up and ran, splashing, and I was among them, giggling in the water.

Chapter Forty

W e stayed on the beach deep into the night. We stayed until stars flashed above our heads, and the music at the bar turned just a notch louder, until more cocktails flowed, our bodies moved to the rhythm. I found myself talking to Dave, dancing with Jessica, and giggling with Olga.

A huge bonfire was lit just a few feet away from the bar, and as I sat close to it, my chin resting on my knees, the person I had tried to avoid all day appeared by my side.

"Can we talk?" Alice asked.

I turned to her and watched as the warm light played on her skin. Sand stuck to her neck, and her blonde hair curled from the sea salt. I glanced at Olga, who stood a few feet away, and she smiled and showed me thumbs up.

"Okay."

Alice stood up and slowly moved into the shadows, walking away from the light of the bar and bonfire. She sat down in the darkness, and I followed her lead. The sand was still warm from the scorching sun.

I looked straight ahead but could feel her eyes on me. I had nothing to say, so I waited. I wondered why I was there, when she finally talked.

"I'm sorry, Emily."

I shrugged. "Okay."

She smiled, a shadow of that mischievous smile I loved playing on her lips.

"I'm sorry I left you."

"Okay," I said again, and when she kept silent, I continued. "Don't worry, it was so long ago it doesn't matter anyway."

She turned to the ocean, and I moved to stand.

"Please, stay," Alice said, and her fingertips touched my wrist.

I jerked my hand back, cradling it close to my chest. She saw it, and her face fell. But I sat back.

"I want to explain myself," she said and took a shuddering breath. "I died that day with him. I died with Jake."

I was silent.

"Police called my parents, and when they found out, they drove to that little house we were renting. My Mom, she ... isn't the same anymore, none of us are. My Dad tried to stay sane for both of us. When they took me from that house and drove me to the hospital, the car was filled with shuddering wails. I honestly thought my heart would stop beating. I could not believe it. In the hospital, my parents didn't allow me to see the body. I didn't even get to say goodbye."

Alice was looking into the depth of the dark ocean; it was whispering just a few feet away.

"My parents took me back home. I remember I watched my father's face as he drove us, silent tears running down his cheeks. I had never seen him cry before." She shook her head. "I thought about Jake and could actually still believe that he was waiting for us at home. That he would hug me and Mom, whisper about how silly we were. The house was empty when we returned. I fell into a very dark state, I took painkillers to numb that excruciating pain. My dad always watched me taking them, they thought I might overdose. And I thought about it, it would be so easy, just to stop hurting, to be with him."

I nodded as I brushed my cheek. I didn't mean to cry. But it was so unfair, he was too young, too kind, too everything good that a person could be.

"I'm sorry," I said.

She turned her eyes to me. "You know, I've thought about you every day since that day. In those first days, it was too dark, and I searched for your face in the fog for comfort. I was disgusted with myself. I blamed myself for not being able to handle Jake's plan. I wanted you all to myself. I talked to him in my mind for days, asking for forgiveness."

"Did you, for a moment, think about the real me? Not the imaginary me. The real, living me. How I was hurting too, how I was alone? You and Jake were my world, Alice. And the two of you were torn out of my life in a second. Did you ever consider that I'd just lost my dad too—I'd barely gotten past that. Did you ever think about how I was feeling?" I asked, becoming angry.

"I—"

"You left me, Alice, to slowly rot from my grief," I said, my hands were shaking, and I hugged myself to stop the violent shivers going down my arms and spine. I stood abruptly. "I fell in love with you, you know, I wanted to break up with Jake that day. I wanted to be with you. I could not pretend anymore. That triangle he invented was broken from the beginning. Because I only loved one of you, and it was you."

She looked at me as though I had punched her.

"But I should have chosen Jake, he was never as self-absorbed and selfish as you. I just know that he would never have hurt me like you did. You fucking saw me from that window, didn't you?" I asked, standing above her, trying to measure my voice, so the people by the bonfire would not hear me.

She nodded.

"I always knew it was you behind that curtain, and that was the cruelest thing anyone has ever done to me, Alice. You had a choice, and you decided to hurt me. I thought maybe you loved me too, after all those moments we shared, I imagined that you cared. But I was so wrong. We don't need to discuss anything, I understood long ago that I was mistaken. And I've had my share of talks in my mind with you, and Jake —I begged for him to forgive me too. So please, Alice, let me go."

She spoke again before I could storm off.

"I hurt myself a week after Jacob died. I didn't mean to, but I managed to overdose. My parents decided that it was better for me not to see you. When I saw you by the window I got scared. I could not talk to you at that moment. I was delirious, barely standing, an IV was hooked to my arm. I realized that it would be better if I stayed away. And I saw that you were not alone."

I snorted, gesturing to her. "You see, you didn't even think about me. How I was feeling."

"I was too weak," she whispered.

"Yeah, and I was not," I said, shaking my head. "You didn't think that I was fragile, that I could be broken, did you?"

"You were always strong."

I laughed. "You're cruel, Alice."

I turned and walked away. I didn't want to understand her. I was selfish too, for myself who could barely breathe for those first months, who was slowly losing myself in the darkness. I didn't want to understand her reasons.

Chapter Forty-One

When we finally returned to the hotel, I looked at my phone. There were forty messages from Miranda. I called her back.

"What the hell, Emily?" she asked instead of greeting.

I told her why we were here, about the talk today.

"What is she hoping to gain? Forgiveness?" Miranda asked. "She can go kiss my beautiful ass, she abandoned you. And I don't give a damn that she tried to hurt herself. I'll never forget those first few nights of screaming. I can still feel that sound under my skin. It was you by the way. Screaming in your sleep."

I remembered those nights, my throat was torn from the sounds that kept escaping it. I lay there at night and tried to breathe, my pillow wet from tears, my fingers squeezing the sheets as if it was the life I tried to hold on to.

"Brian says he always knew Alice would come back," Miranda said.

I smiled. Brian always made those little remarks about my future.

"He didn't tell me," I said.

I heard Miranda asking Brian why. "He says that you'd wait for it."

"No, I would not," I said.

"He doesn't believe you."

Well, he was right. Alice was one massive unfinished chapter of my life. I never had the chance to know why it all ended like it did.

A light knock on my bungalow door pulled me away from my phone.

"That's Alice," I heard Brian saying to Miranda. Miranda groaned. "Please be careful, Emily. Love you."

I ended the call and threw the phone on the bed. I didn't even have a minute to take a shower.

"What?" I said when I opened the door.

It was Alice. Brian was always right.

"Can I come in?" she asked.

"Why?"

She took a shaking breath and rubbed the back of her neck.

"I want you to know ... I'm trying to explain myself. I need you to understand." She looked at me, her eyes filled with moisture. "Please."

"Okay, come in," I said and opened the door wider.

Alice held two small bottles of wine in her hand. She gave them to me, but I only shook my head. I didn't need more alcohol. And I didn't want to drink with her.

She crossed the room and went outside to the shimmering pool.

"Why are you doing this, Alice?" I asked when I sat on the chair opposite her, moving it back as far as possible. "It was so long ago. Why did you drag me here? Back into your life."

"I wanted to help you."

"Oh, yeah, help, okay."

"Please let me speak. I've prepared this speech for years."

"Go ahead," I said and gestured for her to speak, leaning back in the chair.

"Before Jake's accident, I was so in love with you, and so afraid to lose you and to hurt him. I wanted to talk to him, but I knew he was in love with you too. How could we share you? I guessed it would lead to you deciding who you wanted to be with, if anyone. It was a difficult time because I was betraying my brother, loving you, wanting to be by your side every second."

Alice dropped her head into her hands.

"After he died," she said and looked up at me. "I need you to understand me here, Emily. I was empty, a shell. I stopped existing. I could not function. I was disoriented, drugged, hurting. I could not care for myself. My parents cared for me, bathed me, fed me. I barely existed. There was no energy to deal with the world. I think now that maybe on some subconscious level I didn't want you to see me that way, but I'm lying. That living corpse could not face you. And I am so sorry for that, but I just couldn't."

Her voice was shuddering, and she swayed back and forth as she talked, streams of tears slicing her cheeks.

"I needed you to know because I still see your face as I stood by those curtains. I saw how I hurt you, but I ..." Her voice finally gave way, she took a shaky breath. "I didn't do anything. And I'm so sorry."

"It was hard for me too. You must know that. But I guess I've never wanted to imagine how it was for you. I've hidden behind my grief, anger, and my broken heart for so long. I do know I could have returned too, I could have found you again," I said.

I had thought about finding her after a few years. But I had been too angry.

Alice shook her head.

"No," she said.

"No." I agreed. "How did you find your way back? Time?"

"I'm not sure I did find it. But yes, time. Do you remember that I should have started working for a big company?"

I nodded.

"They waited for me for a year. Can you believe it? But in a year nothing had changed for me. They sent me an email explaining that they had hired someone for my role." She looked dejected for a moment. "I only read that email two years later." She paused, looking at me.

Alice continued, "I picked up a brush and started painting again exactly three years after the crash. I painted Jake's face. I charged my phone for the first time in three and a half years. I opened my laptop and saw that the freelance website had changed its name after four long years. I moved to Sri Lanka five years after Jake died. I took on all projects that came—big and small—and worked my way up on the new freelance platform, one project after another. I was living in a rented bungalow deep in a small village, far from the tourist crowds, alone, finding my way back."

I took one of the two bottles she left on the table and opened it, taking a swig of dry red. It had taken her much longer than me to start living again.

"I'm sorry," I said, looking up to the sky.

Alice took the other bottle and gulped some down.

"It's so messed up, we keep apologizing to each other, while all we tried to do was survive the loss," she said quietly.

We stayed silent for a long stretch of time.

"Why Sri Lanka?" I asked.

"Do you remember Jake's favorite shirt?" she asked.

I searched my memory. There was a black T-shirt Jake always wore at home, it was faded, with a white outline of an elephant, and letters above the animal. It said *Sri Lanka*.

"Oh."

"People are kind here, they don't know about your past—you have a clean slate as soon as you get here. It helped. I could not stay at my parents' house anymore, not because I didn't want to. I would have lived there, in my childhood room forever. But when they spotted small signs of my awakening, they asked me to leave. They suggested going to Eastern Europe, but it would be too much, there were too many memories. So here I am."

"What about Benjamin?" I asked.

Alice turned to me, the weight of the world written all over her features. But when I asked about him, the corners of her lips raised.

"He's patient, kind, and understanding. He doesn't judge when I cry at night, he doesn't try to fix me. It's not like he's attracted to something that is broken in me, it's like under all of that he found that hidden part of me that existed before."

"Do you love him?"

Her smile faded.

"I don't think I'm capable of loving again, in the sense you're asking. I care deeply for him, but love, it's not something I can do anymore."

I finished the small bottle in my hand and rubbed my forehead, the words echoing in the back of my memory. I had said almost the same sentence to Arthur not so long ago. I stood up and walked to the pool, looking at the blue lining.

"I'm not sure I can forgive you, but I understand," I said.

"That's all I'm asking for."

She stood up, placing the bottle on the stone floor.

"Jake knew how I felt," I said, my eyes still on the water. "That last night before he ..."

I took a deep breath.

"He knew I chose you," I said quietly. "And every day for the rest of my life I'll wonder if things would have been different if he didn't know, or if I chose differently. If I went through another door that night and stayed with him. He hurt, and you hurt. But at that time it was clear to me: I wanted to be with his sister. He knew I betrayed his trust, and the next day it all ended. I didn't save him."

My last words were a whisper, but they were the truth I had learned to live with.

Alice stepped closer to me.

"It's not your fault," she said. "It was an accident. He went to that market like he did every Saturday. He would have gone anyway."

I nodded.

"I didn't see him that morning," Alice said. "I went for a run, and he was already gone when I came back. The last time I saw Jake was at the bar the evening before, the understanding was written on his face. And I just can't forgive myself that when he was driving that day, he was hurting, because of me."

We stood silent, watching the shimmering light on the walls of the pool.

"I didn't get a chance to talk to him," she said quietly.

"Me neither."

"Ben suggested that I go to therapy, and I've been doing it online for three months. It helps, the grief doesn't go away, but she helps me see that the accident was not my fault and that I just didn't have the time to make things right. And that if I could relive the night before with all the knowledge I have now, I would have acted the same. She suggested it would be good if I speak to you," Alice said.

"She suggested for you to plot all this?" I asked incredulously.

She laughed. "I guess she meant to call you, or text."

I laughed too. "It would have been easier."

"Would you have replied to me?" she asked.

I looked at her, and then back to the water.

"Of course."

"I didn't think you would."

We stood for a few more moments, the sweet sound of waves just behind the wall of greenery, the bright moon that dimmed the stars, the turquoise water at our feet.

"I'm sorry I dragged you here," Alice said, almost in a whisper.

I shrugged. "It's just a blow to my ego, the team seems happy."

"Emily, Ben loved your app. He saw me using it and asked about it. I sent him the link, he installed it, and after a week I asked if he liked it. That's what he called my insisting.

He used it for a few months and one evening he asked me what I thought about his company buying it. I said it was a great idea. I didn't persuade him or trick him. It's extremely difficult to trick Ben. You deserved it, your app is great, and your team did a great job. Please don't think that I schemed it all just to see you."

"He really liked the app?" I asked.

She laughed, the familiar notes I had forgotten. "Yes, he loved it. He would not acquire it if he thought differently."

"Thank you, I guess?"

She smiled at me, bowing her head slightly.

"Just so you know, if not for this app business, I would have called or texted you eventually," Alice said.

"Yes, therapy suggestion."

"I'm still human, Emily. Besides the guilt, grief, and the dark baggage I carry, I was simply curious how your life is."

"Fair enough," I said and smiled.

"I'd better be going," she said and turned to the door.

"Does Benjamin know who I am?" I asked.

"Not really, he knows we went to the university together, hung out a few times. He doesn't know the details of my past. The past stays in the past, he says, it's the future that matters."

I nodded. Only a person who doesn't have such horrendous events in his past can so easily brush it off.

"Good night, Alice."

She stopped, her hand on the door frame, and looked back at me.

"I'm glad you're here," she said.

After a long pause, and after I heard the click of the door, I muttered, "Me too."

Chapter Forty-Two

It was easier after the talk the night before. I didn't wake up feeling heavy. The difference between me and Alice was that I shoved all my feelings and memories about the accident and the time around it deep down inside myself. While Alice lived with them openly, just covered enough from the outside world, if you got closer, you could see everything.

I had texted Arthur the day before, but he hadn't replied, he was flying to Tokyo again. He said the project with the Japanese was coming to an end, and it was only one or two more trips to get everything straightened with them.

If Miranda knew about my long talks with Alice, she would have been so, so angry. Even if I could eventually forgive Alice, Miranda would not. She said to me once that memory was a funny thing, it blocked and muted the traumatizing experiences sometimes. Miranda said my brain chose to forget that time, and it was a blessing. But she remembered those first few months vividly. In the places I remembered a murky darkness, she remembered screams.

But looking at a sunbeam playing on the wall of my bungalow, I chose not to remember again. I picked up my phone and saw that Olga was online. I texted her asking if she wanted to go to the beach.

See you there in ten, a reply pinged back.

I changed into a swimsuit, brushed my hair, and splashed cold water on my face. Looking up at the mirror I noted my skin; it was absorbing the sun with the speed of a tanning salon. The nose ring I had never stopped wearing glistened with a bead of water. I dried my face and stepped outside, the sound of the ocean within my reach.

Olga was already waiting for me, her body wrapped in a sports swimsuit, long lean legs stood on the grass that stopped a few feet away from her, giving in to the sand.

We slowly walked down to the beach and my breath hitched in my chest. It was a serene morning. The waves caressed the shore, white foam marking the line between sand and sea.

Olga elbowed me lightly, pointing to the left. Farther down the beach sat a pair, Benjamin was sitting with closed eyes, his face to the water. Alice was curled by his side with a book. They didn't see us at first, and when I looked at them, it was the scene I would have imagined for her when I first met her—sitting on the beach with a book, the future wife of a CEO of a massive company, her blonde hair flowing in the wind. I didn't imagine her tangled in the sheets with, well, me.

When Alice looked up at us, her face lit with a smile and she waved. She said something to Benjamin and he opened his eyes, gesturing for us to join them.

"Do you guys swim?" Olga asked when we reached them.

Benjamin stood up, brushing the sand from his calves.

"Alice?"

She shook her head and pointed to a book. "I'm fine, go ahead."

When they walked to the water's edge, Olga turned to me and winked.

I sat on the edge of a mat and looked to the horizon. I thought about Arthur and wondered what he was doing now. Reading? Scanning work charts? Trying to sleep? He flew in business class, so it was not torture. I smiled as I imagined him complaining about the plastic food and all the stewardesses flirting with him.

"What are you thinking about?" Alice asked. "You're smiling."

I turned to her and met her eyes.

"Are you planning to live here?" I asked instead of replying. "Like, forever?"

"I don't know, I don't plan. We are searching for a villa to buy here, and I'm sure I would love to make it a permanent residence. But even though Ben tries to stay away from the operational part of this job, he's often needed there. I don't want to return to America, but we'll see, I guess."

I could not grasp their relationship, did she love him? Or was it gratitude and comfort? Was she bisexual or gay, and faking it?

"Are you happy?" I asked.

I watched closely as her eyes turned to Benjamin, and back to me. "I'm learning to live again, Emily."

I nodded. "Doesn't he want to start a family, like all those CEOs with an infinite number of kids?"

"No. He thinks that the planet is already too crowded and is a dangerous place to live in. It was a topic we talked about over and over again because I kept repeating that I never want kids. Never. And he agrees."

I nodded. Alice was sure about being childfree even all those years ago, and now her words proved that she only cemented this belief.

We watched Benjamin and Olga talking in the water.

"I drive now, you know?" I said.

And Alice laughed. "No way."

"Yes, I drive a 1969 Ford Mustang. It was the car my dad left me."

Alice fished her phone from the small pouch bag and typed something, a grin spreading all over her face when she saw the results. She showed me a Google page with images.

"The black one."

"Of course," she said and zoomed in on the image. "It suits you."

"Thanks."

She looked up at the blue sky.

"My yellow Beetle lives in my parents' garage now. I just could not part with him. I think he is bored to death out there, waiting for my return, that may never come."

"He?" I laughed.

"Beetle was always a he," she said, smiling.

Benjamin walked toward us, water dripping from his shorts, and sat down next to Alice. He wrapped his arms around her, and she giggled when his wet beard brushed her chin.

She was learning to live again.

Chapter Forty-Three

"So tomorrow we are going to Sigiriya," Benjamin said. "We'll be away for two days, so pack accordingly. We are going to visit tea plantations, a Buddist temple, local Switzerland, and of course, The Rock."

Everyone cheered. My feet were itching to see the island, to explore. My eyes met Alice's and she smiled at me.

"Today we need to discuss the details of the app, things that we want to save, what to change, and where we are going. How we see the future additions, marketing plans, features we need to work more on, and what parts we can let go of," he said. "I booked a separate office room for us in the local coworking space, so please be ready to leave in two hours."

We finished our breakfast, the terrace framed in white curtains had been ours every day, the only place to seat an extensive group. I stood up and walked back to my bungalow under the morning sun that was already slowly baking my skin.

My phone vibrated when we were having breakfast, so I had to turn down Arthur's call, texting him that I'd call in twenty. Then as I sat on my bed, my call went unanswered. A few moments later a text came that he was in another meeting already.

We kept missing each other, and I longed to hear his remarks. His texts were shorter than usual, the jokes gone.

I went to the shower. It seemed I needed to let it go and accept that I would always have sand in my hair and stuck to my skin. But the constant humidity, I was not used to it. I wanted to wash it away every minute I was outside.

I stepped out of the shower, the calming chill on my wet skin from the blasting air conditioner was a relief. I walked back to my suitcase to find something to wear to the meeting, when a light knock on my door stopped me in my tracks. I was naked. So I rushed back to the bathroom and wrapped a white towel around me.

"A minute!" I said loudly.

I opened the door prepared to see room service, but familiar stormy eyes widened when she saw me in a towel. I was sure Alice didn't mean to look at me that way, but her gaze followed my body down and up, stopping for a second at the base of my throat.

"Oh, sorry, I didn't mean to interrupt ..." she said and lifted her hands with two plastic cups. "I went to the shop outside the hotel, they sell freshly squeezed juice there. They are great to battle the heat, but I see you are battling it with a shower."

She smiled.

"Come in," I said.

Alice walked in, and I touched her lower back to guide her inside. It was such a fleeting contact, I didn't even think about it, my hand going there on its own.

"Oh, sorry," I murmured, hiding my hand behind my back.

Alice stopped, and turned to me, tilting her head. "It's okay."

It was not. Not now.

"God, it's freezing here," she said, sucking her breath in and looking at the blasting air conditioner. "I'll wait outside."

I nodded, and rushed to my suitcase, grabbing my underwear and a light flowy dress. I closed the door inside the bathroom and pressed my back to it. My heart was hammering in my chest. I was embarrassed with myself. Why on earth would I touch her? Why didn't she dismiss it but look at me as though she wanted to say something, those eyes scanning me. I was aware that I wore nothing but a towel at that moment.

I put a dress on and turned to the mirror, fixing my hair with trembling hands.

"Is it okay that I'm here?" Alice asked when I joined her outside.

"I don't know," I said honestly.

She looked away, a shadow of sadness crossing her features.

"I should probably go," she said and started to stand up.

And again my hands were out of sync with my mind, because I watched my fingers gently clasping around her wrist. There was a delay between what I was seeing and reacting to it.

I looked at my hand as if it were something foreign, and then I released her, dropping my hands to my lap.

"Stay," I whispered.

Alice sat back, her eyes on me. And suddenly it was all too much. I sprang up and walked to the other side of the pool terrace. I put my hand to the cold damp stone of the wall and closed my eyes. The memories were rushing back, the moments I had blocked. My fingers were curling into a fist when I remembered how we sang inside the yellow car, how a crooked snowman grinned at us, the smell of hot cocoa, my back to the wall outside the club, her face inches from mine, our first kiss, her hot body pressing into mine, skin on skin. The rush of emotions, the longing, the fucking love that broke my heart.

And there, on the other side of the planet, my body kept reacting to her, as though there were not seven years between those moments and the present, as though it started to remember, as though it dismissed the pain, the loss.

I whimpered.

Warm arms wrapped around me, pressing me close. The long-forgotten smell of vanilla on Alice's skin rushed back, her hair tickling my nose as I buried my face in her neck. I hated how my body remembered her, how it fit, how my arms circled around her waist.

I was breathing hard.

"It's okay," she whispered. "It's okay, it's okay, it's okay."

She brushed the skin at the top of my spine as I tried to breathe. We didn't move as we stood.

"I'm so sorry," Alice said quietly.

I stepped back and went to the lounger, where Alice had sat before, two cups at the foot of it. I took a swig, and as the sweet taste exploded in my mouth, I exhaled. Then I looked at the cup in my hand, and the second on the floor. They always brought me something, Alice and Jake, coffee, cocoa, chocolate.

Alice sat on the lounger and folded her legs in a lotus position, taking the other cup.

"It's good," I said and shook the cup in my hand a little.

She smiled and my breakdown slowly melted away.

My team packed into the bus and Nirved drove us to a coworking space in the neighboring village. The building looked more like a spa than an office. The outside Zen Garden, and small open space inside, various hammocks on the trees, it was far from the usual office we all were used to. There were three meeting rooms inside, instead of a window in each, there was a simple glass wall that looked into the lush greenery outside. The furniture looked new, the office chairs comfy.

All of us sat around a table and I looked up at the air conditioner. It was blasting cold air and I scooted closer to it. One of my colleagues plugged in a laptop, and the screen was projected onto the wall. It was a presentation we had all worked on, our vision for next steps, and current problems.

I stood up and looked around the room, all eyes turning to me. We discussed it over and over before coming here, before talking to Benjamin. He was looking at the screen with the first points. Alice was not by his side, she had stayed in the hotel.

Olga nodded, and after taking a deep breath I started talking, the speech I had prepared long ago.

Some time later we forgot that we were on the island, that the trees behind the window were different than our usual, that the birds that peered into the room were brightly colored, and my team started working, tuning back to our usual routine. We operated as a well-oiled mechanism, all parts supporting each other. Benjamin was quiet for some time, studying us, looking closely. But it was not long before he joined the discussion.

I looked around, confident at our progress. I was so proud of the people that surrounded me, of my team.

Chapter Forty-Four

W e had to leave at four in the morning for the two-day tour the next day. I had barely slept that night, because, after hours in the coworking space, Nirved drove us to Galle. We walked around the Dutch fort, its lighthouse and architecture so different from the Sri Lanka I had seen up to that point. A table was booked for us, and we sat in the fancy restaurant, but as it always was with my team, the food didn't stop us from discussing work.

We picked up where we had left off in coworking as though there had not been two hours of walking in between and continued discussing the newest feature Benjamin had suggested. I thought he would protest, work-life balance being an important part of his new life, but as he dug deep into coding with one of our developers, I got the idea that even though he stepped away from the operational part of the job, he missed it.

When we returned to Nirved's bus, Alice was already inside.

"Hey, how are you here?" I asked, climbing in.

"I took a public bus," she said. "It's always an adventure."

As we passed Galle bus station, all of us glued to the windows, the variety of colors, decorations, and the homemade tuning of each bus stunned us.

Jessica sat by Alice's side and started asking questions about tickets and fares.

Nirved took us to Unawatuna beach, and not long after my feet touched the sand, Olga found me and turned us toward the bar.

The wall of reservation around her was quickly melting in the sun, and I liked the lively person who was appearing. She was easy to be around. Traditionally, the whole team found its way to the bar, and finally, the talk that had started in coworking was trickling to an end.

I walked away and tried to call Arthur, but the Wi-Fi was awful, and eventually, I sent him a text, because I hadn't even been able to upload a photo. I told him about the day, and that I missed him. But before the message was sent the signal disappeared, someone had turned off the Wi-Fi in the bar.

We returned late to the hotel, and when I finally had good reception, it was too late to call Arthur, so I sent the text and laughed at the video he had sent me. He was in a comics shop, making a detailed review of the latest editions. Imaginary review because he had no idea what the comics were about.

So, when I finally went to bed, my backpack ready for a two-day trip, I was asleep before my head hit the pillow. And when my alarm roared in the darkness, it was so disorienting and almost impossible to wake up that I had to drag myself out of bed. I pulled my still sleeping body into the bathroom, brushed my teeth, splashed cold water on my face and, as it did nothing, I gathered my hair into a ponytail and shuffled to the door. I looked back at the bungalow. It would sit that way for two days, with most of my clothes and toiletries hidden back in the suitcase I had left in the closet.

I was not alone in the early morning/late night misery,

because when I stumbled to the bus, Dave was already sitting inside with closed eyes, his forehead pressed to the window. I climbed in, and went to the back row, slumping in the corner seat. Everyone packed inside and, when I closed my eyes for a second, just to open them to the quiet engine rumbling, the bus was already slowly moving through the dark streets. I turned my head to the right and saw Alice's head resting on Benjamin's shoulder, his protective hand around her. It was quiet on the bus, and I watched them for a few seconds. They looked good together, and I wondered if it was as real for her as it was for him.

I folded my jacket and placed it against my cheek, creating a cushion, and closed my eyes. I remembered the video from Arthur and laughed quietly.

When I opened my eyes, it was much lighter outside, the rushing traffic honking at us. I looked around and saw that most people were awake, Olga was reading on her Kindle, one of our developers was tapping his leg and shaking his head to the rhythm in his earphones, Jessica was glued to the window, Dave was still sleeping, and Alice sat upright by my side, reading. Benjamin had his eyes closed, massive wireless headphones on his head.

I looked at Alice's screen and noticed a familiar frame of an app. It was our reading app.

"What are you reading?" I asked.

"This month I was matched with a domestic suspense. God, it's chilly," she said.

Our app was a subscription-based Tinder-like reading app. You fill in preferences, and the more you read and rate books, the better the match you'd receive. Deep analyzing algorithms made the process similar to interacting with a real person.

I nodded and looked down, my heart skipping a beat when I noticed that my knee was pressed to hers. Alice was sitting next to me, but when I acknowledged the parts of our bodies that were touching, the shoulders, bare arms, it was as though I had turned to her in my sleep, and she ... she had scooted closer.

I straightened my spine, crossed my arms over my chest, and pressed my knees tightly together. Alice looked for a second to the place where my knee was pressed into hers and looked back to the screen, her face betraying nothing.

"Good morning, guys," Nirved said loudly from his seat. "We will stop for breakfast in ten minutes in a village."

People murmured in approval. And the next ten minutes I stayed plastered to the window, sharply aware of all my limbs, and making an effort to take up less space, so as not to touch the person by my side.

When we got off the bus I stood and stretched my arms over my head, cracking my spine, and looked around. It was much hotter there than in the bus, and even hotter than in the village our hotel was placed in. We were farther inland, away from the cooling effect of the ocean. We stopped by a local two-story house, and a family greeted us. The man looked strikingly similar to our driver, and it appeared that we arrived at Nirved's brother's house.

The table was served with unfamiliar dishes, and as we sat around Nirved started pointing to potato, chicken, and egg curries, different kinds of hoppers made from rice flour, and Pol Sambol, a coconut condiment. The spicy variety of tastes was an unusual start to the day, and I managed to snap a photo of the table before we started. I would send it to Arthur later.

As usual, I waited for the tea, and as always it had a rich flavor. I noticed how Alice glanced my way when I took the first sip.

"So, you are into tea now," she said later when we walked back to the bus.

"Kind of, yes. And you?"

"I stopped drinking tea for years after ..." she said, her voice sounding quieter, "Jake died."

I nodded. "At first the tea was one of few reminders that both of you existed," I said and turned away abruptly, walking to Olga.

I didn't want to see her reaction, I was mad at myself for even saying it. I was really into tea, even if Alice was the one that showed it to me. And later I drank it in gallons trying to capture the fleeting memory of the many times I drank tea with both of them. But later, much later, it turned into something that I enjoyed for myself, not connected to anyone, a hobby and meditation.

"Honestly, I would kill for a latte and a butter croissant," Olga whispered, rubbing her stomach. "It's just too much for breakfast."

I laughed. "Agreed."

When I climbed back to my seat and Alice sat quietly by my side again, she didn't say anything. I took out my headphones, turned on the noise cancellation function, and played the downloaded playlist of my favorites on shuffle.

Minutes ticked by as I watched the Sri Lankan countryside out of the window, songs turning from melodic to dance, from sad to fast, and, when a heavy metal song blasted in my ears, I looked at the time on my phone. I caught Benjamin looking at the screen before I turned it off. Alice was sleeping on his shoulder, and he quietly pointed to his wrist, asking the time. I turned on the screen again and showed it to him, he nodded, noticing the song title. He pointed to his ears and showed me thumbs up. I smiled. I tried to imagine both of them shouting to many rock songs Alice loved to listen to, and could not. He was just so different. But I was not sure Alice changed a bit, below the layer of sadness, I assumed the girl who loved bellowing to the songs in her small yellow car still existed.

Chapter Forty-Five

Sigiriya was a massive rock fortress lost in the jungle. While we climbed what felt like thousands of stairs under the curious gazes of monkeys, the heat slowly burned my skin away. Nirved kept repeating to us to keep a firm grip on our phones, sunglasses, hats, anything that could be lifted.

"Monkeys just seem cute," he said. "They are jerks, they steal stuff."

When Jessica laughed, he turned to her with a serious face. "I'm serious, they stole the latest phone from a previous group I took here."

She nodded solemnly and tightened her grip on her phone. Monkeys' eyes followed our ascent, and when a big boulder stopped us in our tracks, Benjamin climbed it first and stretched his hand to the next person. One by one, we climbed it, and when I was the last one standing, a familiar hand gripped my palm. Her hand was warm, and silky skin grazed mine. It was so painfully familiar that I looked up into her eyes. I could see the moment our hands met, her pupils going wider. I noticed that when I was up, she didn't release my hand immediately and that she brushed it with a featherlight touch of her fingertip.

Before I could say anything, Alice disappeared to the front of the group, talking to the tour guide.

We studied the frescos, the palace on the top of the rock, all the way listening to historical facts. The guide spoke in a flowy rhythm, as though he was reciting a poem, and sometimes it was difficult to understand what he meant. As he lectured us, my mind kept wandering away.

When we got to the small hotel lost in the jungle, I was tired, my body craving a shower. So when Nirved asked if anyone wanted to see traditional Sri Lankan dances in the evening I was the first to say that I'd stay.

Alice chose to stay too, along with Dave and one of our developers.

There was no Wi-Fi in that hotel, proudly labeling itself as a digital detox center. When I opened the door to the room and noticed a second twin bed, I remembered Benjamin saying that the hotel was too small to provide everyone with a separate room, so we were placed in double rooms. Later someone would join me here. I wanted to text Olga, saying that I saved her a place, but when I turned on the screen of my phone there was not a single bar. A real digital detox.

I dropped my backpack on the bed and rushed to the shower, finally stripping myself of the damp clothes and standing under heavenly rivulets of cold water. It was strange how little I needed, and how the simple shower felt like a luxury.

Twilight coated the trees when I ventured outside. The hotel sat on a small hill, a river flowing at the foot of it. The buzz of the jungle was so loud and alive that when I walked to the edge of the trees, the noise was so overwhelming that I just stood there, watching the darkening space, unable to process. When I finally turned away, I saw that I missed someone reading in a hammock nearby. Alice.

I walked to her.

"I'm starving," I said. "What about you?"

She laughed.

"Good luck with finding food here. There isn't a living soul besides us and a snoring developer, Dave went to the river. I tried to find a kitchen, but it's locked, and since we're far away from any village, we can't even eat out. The group will go to a restaurant after the performance, so I guess we're on our own. I have a few protein bars in my room. Do you want the most non-Sri Lankan food possible?"

As if on cue, my stomach grumbled.

"Let's go," she said, taking my hand and leading me inside the building.

Alice froze a few steps later, looked at our hands, and then up at me. And it was like a long time ago, when the noise of an outside world dimmed, leaving only the two of us. She didn't let go as she turned, opened the door, and led me inside.

"Did you notice how our bodies seem to be drawn to each other—like they don't remember that it's over?" I asked when she eventually let go of my hand and I was standing in her room, the twin of the one I was staying in. My heart hammered in my chest as my hand lightly tingled.

She didn't reply as she dug in her bag, taking out a few shiny bars.

"Alice?" I whispered and she lowered her head.

For a few seconds, she stood like that, her face hidden under the veil of blonde hair.

"Yes," she said quietly and walked to me. "I did notice it. I'm trying to fight the urge to be close to you all the time you are here. I'm trying to control my body, and you are making it impossible. When I pull away, you reach out. It's like a crazy dance we are trapped in."

Alice lifted her hand. It was trembling, but she caught a strand of my hair, and then released it. I closed my eyes, and she touched my cheek, the tip of my nose, painting a slow line on my lower lip.

She was closer, I could smell the painfully familiar vanilla smell.

"I have to go," I said, and stepped back.

She was looking at me, a hand dropping to her side. She was so eternally beautiful, magnetic, that it took my breath away. And now she stood there, so close, a storm of emotions raving in those gray eyes.

"I have to go," I repeated and dashed to the door. But I turned back, my hand gripping the handle.

That time, I was seeing not the flashes of the past, but the glimpses of the future if I just took a step in her direction. I could almost feel her lips on mine, the frantic movements of pulling our clothes off, my shivering skin when it met hers, our bodies pressed together, her fingers on my breasts, my hand finding its almost forgotten way between her thighs. A light moan on her lips, as my fingers slid on the slick of her wet flesh.

It felt so real, the possibility just seconds away. So I opened the door and closed it behind me.

Later there was a light knock on my door, and when I opened it, two protein bars lay on the floor on a paper napkin.

Chapter Forty-Six

I woke up when someone entered the room and went to the bathroom. It was dark outside, and I had been out for hours. But when I looked at my phone screen, I saw that it was only midnight.

I heard a thud and a low cursing in Ukrainian. Olga. I waited for her to return and asked about the evening.

"Well, the dancing show was weird, but the restaurant afterward was surprisingly good. We brought you food because we realized too late that you'd be starving here. Everyone was exhausted, so we called it a day pretty early," Olga said. "We should be down at reception tomorrow morning at half-past eight."

"Okay, thanks," I said.

She looked at her phone and made a slow circle around the room.

"No chance," I said, "this place is either a completely digital detox or a tomb."

She sighed and returned to the bed. When she climbed in, she whispered, "Can I ask you a question?"

"Sure."

"Why is Alice so sad all the time? I mean she hides it well. Did you notice the moments when she's present, as though she is falling? Her features freeze, but Benjamin is always close. He brings her back to reality, placing his hands on her. The way she drops her head onto his shoulder is like she's fighting for a breath, and he helps her breathe," Olga said and turned to me. "When I think about it though, all those times I've seen Alice that way, you were not around. It's as though your presence makes it easier for her."

Her last words echoed in my mind.

"She had a brother, Jacob. They were really close. He died in a car crash when we were studying and Alice took it really hard. I didn't see her after the accident. She just disappeared from my life, they both did," I said quietly. "There was a lot of love and guilt involved at that time."

"I knew it was grief I was seeing," Olga said.

I nodded into the night. We stayed quiet, the raucous noise from the wildlife outside taking the place of dialogue. The birds, insects, all the animals, they were wide awake outside the hotel walls.

In the morning, throughout the traditional breakfast, I was sharply aware of my location in the room regarding Alice's. When she took a step in my direction, I took two backward.

The hotel and kitchen boasted workers at that time, the deserted place of the previous day was full of life.

But as much as I stayed away, my gaze kept returning to Alice. I watched her closely, and our eyes met often.

"We're going to the Temple of the Tooth now, so your knees and shoulders should be covered," Benjamin said.

"Men also?" Dave asked, shoving a bun into his mouth.

"Yes, but you can wear shorts, they provide a semblance of a skirt to tie around the hips," Benjamin said.

So, when we were all standing with our bags around the bus, almost everyone was wearing shorts. I had a shirt to cover my bare shoulders, tied around my waist. As for the knees, I'd use the skirt they gave at the temple. I'd googled the rules of entering sacred places before the trip, and almost everywhere you could find a skirt to borrow.

I shoved my backpack into the trunk of the bus and walked to the door to climb inside when Alice joined us. She was wearing a white flowing dress that fell to her knees, the upper part hugged her waist and breasts while the lower part showed just a hint of the outline of her bottom. Her hair was curled into natural waves. Something glinted on her chest, and, when I looked closer, I saw the moon pendant.

Benjamin smiled at her and kissed the top of her head. Someone pulled my arm.

"Climb inside," Olga hissed. "Stop staring."

I took my place at the back of the bus and pressed my forehead to the glass. Alice was teasing me. The modest white dress with just a hint of sexiness could plausibly have been for someone else, but the pendant was solely for me.

She knew I saw it, because, as always, our eyes met. I looked away first.

We were booked for a private tour of the Temple, so when Nirved dropped us at the parking lot, a smiling man welcomed us. He shepherded us to the flower market, where all kinds of lotus flowers were sold separately or woven into the intricate bouquets. White, yellow, purple, bluish, the colors mixed, and I was mesmerized by the kaleidoscope around me.

I chose a small bouquet of pink lotuses, and gingerly touched the petals. They were like liquid silk.

When I returned to the group I scanned the crowd, immediately finding the woman in white holding the white bouquet, silver glinting on her chest. The dress was different, but I remembered the Thanksgiving dinner when I felt attracted to her for the first time, not as a friend, but as something more.

Seeing her pulled all those forgotten memories to the surface, revealing the rawness of it. I rubbed my eyes and turned away.

The Temple was a popular tourist attraction, so when we left our shoes outside and squeezed in, following the crowd, the magical feeling from the flowery market was erased as we walked one pressed into another. The holy reverie was gone as there were so many people, that even our guide was shocked. I felt dizzy and stifled and when we finally ventured outside, my shirt plastered to my skin.

I gladly dumped the borrowed skirt and walked to the nearest tree, pressing my palm to the trunk, the coolness slipping into me under the shade.

The next stop before the long way back to the hotel was a tea plantation in Nuwara Eliya, a city surrounded by green hills. It was the coolest place in Sri Lanka, and it felt like a balm to my skin when we stepped out of the bus. What followed was a tea tour showing the whole process from collecting the leaves to its finding its way into our cups. When a young woman was describing the types of tea, I caught each word and then marched to the shop and bought every type they sold there. It was time to get Miranda into tea drinking. And what was a better way than with the tea that grew on a nearby hill?

As I walked first in the group, soaking in the details, the smells, for the first time in the trip I was not aware of who was looking at me, whose eyes followed my every step. I felt lighter here. When after the tasting I walked away for the duration of the free time we had, and slowly went up a hill, it was the first time in the whole trip that I felt what I had thought traveling should feel like, the connection with the place. I ran my fingers over the leaves that would become someone's drink soon, and I hoped that someone would be as happy as I was at that moment.

When I returned to the bus and climbed inside, I saw Olga sitting in the seat next to mine. Benjamin and Alice were at the front, and I didn't look in her direction. Olga smiled at me and looked back at her book. When the bus was backing away from the tea factory, the hills disappearing from the view, I found myself gently touching the glass, as though I was saying goodbye.

As we drove by cottages that looked so out of place there, Nirved explained that that part was called Little England and I smiled to myself. If real England looked like this part of Sri Lanka I thought Arthur's childhood would have been much happier.

I looked at my phone, the signal bar disappearing and returning as we followed the winding roads. I texted Arthur three words.

I miss you.

I imagined the message flying across the world, landing on his screen. But as I stared out the window, the signal disappeared and didn't come back.

Chapter Forty-Seven

My bungalow was a little heaven when we got back. I dove into the pool and floated at the edge. I needed some time to myself after hours on that bus.

There were five missed calls on my phone when it finally found a signal—texts from Arthur, an angry tirade from Miranda. When I tried calling him, the call went unanswered.

The next day we'd have a work day, going back to the meeting room in the coworking office. The day after would be the last of our trip, free time.

I let go of the pool edge and sank to the bottom, the light playing tricks under my closed lids. When I emerged I knew what I had to do. I pulled my wet hair into the bun, draped a tunic over my shoulders, and marched outside, to the bigger bungalow on the other end of the hotel grounds.

I knocked lightly and when the door opened, I saw surprise in Benjamin's eyes.

"Is Alice here?" I asked.

"Yeah, she's in the shower. Come in," he said, gesturing inside.

The faint smell of vanilla was inside the room, and when I

sat on the leather settee Benjamin sat across from me. He tilted his head to the bathroom, and when he heard the water he turned to me.

"She's fragile, Emily," he said quietly. "It's like she's made from the thinnest porcelain, so thin it's almost impossible to touch it without breaking it. And I know that you have a past together. I don't know the details, and I don't want to know, but I know it involved her brother."

Suddenly my throat felt dry, and I rubbed the skin under my chin.

"Do you know how it all began? When I saw her using that reading app for weeks I asked her about it. She said that her old friend had created it and that she was proud. I asked her to send me the link, and when I downloaded it and used it myself I saw the potential. But one simple question made the decision for me. I asked Alice what she thought of me acquiring it, and not only marketing it, but adding it to the pack of apps that goes into the default set of apps on the majority of new phones. She shone, Emily, for the first time since I had met her, she smiled so brightly—it took my breath away. I loved her from the first second I laid eyes on her, and it took time for her to trust me. But when I saw that I could make her so happy, just by buying the app of her old friend, of course I did it. I knew a woman was this old friend, and it made the perfect sense. Until I saw how she looked at you. You were much more than a friend," he said and sighed, clasping his hands in front of him, leaning closer.

"That was my mistake, and I see it now. But then, she lit from the inside when I told her about the process, she was alive again. Did you know that she screamed at night before?"

I shook my head, remembering Miranda's words.

"She stopped screaming after I suggested buying the app. She was so gentle with me, so pure, pulling me like a magnet.

Alice stayed close, and I was elated. But she never looked at me like she looks at you," he said and stood.

"So, whatever you came to tell her, please be gentle. If you came to take her, so be it. As long as she's happy. But please care for her, she won't survive alone. She's just too delicate for this world. It hurt her, and she didn't heal." His voice was shaking, and he looked up at me. "Promise me. Promise me, Emily. Because she won't get through another hit."

I felt my tears burning my skin. The love of that man was so strong, so protective, so powerful, that it took up all the space in the room, the island, the world.

"I came to say goodbye," I whispered the same moment the water stopped running in the bathroom.

I saw a relief on his face, how his shoulders relaxed, following the guilt. He loved her, and the conflict between her being happy with me and the chance to be with him, tore at his heart.

He stood up and walked to the bathroom door. He took a deep breath and knocked.

"Emily came to see you," Benjamin said.

There was a pause in the movement, and in a few moments, the door opened. But what gave me hope was where Alice looked first, she looked at Benjamin. He smiled and scooped her in his arms, water still dripping from her hair and onto his T-shirt.

He kissed her cheek and let go, only after that did she look at me.

"Can we talk outside?" I asked, standing up.

"Sure," Alice replied.

"We'll be on the beach," I said to Benjamin and he nodded.

We walked quietly through the gently lit path of the hotel, the sound of crashing waves getting closer and closer. Tonight, the ocean wasn't calm, the waves bigger, the worry of a mass of water palpable just a few feet away.

Alice didn't ask me anything all the way. She was waiting.

"Whatever it is between us on this trip, it has to end. There is no us anymore, and there hasn't been since that moment at your parents' house. I know you explained, and now I understand. But I can't forgive, okay?"

I was standing close to her so she could hear, but my every word was met with a wind that carried it away. Alice was looking at me with her huge eyes, left hand squeezed into a fist and pressing it to her chest.

"You keep pulling me back. You taunt me, and I don't trust myself with you. I just can't stay at a distance when you are so close. I don't want anything to happen, but even though I didn't forgive, my body seems to be attuned to yours, as though it forgot about the pain it was in," I said, my voice straining.

Still, she said nothing.

"Benjamin loves you so much, and my stay here just hurts him. I don't want to see you again," I said.

"You're lying," she said quietly.

"No, I'm not. Because the longer I stay the stronger the pull. And I can't resist it. I can't resist you."

It was fast. Alice closed the distance between us and pressed her lips to mine. But before my fury set in, there was a moment when it all rushed back. It was such a familiar feeling, her lips on mine, fervent. I sighed as she pulled me closer, her hand getting lost in my hair like it had a million times before. Her lips were gentle, and I welcomed her. I kissed her back. And then my anger kicked in.

"No," I said, stepping back.

My lips still buzzed from her touch, my stomach still roiled, my heart thumped louder than the ocean.

"No, Alice. I'm sorry, but I told the truth. There is no us anymore," I said.

She pressed her hand to her heart as if she could stop it from breaking with her fingers. I brushed something wet from my cheek and turned to go.

"I'm so sorry," I whispered.

I left her out there. I left her alone on the beach.

I curled into a fetal position on my bed and cried, my heart swelling as my body shook. How much *did* I lie? How much *did* I want to go back to her, to repeat that kiss? She kissed me like before, with all her love, but I was a new person.

My phone buzzed with calls from Arthur and Miranda, but I could not bring myself to answer. I cried for the love that died for me, but that lived for her. I cried for what would have been a perfect love story, and, because it all started with Jake, it all ended when he was gone.

I cried until my tears dried out, until my sobs went quiet, then I shifted to another pillow, and fell into the abyss.

Chapter Forty-Eight

I missed breakfast deliberately, calling room service. As I said the day before, I couldn't see Alice anymore.

I walked to the bus and sat by Olga's side. She looked at my face and smiled gently.

"Everything is going to be fine," she said quietly.

I nodded. As it was a work trip, Alice wouldn't be there.

Nirved sped us through the streets of Sri Lanka to the coworking center and, as we filed into the office, the meeting started. My colleagues discussed the future tasks, while I listened, trying to avoid looking at Benjamin. I felt guilty for that second when I kissed her back. It was extremely difficult to focus on work because I didn't want to be there anymore. I wanted to be away, to go home.

Finally, when I gathered the courage to look at Benjamin, he was looking at me. He nodded lightly and stood up.

"Guys, when I first used the app I noticed the small details that were carefully woven into it. And now that I've met all of you, I see that it could not be different. With such a dedicated team, something beautiful was bound to happen. I hope I've shown you the pros of working remotely, of traveling while working, and now, with pride and confidence, I transfer you to Samantha, who will manage the project further. She's great, you'll meet her in the office soon for a few meetings when you're back, and then we're going remote. It was great meeting you all," he said and looked at each of us, his eyes lingering on mine. "And I hope you'll have more ideas, more new fascinating projects, if anything comes to mind run through Samantha. She's skilled at picking up the gems of ideas. I'm proud that you joined my company."

Everyone stood up and clapped. All drama aside, Benjamin was a great leader, thoughtful and encouraging. And I saw in the faces of my team how the trip influenced their professional confidence and, as I clapped, I was proud of them and grateful for him.

We left the coworking space shortly afterward and Nirved drove us to the nearby beach restaurant. The setting was simple, plastic chairs and tables, brightly colored paper tablecloths, but it stood at the foot of the ocean. The night storm changed to a calm whisper. I nervously looked around, but Alice was nowhere to be found. I heard Jessica asking about her, and Benjamin replied that she was not feeling well.

I didn't want to face her after the day before. It was hard already, draining. I'd tried to forget and move on, but then it was all rushing back.

I would do my utmost to avoid her until the end of the trip. I had nothing left to say.

When we sat around a table, which was assembled from four plastic tables, and a variety of brightly colored fish was served, the waiter explained that it was caught only that night.

I looked at Benjamin. He was different, and as hard as he tried to be cheerful, I saw how his hands trembled. He wanted to be with Alice, but he needed to be with us. So, when our eyes met, I lightly turned my head to the exit and whispered: "Go."

He looked at me a moment longer and nodded. He stayed for twenty more minutes and then stood up.

"I need to go; Alice isn't feeling well today and I'm worried. Is it okay that I leave you here? Nirved will drive me back to the hotel and will return for all of you," Benjamin said.

Everyone murmured an agreement and wished Alice well.

"Thanks, see you later."

"He's such a gentleman," Jessica whispered when Benjamin disappeared around the corner.

"Is there a chance you're the reason why Alice isn't well?" Olga whispered in my ear.

"I don't want to talk about it," I replied, shaking my head.

I focused on the moment, on the fish on my plate, on the conversation around me. Everyone was talking about the things they liked there, later the discussion flowed back to work, and in that exchange, I took a bigger part. I was there for work in the first place.

It was twilight when we exited the restaurant, and I asked if anyone wanted to go to the bar. I wanted to stay away from the hotel as long as possible. Because I hurt Alice yesterday, and I didn't trust myself not to try to fix it. She had Benjamin, he'd care for her.

I asked Nirved for directions to the closest beach bar, and we walked by the water's edge barefoot, talking about nothing in particular. There were five of us, and as they told me the countries they wanted to visit, I thought about how I wanted to be back home. Out of the sheer mess. So when a jolly-looking bartender poured us shots, and then one more round, and one more, it was a relief, the alcohol taking the edge off reality, the sounds of the ocean turning louder, the stress muting.

After hours on that beach, we finally called Nirved to pick us up. The world tilted when I was climbing into the bus, and I slipped, a jolting pain on my wrist bringing me back.

I needed to sober up, or I needed to get to my bed, fast.

As Nirved looked back at us from his driver's seat, he shook his head and drove in a different direction from the hotel. He called someone and quickly said something unintelligible.

The bus stopped at the closed shop, but a sleepy man appeared by its door. Nirved asked us to wait inside the bus, and he hugged the man and walked inside the shop. A few minutes later he appeared with five cups of a yellow substance. He climbed inside and gave each of us a cup.

"Drink, you'll be sober before we get back to the hotel," he said.

We did. It was a mix of juice with a hint of spice and something hot tickled my tongue. I closed my eyes as he drove us back and sipped the concoction. It was refreshing and cleared my thoughts.

"Wow," Olga whispered by my side as she sipped from her cup.

We giggled.

Nirved was right, I sobered up by the moment we got out of the bus. As Jessica asked him what was inside the drink, I bid everyone goodnight. With sobriety came a strong need for a shower. I had sand everywhere, again. It clung to my body, the skin moist from the humidity.

As I walked by the hotel lobby, I saw the familiar shape of a man sitting at the hotel bar. Benjamin's head was lowered, his fingers clutching the glass in front of him. My heart ached for the man, but the best here was for me to get away as soon as possible. My plan for the next day was to stay in my bungalow and read. I couldn't run the risk of bumping into Alice.

So, I sped up past the lobby, hoping Benjamin didn't see me.

When I was inside the bungalow, I fished out my nightie

and went straight into the shower, discarding my clothes as I went.

It was heaven, the cool water flowing down my face, neck, and body. I stood there turned to face the faucet, my palms on the tile in front of me. I thought about Arthur, and how maybe it would be possible to have a phone call, not the delayed texts that came out of order, making it difficult to understand.

So, when I was finally out of the shower, I put on my silk nightie and went to the bedroom. I clutched my phone close to my ear, listening to the call going unanswered again.

I texted Arthur asking if he was okay.

As I tapped the Send button, the front door to my bungalow opened. I had made a bad habit of not locking it, after seeing how safe the hotel was.

Alice walked into my bedroom. She was swaying a little, a light gray kimono similar to the one she wore years before was draped around her frame.

"Alice," I sighed.

And the thing with her was that I could not feel angry for the intrusion, and with a pang of my heart I realized something warm was spreading inside me at the sight of her.

"I don't believe you," she said quietly, her voice soft.

But before I could reply she walked to me and pressed her finger to my lips.

"Please let me speak," she said.

Before she removed it, she looked at my lips and sighed.

"I was elated to see you. I thought I would apologize, we'd talk and everything would be peachy," Alice said, and I realized she was a bit drunk, her words slurring. "When I saw you, it was as though the years turned back. I realized I still loved you. You morphed into this new sophisticated person, stronger than before, and even though I was still in love with the old version of you, I fell for the new one too. But as the days went by, this new version opened to me, as much as you fought, the little signs betrayed you. You watched me, and those accidental touches ..."

I was breathing in the sweet vanilla because Alice stood so close, and when she lowered her gaze, she smiled softly. Her fingers gently touched the skin on my neck, sliding down to my collarbone, and slowly, to my breast. She circled it, barely touching the silk of my nightie.

"Don't tell me you don't want it, it would be a lie," she whispered, as her fingers closed on the bump of my nipple.

She was right, I knew how it would feel, her lips grazing my skin, how she would melt, how her lips tasted on mine after she devoured me. We had had it all before, but it was all in the past.

"I'm yours, Emily."

Those words set something loose in me, because there was me, and there was the girl that got left behind. And she craved for it, the nights she screamed herself to sleep, not because of the death of a brother, but the loss of a sister.

"I love you, Emily. Please take me back, we can figure it out. Don't deny this," she said, and lowered her hand, lightly rubbing it between my legs. Even through the shorts, I felt the fire.

And for a moment the me from the past prevailed, she wanted to touch Alice, to cut the distance and drown in her. But I was not her anymore.

"No," I stepped back. "I loved you so much, with every cell of my body, with the unending vastness of my useless soul. But you left me, in your pain, you left me there alone. And from that moment the crack in my love for you only grew larger, I barely survived the agony. I would have given everything, and I mean it, *everything*, to have you back. I would be yours, completely. But with your absence, you killed my love, Alice. You left me and my love didn't survive it."

She was crying, her eyes never leaving mine, as pools of gray overflowed with pain.

"I'm sorry, but what you see now in me is my body remembering what it meant to touch you and be touched by you. But as my body responds, my heart is shut," I said.

She wiped her tears with a swift motion. And then she untied the kimono and dropped it to the floor. My eyes dropped to her breasts, the familiar lines, the images of the past rushing back.

"If it's only your body talking, I'm okay with it, you can have me. If it's only just this once, please," she whispered, "please, touch me."

Light steps sounded from the front door, and someone entered the room. Someone tall, with a black leather bag in his hands, someone whose eyes found mine, a familiar blue.

"The door was open, so I ..." Arthur said, but then he looked around. "Oh."

I saw his gaze following the trail of my discarded clothes on the floor, the one I had left before going into the shower, on the woman who stood only in minuscule jean shorts close to me. I watched his gaze following her naked back, and when she rushed to pick up her clothes, he saw her face.

A dawning understanding clouded his bright eyes. I saw how his jaw tensed.

"Sorry for the interruption, you can continue," he said and gestured to us, "whatever you were doing."

Arthur turned around and walked away, his stride wide.

"No, no, no, no," I whispered and rushed to him. But he was fast, so I had to run to catch up with him. Something cut into the bare sole of my foot, but I kept running. Finally, I was in front of him and placed my hand to his chest.

"Please wait," I said, breathing hard, "let me explain."

He shook his head. "There is nothing to explain, Emily. I saw what I needed to see, it was Alice, right?"

I nodded. "But ..."

"When would you tell me? Or judging by those texts you wanted to keep us both. How would it work?"

"No, it's not what you're thinking—"

"God," he whispered as he shook his head, "I thought we were something. I believed in our future. What a fool."

Arthur rubbed his eyes and opened his bag, he fished a few sheets of paper and thrust them into my hands.

"You can read them or burn them. Goodbye, Emily."

He turned and started walking away.

My chest burned, but as I tried to say something, anything to stop him, my throat closed bringing up only a whimper. But I ran after him, the soles of my feet screaming.

"Arthur, please, let me explain."

He stopped and turned to me. There was so much pain in his eyes. He dropped his head.

"Just read the pages, Emily. And afterward, you know where to find me."

He started walking again. And that time I stared at his back, wet tears running down my cheeks.

I looked at the pages in my hand and walked to the nearest lamp, hunching down to see the words.

It all blurred, as I tried to make sense of the words. Trust, relationship, closeness—the words that jumped at me.

I stood up and limped back to my bungalow, the numb daze clouding my vision. I was so tired, and my heart hurt, and I still could not believe how fast it had all happened, and how unbelievably stupid it all was.

Alice was sitting on my bed, clothed.

"Now I understand," she said quietly. "There really was no place for me anymore in your life, because you are already in love. And, as we learned earlier, you can't love two people at the same time."

I sat on the settee and dropped my head into my hands.

"Oh, God, you're bleeding," she whispered.

When I lifted my head, I saw a bloody trail on the tiled floor that stopped right at my feet. I didn't care.

"Come," Alice said gently and took my hand, she pulled me up, and led me to the bathroom. She sat me on the edge of the tub and found a medical kit under the sink. She sat on the edge next to me and helped me flip the leg into a bathtub. I was like a ragged doll, the tears still falling.

Alice cleaned the wound, then applied something that stung and bandaged my leg. All that time I sat quietly.

"I'm sorry," Alice said finally. "I didn't know he was coming, I didn't know you loved someone, I just wanted you back. I still want that."

She looked at me.

"But there is no way, am I right?" she whispered so very quietly.

I shook my head. "I'm sorry it all happened; I'm sorry about a lot of things. It started from when I betrayed Jake by loving you, I'm sorry that when he died it almost killed us both, I'm sorry it killed my love. I thought I was not able to love anymore, but then Arthur came, and it all slowly changed. I'm sorry I can't love you back. I'm sorry you are feeling this way for me. I'm sorry for Benjamin, he cares for you so deeply, and I just hope that you can figure your way out of the past. I'm just so, so sorry. Please, let me go, Alice."

She sniffed by my side, and then she flung her arms around me. For a second I thought she was going to kiss me, but she didn't. She hugged me.

I buried my nose in her hair, knowing that it would be the last time. I hugged her back.

Alice was the first to let go. She stood up, and looked back at me. Tears were pooling in the corners of her eyes.

"I'm sorry I wasn't around when you needed me the most. Goodbye, Emily."

That was the second time someone had bid farewell to me that night, but that time it felt lighter, the release both of us needed.

"Goodbye, Alice."

She looked at me for a moment longer, then turned away and disappeared into the hallway. Seconds later the front door quietly shut.

Chapter Forty-Nine

I limped back to the bed and sat on the edge. I took Arthur's papers and started to read.

Dear Emily,

You don't know this about me yet, but I journal. Every morning I write my plans, my thoughts, and the things that worry me in a dark blue notebook. By now you know almost everything about me, but I assume I don't know as many things about you.

So now as I sit on my second flight after the connection from Tokyo to Colombo, I am so nervous that I decided to write. You probably won't even see this letter. I hope you won't see it, because I'm coming to Sri Lanka to tell you all this in person.

Don't you think it's crazy? I assure you, I'm not the stalking type, but when you told me the love of your life was there, and when your texts and calls dwindled, when I couldn't reach you, I was worried sick. I didn't want our relationship to die because of some misunderstanding or miscommunication. But with every call you didn't pick up, I had a dark vision of you and that blondie, together.

I'm not the jealous type, either. But you loved her so much, I remember how you told me your story.

But she left you. Even if it was in her greatest pain, she still left you.

And I hope you won't be manipulated back into that relationship. And even if you decided to go back to her, I need you to know how I feel about you.

So, as I'm saying that I'm not a stalking or jealous type, I'm still flying to see you on your working trip. God, I'm pathetic.

And even as I fly in first-class (you would call me posh again), I'm feeling uneasy, because I'm scared. The fear is gripping my insides, making it difficult to take a breath. I worry that I might be too late.

I promise you, I'm not a person who overreacts. But you loved her, and the only thing that broke your relationship was the death of Jacob. I honestly think that if he was still alive, you three would have figured it out. I think you'd still be with Alice. And now, she is the reason you are in Sri Lanka. And I'm sure she didn't plan all this just to drink tea with you. She wants you back.

And before you decide anything, I need you to know one thing about me you still don't know. I fell in love with you.

Here, I wrote it down, now I just hope I'll have the courage to say it to you when I see you. Even if I don't, I still can give you these pages. Maybe I should highlight the words so you won't spend time reading all my gibberish.

<u>I love you.</u>

I won't explain here how it started with small things, with your laugh, with the tilt of your head, how it was easy, and so so warm inside me.

And if this work trip was just a normal trip I already had a plan for us. If you want to travel, I will travel with you. I'm wrapping up this project and then I'm free. I vowed not to take this kind of work again because it's all-consuming. Before I met you it was fine, I hid behind the work, I made myself busy, hating the time I spent at home. Because home, I was told, should feel different. Not an empty place to binge-watch series. Home is where your people are.

Call me romantic, or a fool, but I wanted to make a home with you. Yeah, yeah, it's too early. But I think we can do it. If you want to, of course.

Before the trip, I had a chance in building a life with you. Do I have it now?

I hate Alice, even though I've never met her, I hate her. She had you, and she blew her chance. But, and I may be just a hypocrite, I think that whatever happens, I won't betray you. That if something similar happened to us, I would never turn my back on you. But there is no way of knowing that, right? So whatever happens between us, I promise I will do my best to stay close.

Because, unlike Alice, I know what my life is without you.

I can live it. But with you in my life, it's so much brighter.

And I hope that you feel just a fraction of what I feel toward you. Because it will be enough. I might stand a chance against her.

I traveled the world, and I'd be so glad to show my favorite nooks in places I've been, and to discover so many more new ones together. I'll work remotely. No more stifling offices and ties, I'd need to make more calls than you, but now the world is so digitized that the companies don't need my presence, providing online support will be enough.

So, whatever you choose.

And one more thing you need to know about me. We never discussed this before but I'm not sure I want kids, Emily.

I hope I will tell you this after you choose me. But if for some inexplicable reason you are reading this instead of me telling you, I just hope it won't be a deal-breaker. Just talk to me, Emily. If your goal is to be a mom eventually, I will choose a life with you anyway. But my gut tells me that that's not your goal. Am I right?

My hand is steadier now. It's always easier to write, to sort out my worries. But the lousy thoughts are still gripping my mind. I haven't heard from you for some time, and now I imagine as I come to your bungalow, the two of you together. My mind paints various poses, your wild love revived after all these years. It would be a major turn-on, if it wouldn't break my heart. So if by any chance this is the real-life scenario, I'm sure you'll hear the crack.

God, even imagining this hurts so much. Great, now I'm in misery again.

But we are starting to land. And soon I'll see you. Hopefully, you'll smile at me, because I love your smile.

And I hope with all my heart that you are going to choose me.

Love,

Arthur

By the time I finished, I was sobbing so hard that the pages were wet from my tears. His fears had come true, it happened exactly as he dreaded. He thought that I was having sex with Alice, our clothes on the floor, her naked body so close to me.

Arthur needed to know the truth. Because I had dreamed about our future too, because I had plans, because he made my life lighter. And as he was talking about home, I realized it even before I came to Sri Lanka. Arthur *was* my home.

So, I stood up and took out my suitcase from the wardrobe. I opened it and started packing. It took me fifteen minutes to stuff all my things inside. I changed from my nightie to a white shirt and jeans and left the bungalow. I didn't look back.

The hotel was deserted, the bar closed for the night. And I wondered for a moment what would happen to Benjamin and Alice. But it was not my place to know anymore.

There was no one at reception, and my heart sank as I looked outside at the usual spot where a few taxi cars usually stood was empty. I looked around trying to find anything, a card with a taxi number, anything, when I remembered that I already had one number on my phone. Nirved.

My hands were shaking as I called him. It was long after midnight and I prayed he would pick up.

"Hello?" Nirved said and continued speaking in Sinhalese, his voice groggy.

"I'm so sorry for disturbing you so late. It's Emily, the one from Benjamin's group. I need help. I need to get to the airport, now. Do you know anyone who could take me there this late at night? It's an emergency."

"It's a two-and-a-half-hour drive," Nirved said.

"Yes, I know, I'll pay. I just...need to catch someone before he flies away."

"What about Miss Alice?" he asked.

I wanted to laugh and cry. Was it really so transparent?

"Our story ended a long time ago."

He was talking to someone in a language I didn't understand.

"Okay, meet me in ten minutes at the hotel entrance."

"Thank you, thank you, Nirved."

He ended the call. My heart was beating fast. I just hoped that Arthur went straight to the airport. I didn't call him, nor did I text him. I wanted to explain everything while looking into his eyes. I just hoped he didn't give up the future we imagined so fast.

I looked around and saw a bell on the reception desk, how did I miss it before? The noise of the bell was so deafening, I thought it would wake everyone in the vicinity.

A smiling woman appeared in a hidden doorway, I had woken her up.

"So sorry for disturbing you, but I need to check out."

"Now?" she asked incredulously, her brows rising.

"Yes, the bungalow number seven," I said and placed the key on the counter.

She took the keys and wrote something down.

"I hope you had a pleasant stay with us, and hope to see you back soon in our hotel," she said, still smiling.

"It's a paradise here, thank you very much."

I turned to the exit but stopped at the sight of a printer.

"Can I please have a few sheets of paper? And a pen if possible."

She nodded and gave it to me. Just as I got outside, in the lush darkness of the night, a small car rushed to the hotel entrance and stopped. Nirved looked at my bag and helped me to put it on the back seats—because the trunk was minuscule.

As soon as I sat down inside, the small engine roared and in a few seconds, we were speeding through the still sleeping roads.

It was almost impossible to sit straight in the car, as Nirved drove the dark streets. But as soon as we hit the highway I took out a pen and paper and started to write.

Benjamin,

I'm sorry I left earlier. But we didn't have any work plans for the last day, right?

I'm so sorry for coming into your life. I'm sorry for ruining the peace you found on this paradise island.

You need to know that I'm immensely grateful for your help with my project. You are a great leader, and I am proud to know you. Thank you for acquiring the app and for your professional guidance.

I wanted to talk about Alice.

Alice. I loved her so much seven years ago. But when her brother died, she disappeared from my life. She told me on this trip that the death of Jake nearly killed her. You can ask her to tell you about Jake sometime, you'll see how she lights from inside. They were the most kind and caring people in my life, the three of us were close. If you want, you can ask Alice to tell you our story.

But our story ended a long time ago. When Jake died, Alice was gone too. On this trip, she explained to me why she disappeared, all her pain.

And I told her the truth—my love died that year they were gone.

I don't think she still loves me. I think I'm a strong reminder of the short happy time we had together with Jacob. When we were all happy. It was almost eight years ago.

I saw that she cares about you, when she enters a room her eyes go to you first. As though she needs to know that you were there. As though your presence brings her comfort and balance.

I hope you two can find your peace. And as you said to me, be gentle with her. She still grieves, and I think she will for a long time. They had the strongest bond. You should have seen them together. They were golden. And now Alice still struggles to live without Jake.

My part is over in this story. I'm leaving and I won't be back in her life.

If you ever want to discuss anything business-related I would appreciate that we meet somewhere neutral, and without Alice.

I wish you two to be happy.

Goodbye.

Emily

I folded the paper and put it on the dashboard.

"Could you please give that to Benjamin the next time you see him?" I asked.

"Sure," he said. "Are you running away or are you chasing something?"

I smiled. "I'm chasing my future."

Chapter Fifty

When we finally arrived at the airport it was crowded. Back in the car, I checked for the earliest flights back to San Francisco. There was one leaving at six in the morning, with the short connection in London. I tried to buy a ticket online, but the page showed an error every time I went to the payment step.

I thanked Nirved and almost hugged him when we stopped at the terminal.

I ran. I ran to the ticket office.

"I need a ticket to San Francisco, I saw there is a flight at six," I said, my heart in my throat.

The woman looked at her laptop and started typing slowly. After what felt like hours she looked up at me.

"I'm sorry, it's full."

"What?" I asked. How can a flight from Colombo be full? "Please check again."

"I've already checked, m'am."

And at that moment I had the stupidest idea ever. I ran again. There was a long line to the security check, and I ran to the end of it. I halted at the last person and started walking the length of the line, but soon it stopped at the open door to the next hall where people were taking out their laptops and liquids, taking off belts, and going through a metal frame.

By that time Arthur would be inside, he had left at least half an hour before me. He would have completed all the checks and would be sitting by the gate.

As I clutched the hope that wanted to spill out, I did something crazy.

"Arthur!" I screamed.

People turned to me with wide eyes, but none of them were familiar. My heart sank as I stood on tiptoes, but still, the view was blocked. A security guard walked up to me and asked who I was searching for. I gave Arthur's details, and as the man walked right to the checkpoint, peering at each one, asking if he was Arthur, but none of them were.

I was too late, he was already inside. Or in any other place. He could have checked into the hotel for the night or gone to a bar. But bars in the village closed early, and the hotels grew dark at night. I thought he would be there.

Arthur said I knew where to find him. His house.

The guard turned to me and shook his head. I mumbled my thanks and grabbed the handle of my suitcase. I didn't know what to do. So, I turned and walked slowly to the rows of seats.

I gasped when I saw a familiar shape hunched in the far corner. Arthur was looking outside, wireless earphones in his ears. His look was frozen, absent, it was as though his figure was carved from marble.

I ran again, leaving my suitcase by the nearest seat, I almost tripped on someone's shoes. But in a few moments, I stopped in front of him.

His eyes widened in surprise and the corner of his lips went up for a second. Arthur pulled off the earphones and stood up.

Before he could say anything, I hugged him so fiercely that he stumbled back a little. I pressed my head to his chest and felt his heart racing.

When his warm hands pressed into my back, when they got lost in my hair and rubbed the base of my neck, I exhaled. I didn't notice that I was holding my breath, waiting.

"Why are you here?" he asked quietly.

I let go of my hands and looked up at him. "You have to hear me out."

I told him everything, bared my soul. I told him about the kiss, about the part of me that kissed her back. I told him how I had lived with that old part of me over the last few days, just to realize that the love was long gone. I told him about that night, how he misunderstood things. How Alice still grieved and that seeing me brought back memories of Jake.

"I think she thought if we got back together that the feeling of him would be closer. She wanted to seduce me," I said.

"If I didn't enter the room would you ..."

"No. Do you remember her face?"

Arthur shook his head.

"She was crying because I'd said that everything was in the past."

He scooped me up in his arms and swayed lightly.

"You're wrong on one thing, Emily. Alice didn't do all of this to remember Jake, she still loves you, she never stopped."

"Maybe, but I stopped."

We stood silent for a long time.

"Do I still have a chance for a future with you?" I whispered.

His laugh was warm.

"Maybe."

I hit him lightly on his chest.

"Because what I wanted to tell you was that I realized that you are my home," I said.

He was smiling so widely it lit my heart.

"Is this a feeble attempt at saying *I love you, Arthur*?" he joked.

And when I felt my cheeks grow crimson, he continued. "Because the things that you read in those pages are true."

He stepped close and put a thumb on my chin, lifting my head a little. "I love you, Emily, and I want to be with you."

And before I could reply, he kissed me, deeply. My knees grew weak, and he held me in his arms.

"Yeah, I think I'm in love with you, too," I said, just inches from his lips.

His laugh was loud and genuine.

"God, I missed you, Emily."

Epilogue

More than three years have passed since that fateful night in Sri Lanka. I would like to boast about my many travels, the countries we have visited, and paint pictures of us working on the beach with toes dipped into the white sand.

Instead, soon after we returned to San Francisco, the world was shaken by a new kind of virus.

My fear of it was dimmed by a new wave of happiness, when more often than not I woke up with Arthur in his house. When people went crazy we stayed away in our own bliss with the hunger we needed to quench, the rawness of the feeling so powerful.

So, when I was finally ready to talk about all that had happened, the only way we could meet with Miranda was by video.

When my lease was running to an end, Arthur asked me to move in with him. I agreed because I had essentially lived with him since that first day we had come back from Sri Lanka.

As we were forced to stay at home during the first year of

the pandemic, we minimized taking in the news and maximized lovemaking.

I had a lot of work because, when the pandemic hit, the downloads of our app grew tremendously. Arthur spent this time cooped up in the house setting up his business website, social media, and he consulted online. It was a good time for him to slow down his working process.

As I didn't have a family to worry about, and Arthur's family was trapped up in their mansion in England, staying away from people, all we could do was watch how stress and anxiety ate away the world.

We spent the next year traveling America. Arthur showed me how big, diverse, and interesting our country really was. We flew to big cities on the East coast, and we went on short road trips because working on the road proved to be more of a nuisance than anything.

One evening, after we returned from a trip and were splayed on his sofa in front of the TV, Arthur turned to me.

"Let's get married," he said. "What do you think? We spent a year caged in the house side by side and didn't want to murder each other, and we like the same things."

I smiled. "That's the most practical proposal I ever heard."

"Have you heard a lot of them?" Arthur asked, his brow raising.

"Plenty."

He chuckled and stood up, just to lower himself onto his knee in front of me. I was wearing pajamas and was sleepy after a shower, but his next words woke me up.

"Emily, I want to share my life with you. You are my life. These two years have been the best of my life because of you. When I thought I lost you that night in Sri Lanka, something in my chest cracked, and it hurt so much that I wanted to claw my heart out. But when you appeared in front of me, I was the happiest man on Earth. I love our life, your laugh, and every second with you. I love you. And among this craziness and uncertainty, I realized one thing, I want to be with you forever. If you'll allow me."

Arthur fished something out of his pocket and showed me a light blue box. He opened it as my heart raced. A beautiful stone lay on a delicate golden band. He took the ring out of the box.

"Marry me, Emily."

"Yes," I said without hesitation.

"Yes? Just like that?" Arthur asked, his eyes shining.

"Just like that," I said as he put the ring on my finger. "You're my home, and I want that future you promised in the letter."

Arthur kissed me, and I kissed him back, slowly.

"I love you," I whispered.

His lips trailed down my neck as his fingers unbuttoned my pajama top, as they slowly slid over my skin. In a few moments I was wearing only the gold ring and I was melting under his touch. It was almost pleasurably painful, this promise of our future.

We got married shortly afterward, by the ocean. I wore a white dress that hugged my body. Miranda curled my hair and I wore almost no makeup. Arthur promised me to try his best to never fail me, and I promised to be by his side, always. Miranda and Brian were the only guests, and the camera trained on us broadcasted the ceremony to the UK. Arthur's friends, with whom he started talking a lot when the pandemic hit, watched us. They would have loved to come, but borders were closed. As we later found out, Arthur's parents were also watching the ceremony. He sent them the link, but he said they would probably ignore it. They didn't.

When a few days later we came back from our honeymoon weekend in the desert, a massive bouquet was delivered, with a letter welcoming me to the family and inviting us to stay when international travel was allowed again.

"They probably found out that my brother can't have children, and they want us to make an heir for their legacy. They never pay attention for the sake of attention, they always seek something in return. Just wait to see their faces when we tell them we don't plan to have children," Arthur said.

We talked about having kids a lot. Arthur said that it was usually women who decided if they wanted kids, but in our family, it was reversed. I never had any inclination, and with an already overpopulated, dangerous, and polluted world, I thought it was not wise to bring a little person into it. And I cherished my freedom, our flexibility, our way of life too much. So the decision came naturally.

But Arthur was wrong about his parents. When we finally were allowed to travel to the UK, Arthur saw how his parents changed in the time he was away. They had grown softer, and even though he still didn't trust them, they were slowly winning his heart.

As for me, I watched his family with the wide eyes of a scientist—the rules, the formal interactions—and could not help but compare it with my family of just Dad and me. They were a family of old money, with the well-maintained mansion that was even filmed in movies and series now. Old money got invested in new stocks and made the family even richer. I could not count how many times I muttered *posh* to Arthur during our stay.

But the ice was melting, and Arthur spent hours talking to his mother, both of them retreating to their rooms red-eyed.

We came back to America with a promise to visit them soon again, and with just a small feeling of being loved. It was new for Arthur, and under his stoic facade, he clung to that love.

Miranda and Brian became famous for their parties, and

when their house was too small for their plans, they bought a bigger one, and it turned into a full-force business, with schedules, themes, and exclusivity. Arthur loved both of them, so soon it was not me who scheduled our visits, but Miranda and Arthur, while Brian and I rolled our eyes at the next crazy idea they discussed. Their podcast bloomed.

Working away with our toes dipped into the white sand didn't work for us. We stayed at Arthur's house to work and took vacations away. We left our laptops in the house and flew away as often as our schedule allowed.

Now, when we had just gotten back from our first trip to Europe, Miranda drove to our house. She was nervous and when she entered the house she let out a long string of profanities. She held a letter. It was from Alice. Miranda put it on the table as if it were hot to the touch.

There was a letter inside the letter because Alice hadn't known how to reach me. She sent one to Miranda asking her to forward the one inside to me.

Sometimes my thoughts wandered back to her. How was she now? Where did she live? Was she happy?

So, when Arthur took the letter and gently pressed it into my hands, motioning me to the bedroom to read it, I did so. My hands shook as I opened the envelope and her familiar curly letters danced in front of me.

Dear Emily,

I owe you an apology for so many things. For dragging you to Sri Lanka, for almost manically stalking you there, for that night, and for hurting you so long ago when I didn't meet you outside my parents' house.

I'm so sorry.

But as I said before, I coped as best I could. And it turned out my coping mechanism wasn't the best thing.

I just hope I didn't ruin your career with that acquisition.

But as Ben has told me, the app is doing great, so I hope that at least one thing I did didn't hurt you. I'm so proud of you.

We live in Bali now. Before the pandemic hit, we left Sri Lanka and moved here. Since that time we have only visited America twice. During the first trip, I went by the little old house Jake and I rented. But it was a house for three, do you agree? It stood empty then, and I could almost see my Beetle and Jake's rusty Toyota in the driveway. I could almost hear the music flowing from the house, and the laughter. We were so happy there. I stood and cried as I watched the dimmed empty house.

My therapist told me it was a good idea for me to visit the place. She was right. It helped.

She helped me to sort out my feelings and guilt. I see how by wanting you back I wanted Jake back. How staying close to you brought him back, the feeling that he was just around the corner. It's true, but I also think it was love. I sometimes wonder what would have happened if you took me back. Would we be happy? Because when I look back now, I see the mess I was, how unstable and damaged I was. I'm still working on getting myself whole again.

But there are events that can't be changed, events that we have to live with the consequences of. I could not change that Jake died, and I could not change my grief afterward—the grief that pushed you away. But even now, after all these years I can't imagine going downstairs that day Miranda and Brian brought you to my parents' house. I could not change that moment.

And I am so sorry for that too.

I don't know anything about your life and it better stays that way. That's why I googled Miranda and Brian (they are finally in the entertainment business, it suits them!) because I knew that after all this time you'd be close to them. Because they saved you.

I hope you found your happiness.

After all those years of pain, I finally found mine.

That night in Sri Lanka I was so ashamed of myself that when I came back to our bungalow I started packing. How could I even stand by Ben's side while minutes before I had begged you to have me? A shudder ran down my spine as I remembered it. I was broken, Emily, and afterward, disgusted with myself.

When Ben entered the room, he didn't let go of me. He never did. I remember how I pressed myself to the wall because I could barely stand. I explained that he needed to let me go because I betrayed him, because I loved another person. I told him that I kissed you and how I had just stood naked in front of you pleading for you to touch me.

I saw how each of my words landed like a whip, but he stood there looking into my eyes.

I tried to prove to him that I didn't deserve him. I felt like filthy lying trash.

Do you know what he did? He scooped me into his arms. I was shaking so violently by that time that the bed trembled when he sat on it with me in his arms. We sat silent for a long time until the shaking finally subsided. He asked me if I would have him. I remember how I laughed incredulously, and that I asked if he had heard what I told him. He did.

Ben said that he loved me from the first moment he laid eyes on me. And that if it was not a reciprocal love, he was fine with it. He asked if he could stay until I felt better, that he needed me to heal. And when I was ready, he would disappear.

I had no power to fight. Ben stayed by my side when even I would not stay by my side. I worked through the guilt with my new therapist. Those were dark months, we moved to another place and started from scratch. I lived separately, but close to Ben. I wanted to offer something to him in return. On many nights I walked to his house and offered him my body, he refused every time, and we just lay in the darkness as I curled by his side.

Soon it was every night that I came to him, and later the nights turned into days. I moved in with Ben, but he still wouldn't touch me. We lived as friends, we talked for days and nights.

You said I was a lesbian, I am, but with one major exception. I fell in love with a human, not with a gender. My love for him grew slowly, yes, but it is so strong now, that sometimes it's difficult to breathe. He didn't kiss me until he saw how I felt, until I loved him with everything I had.

There are different kinds of love. One that blooms immediately, one that binds you to family, one that is easy, one that is hard, and one that grows.

My love for Ben grew in the darkness of my mind, through the pain. His constant presence, care, and protection helped me find the lost part of myself. Without it, I could not love.

One night I woke up to an empty bed, and at that moment the feeling of such a profound dread overtook me that I barely stayed conscious. Ben was gone. I remembered how he promised that when I was better he would disappear. I sat on the bed and looked at the empty space to my right, hollow, frozen. That moment undermined everything I had worked for years because I was only strong if Ben was by my side. And he was gone.

I sat paralyzed for what seemed like hours, in truth it was no more than fifteen minutes. When the door opened and Ben walked in, I dashed to him, almost knocking us both over. I clung to his shirt as I was drowning. As I sobbed I asked him not to go, that I could not live without him, to please, please stay.

Apparently, he could not sleep and just went to the ocean to take a breath. I was so ashamed, but he looked happy. I said that I remembered his promise of disappearing when I felt better. He hugged me tighter and whispered that he wasn't going anywhere until I asked him to.

That night showed me the power of my love for him. In those minutes when I sat alone my heart was breaking, but when he rocked me in his arms, it mended itself.

The next day he proposed a second time. It was the happiest day of my life.

I wished Jake could attend the small ceremony we had, and in a way, I think he was there, I felt him. He would have loved Ben.

I think about Jake a lot, and often try to imagine the life he'd have had now. When traveling is easy again Ben and I plan to duplicate the trip I took with Jake to Eastern Europe.

You may wonder why I'm writing all this, for you. You said that our story ended years ago when I didn't go downstairs to meet you. It would have been easy just to open that window and call you. I used to torment myself with what-ifs. One major what if was what if I had called you, what if I emerged for a second from that dark swamp and called for your help. I think we'd still be together. Can you imagine us both being thirty-something, living together, loving each other? I can.

But maybe it was never meant to be. One part of me always loved you, while the rest of me is healing, and living, and loving my life now. I'm proud to be the wife of the person I can't live without.

I hope you love and you are loved.

This is a letter of goodbye, Emily. Finally, I'm at the point where I can truly say that our story is over. You got there much earlier than I did. But it's time to let go of the past.

I'm letting go of the part of me that loved you with this letter.

Goodbye.

Alice

I pressed the letter to my chest, the smiling faces of Jake and Alice in my mind, that Thanksgiving almost eleven years ago.

"Goodbye," I whispered back.

Acknowledgments

In 2021, I had a dream featuring a brother and sister. The end of the scene where Emily meets Alice in a bar for the first time, and when Jake and Alice pause before leaving—that is an exact replica of my dream. I'm so glad they visited me, and I hope you enjoyed meeting them too.

I want to express my gratitude to the team at Creative James Media who believed in this book and showed constant support throughout this publishing journey.

Special thanks go to my family. Thank you for your unwavering encouragement and for standing by me and my creative work.

To my friends, the cheerleaders of my writing odyssey.

And to you, dear reader, who invested time in exploring this book, I hope it took you on a beautiful emotional adventure.

About the Author

Laura May is the pen name of a Ukrainian-American author. She travels around the world, but her hometown, Kyiv, always calls her back.

For the latest updates on Laura May and her books, visit LauraMayAuthor.com, and you can also follow her on Instagram at Instagram.com/LauraMayAuthor

Do You Wish You Never Met Me is a third book by Laura May published by Creative James Media.

Call to Action

Dear Reader,

Thank you for choosing to explore the pages of this book!

Would you like to receive exclusive discounts, special offers, and early reader copies? Feel free to join my newsletter at LauraMayAuthor.com/newsletter

Your thoughts on the book are immensely valuable to me. If you enjoyed the story, I would greatly appreciate it if you could share your feedback by leaving a review on platforms like Goodreads, Amazon, or any other online store where you made your purchase. These reviews play a vital role in guiding other readers toward this novel.

Your support is truly cherished. Thank you for being an integral part of this literary journey!

Warm regards,
Laura May

www.ingramcontent.com/pod-product-compliance
Lightning Source LLC
Chambersburg PA
CBHW050743190726
48285CB00005B/1513